THE PRICE OF HONOUR

By

Nash Ramji

ISBN-13: 9781697351484

DEDICATION

To Ali and Mariam-Sara.

CONTENTS

ACKNOWLEDGMENTS

Julie Wilson (UK)
Dr Murtaza Hussein (Toronto – Canada)
Moazzam Shamsi (UK)
Mariam (UK).

Author's Note

This is my first fictional work. I have enjoyed writing this book immensely. There has been an abundance of help around me and I could not have done it without help from my daughter Mariam and very many good friends whose feedback from time to time has been invaluable. I therefore acknowledge my gratitude to all those friends who have helped me on this fantastic journey of writing a novel to fulfil my long ambition to be an author. My daughter Mariam without fail constantly encouraged me to continue when there were many days I was ready to give up, as I got exasperated when lost for words of expression, but Mariam continually kept up her words of encouragement. Many times, I would read to her what I had written, ask her opinion on it, she would without fail provide an honest one which helped me focus. She was great. I also at the same time acknowledge my gratitude and thanks to Dr Murtaza Hussein of Toronto, to Julie Wilson whose critique of my very first draft manuscript was invaluable and lastly but by no means least my very dear friend Moazzam Shamsi for proof-reading the book. I salute you all. I am totally indebted to you all for your generosity nurtured with kind help. Thank you.

Preface

This is a fictional story about an ordinary family. The patriarch upholds his traditional cultural values; though very much outdated and anachronistic, he does his best to continue to uphold them even in the face of adversity. To him these values are pivotal in the day-to-day existence of his life. To continue them through his children as they were, he believed the fabric of his culture and society he lived in. The importance of family honour and integrity mattered to him greatly. The novel focuses on a closely-knit family which has a history of long-standing traditions, cultural values and strong bonds with its community. These are underpinned by religion, faith and belief. A strange phenomenon emerges from those values. Family honour is held most high in status. It has an elevated status with the head of the family. Sadly, a dark side emerges with tragic consequences.

Chapter 1

On a bitterly cold, grey, frosty morning in February 1972 Faizali Rehman paced up and down in the hospital maternity ward waiting area. It was very early morning. He looked around, surveying the surroundings. There were a few people about as he looked around. He could smell that strong, clinical, industrial bleach which permeated the air all around the hospital. The cleaners had finished their usual early-morning routine of rigorous cleaning at the local maternity unit in Leicester. The long hospital corridors sparkled and gleamed from the fresh clean. Soon hundreds of feet shedding dust would be trundling up and down those freshly cleaned corridors, taking the shine off as the thoroughfare would get busier during the day ready for another clean and polish the next day. All different people, patients, visitors and different grades of workers from professionals right down to menial task workers delivering services were busy going about their business. The place was like a conveyor belt, well-oiled, producing new arrivals in the world who started their journey in life here too. Who knows? Some may even end up working in the very place they were born.

Faizali Rehman waited anxiously in the waiting area with his five daughters for his new arrival. His wife Mehrunnisha was in child labour as they waited. Tradition was that men were not permitted to be present with their partners during birth. He waited as custom demanded in the waiting area. He paced up and down in a section of the room. Soon the pacing area was defined by scuff marks from his trainers on the freshly cleaned floor. The shine gradually disappeared on the patch as he carried on pacing. Faizali was a small bearded man with a hooked nose. A round face partly covered by thick rimmed glasses with a covering of a few grey hairs mixed with mostly jet-black hair. An oval-shaped *topi* tightly sat on his head; all around it his ruffled hair sprouted. He was dressed in traditional Indian s*halwar kameez* clothes with a thick winter overcoat on. He had forgotten to take it off in his state of anxiousness despite the temperature in the hospital being around thirty degrees centigrade. Tired from pacing, Faizali finally sat down, but no sooner he did a nurse popped her head into the waiting area. Quite pretty looking, she was, early twenties, dressed in a light grey nurse's uniform, white paper cap clipped to her blonde hair tied at the back in a ponytail.

"Hello. Are you Mr Rehman?" she enquired, smiling at him.

Faizali Rehman nervously nodded as he whispered to himself, "Please, Allah, let it be good news."

"Don't look so worried. I assume you are dad?" looking at Faizali. "Well you have a son, congratulations!"

The news made him jump out from his chair like an athlete getting started off his block with a spring in his feet. He turned around in a full three hundred and sixty degree circle, clapping his hands with joy. Raazia had never seen her father do that before. It made her chuckle as she looked at him with a smile. His delight at hearing the good news was palpable. The nurse had to laugh too.

"You seem very happy, Dad?"

"I am. I really am, my dear. You cannot imagine how happy I am today hearing this good news you have given me. I thank God *Maa'sha'Allah.*" He turned to Raazia holding her hand. "Raazia, *betti,* isn't it wonderful news? I truly feel blessed."

"Would you like to come meet your son, Mr Rehman?" she asked. He nodded. "C'mon, follow me."

Thrilled, buzzing with excitement, Faizali, Raazia, Allia, Sameena, Saleena and Sara walked behind in a line following the nurse as she led the way. Sara hop-skipped on a red line painted on the ground. Begum was resting on her bed cradling her infant child in her arms when the family entered the ward. A huge smile on her face as her daughters came into view was followed suddenly by tears as she became emotional. The girls tightly hugged their mother as she handed the infant child over to her husband, continuing hugging her daughters.

"*Salaam alaiykum Bibiji*, *Mubarak ho, arey wah aaj tow kaam hoggia. Allah hu Akbar* (God is great). Finally, glorious news, glorious news my dear Begum *He* has finally blessed me with a son. Isn't that wonderful?"

Begum nodded. Faizali cradled the infant in his arms with a smile on his face. He lifted the child up to his chin, carefully supporting his tiny head, neck and back. As was tradition he recited the *azan* (call of prayers) softly in the infant's right ear then his left. His face glowed like a shining beacon as he proudly settled down on a chair resting his head on its high back. He cradled the infant in his arms for a while. Looking at his tiny face, Faizali continued to smile, whispering inaudibly, offering his thanks to the Almighty.

"*Shukher'Allah, shukher'Allah.*" He continued repeating the same words many times then mumbled something inaudible. "I have waited many years for a son, my dear, and finally the moment has arrived for which I thank *Allah* the Almighty first. I thank you too, my dear Begum. My life is complete today as I have a son."

"*MerriJaan* no more children for us now, I have had enough!" she said.

Begum gave out a huge sigh of relief. At the age of thirty-five, she was overweight, seemingly aged by miles having given birth to six children over the last fifteen years. Raazia began to brush up and tidy her mother's long jet-black hair as she sat on the bed beside her. Using a medium-size black comb, she brushed out all the knots then tied it in a neat single braid. She stroked her back with the palm of her hands, soothing the pain a little. Begum's weariness from the strain of labour was plain to see. The crow's feet on the side of her eyes and lines on her forehead were noticeably pronounced. Faizali, tired of holding his infant son, handed the infant over to Raazia.

"How are you, my dear?" Faizali asked Begum belatedly, slightly bringing his posture forward as he did.

"I am fine, my dear husband. I am tired from the birth. I offer my thanks to the Almighty that was a natural delivery. He was a long time coming out, this one. I thought I was going to end up in theatre delivering by caesarean section at one point. I am glad I did not as I am not as young as I used to be. I can't go through this anymore," Begum said with a robust tone.

A sudden change of mood gripped Begum. She became tearful and emotional as tears filled her eyes, rolling down her cheeks. Using her *dupata* she quickly wiped the tears away. The younger ones began to wonder what was causing their mother to be upset. Display of emotion like this in front of the family was a sign of weakness, she thought. Begum knew she could not. She quickly regained composure. The girls hugged Begum, showing her affection, not exactly understanding Begum's emotional hormonal state.

"I can't wait to get home, my dear husband. I have so much to do at home," she said, breaking away from the sombreness of her brief emotional display.

"You don't have to worry about that, my dear. Raazia has everything under control," Faizali said, pretending not to have noticed his wife's short emotional public display.

"Faizali, we need to decide upon a name for the child. You will need to make arrangements for the boy to be done," Begum said, addressing her husband, carefully avoiding the 'circumcision' word.

"Yes I have, my dear. He will be called Abdel Faizali Rehman. It was my grandfather's middle name. It fits him, don't you think Begum?"

"That is a lovely name, befitting for a Rehman. Raazia *betti* are you all okay at home as I so much worry about you my angels?"

"Yes, Mum, we are all fine, truly we are. Please don't worry," Raazia said. "Now you must rest."

"Faizali have you made the necessary arrangements for the boy's circumcision?" Begum asked again, forgetting she asked the same question a minute ago.

"Don't you worry about that, my dear Begum. As I said, I have taken care of it and you need to rest now. C'mon girls, let's be on our way."

Contented for now that some tasks were taken care of she pushed her body back into the bed, making herself comfortable with her head resting on the pile of pillows stacked up behind her. The younger girls had become loud and noisy. A middle-aged nurse sitting at a table near the entrance of the ward with half-moon spectacles perched on the end of her nose, looked up towards them with piercing eyes.

"Sshhh..." She raised her index finger vertically across her mouth and nose.

"Quiet, girls," Papaji said loudly, responding to the powerful instruction just issued.

The bell sounded signifying the end of visiting time. Abdel was fast asleep in the baby cot oblivious to the many sounds around him. It was time for Begum to catch up on the much-needed rest from her labour.

*

The day became colder as the hours wore on. Temperatures barely made it to zero degrees in the day. The biting winds whistling outside, gusting at fifty miles per hour, made it feel bitterly cold. It was a Saturday. The girls were at home sat together on the sofa, huddled together in front a small gas fire, burning on a low heat, trying to keep warm. The fire looked worn, above the grill burnt with flame marks. Sara, Sameena, Saleena, Allia and Raazia sat on the sofa huddled together with a blanket wrapped round them. As dusk fell the fresh cold air from southerly isobars began to dip the temperatures. Soon the short day passed into darkness. Faizali stepped through the front door into the house shaking his head, making a 'brrrr' sound as he exhaled the carbon dioxide from his mouth and nose. A white cloud of air exhaled made Sara titter.

"Papaji you have smoke coming out from your mouth," she said and laughed.

"Yes *betti,* it's so cold outside."

"Salaams Papaji," the girls greeted him.

"How was *Maghreb* prayers, Papaji?" Raazia asked.

"Just fine, what a cold day though. I shall always remember this day for your brother was born on a day like this. His arrival has warmed me a little as I am very excited, girls," he exclaimed as he proceeded to take his gloves off first, then unravelled his tartan woollen scarf from his neck followed by taking his thick black overcoat off last. He flung them all onto a chair, and then settled down in his chair in front of the gas fire. He rubbed his hands as he leant forward closer to the fire, turning the gas knob up to increase the heat, then extended both hands towards the fire to get them warmed up, rubbing them together.

The house was an old three-bedroom terraced property built in the late forties. The old post-war brickwork made it cold in winter months. The front door led directly into the lounge. A yellow patterned carpet covered the lounge which was sparsely furnished. A long, garish, red-coloured sofa sat in the middle of the room, a black and white television in the far corner of the room, and next to it a wooden sixties-style art deco coffee table covered fully with a huge pile of newspapers piled high but precariously leaning sideways like the leaning tower of Pisa. One flick or a push would have set the whole pile cascading down onto the floor. Maroon-coloured velvet drapes covered the entire length of the wide window. Horrid wallpaper, garishly psychedelic, covered the walls. The dining room was the next room. A long, mahogany, oval-shaped table with clear plastic covering it stood out, occupying nearly the length of the room. Seven dining chairs were neatly tucked under the table. Long drapes similar to the lounge covered the window. Three wooden birds with their wings expanded as though they were flying were fixed on one side of the wall in ascending order. Next to it was the kitchen. It was crowded. Every inch of space was taken up with food and kitchen items as you stepped into it from the dining room. A stale, pungent smell of curry permeated the whole house.

Raazia was fifteen, Allia ten, Sameena nine, Saleena eight and Sara five. The girls were nicely huddled together underneath blankets as their body heat kept them warm from the brutally cold day. Raazia stood up from her warm seat to pick up the pile of clothing off the chair as she spoke to her father.

"Are you ready to eat, Papaji?" Raazia asked.

The sisters adjusted the vacant spot left by Raazia, quickly folding the blanket back over them to preserve the heat inside. She took the items off the chair and hung them on a hook one item at a time behind the front door.

"Papaji, you must be happy now that you have a son?" Raazia asked.

"Yes, I am so happy. Don't forget you are all my dearest daughters. I love you all. Life is something *strange.* You will all get married when you are of age, losing my identity you were born with as you take your husbands' names in marriage. Abdel on the other hand will carry our family name to the next generation. That makes me proud and happy, *betti.* Praise be to *Allah."* He made some odd facial contortions, but elation seemed obviously glowing on him. "How are you, my angels?"

"Fine, Papaji, we are just fine," the girls responded.

Raazia had an odd feeling within her. It was almost as though he now had a different focus in life which oddly meant the girls had been displaced into second-class citizens. Raazia tried not to think negatively but her closeness to her mother made her feel a little secure as she knew her bond with her was much stronger than with her father. She missed her mother. Her brief spell away in hospital seemed like a lifetime to Raazia.

Papaji sat with the girls at the dining table eating

lamb spinach *Sabzi* with *rotis* which Raazia had prepared ready for when Papaji came home. They sat round the oval-shaped table huddled together as they ate, talking. The excitement about the new addition to the family was the talk at the table. Raazia and Allia cleared up the table after they had finished eating. Papaji stood up, as was usual for him. After washing his hands and drying them he went into the lounge. He rarely helped clear up after eating, much to Raazia's annoyance, but she dare not say anything to him knowing full well had she done so Papaji would have reacted swiftly, putting Raazia in her place. He had put the television on, turning the lights off, preferring to sit in the dark, and commanded the children to go upstairs.

"Children, it's time for you all to go upstairs, finish your prayers first, then to bed."

"Papaji it is Saturday night, can we not stay and watch television with you?" asked Allia.

"No, Papaji is tired. I want to relax."

Reluctantly Allia joined her sisters as they proceeded to go upstairs. The temperatures dipped even more as the night wore on, dropping two or three degrees more. It was a bitterly cold night. Papaji sat downstairs with the gas heater on. Raazia and Allia's room had a small portable paraffin heater on low heat. Though it kept their bedroom mildly warm, the strong odour of kerosene lingered in the air. Raazia and Allia prayed *namaaz*, and then each one read a *Surah* from the *Koran* picked randomly. Allia picked the shortest one to recite before closing the book. Before she put it away, she kissed its cover, touching the Holy book to her forehead lightly, and then placing it in a cloth sewn especially for the book to fit snuggly like a glove. Raazia pushed the two single beds together so all five could fit in. They huddled together, trying to keep warm. The girls were thrilled to have a baby brother and the excitement kept their spirits up on this cold night. Raazia switched the light off, getting the younger ones off to sleep by singing a lullaby to them. Once the younger ones were asleep Raazia and Allia carried on talking, whispering so as Papaji could not hear them until they too fell asleep.

Chapter 2

Begum arrived home from hospital, two days after giving birth to Abdel. She hugged all her girls upon arrival. As school was closed for half-term, she looked forward to spending time at home. Besides, Begum knew Raazia would be around to help her with some of the household chores. Begum loved being surrounded by her daughters, Raazia especially.

Begum, as was traditional stayed at home looking after the family. Women going out to work was frowned upon. Men were breadwinners and firmly in charge of providing for the family. Tradition and culture dictated an order and a hierarchy within the family. The Rehmans were no different. Traditional values derived from culture, religion and tradition for a Muslim family living life in the way Papaji had been brought up was how it was for this family. Living in a fast forward-moving modern society made no difference to a long-standing way of life, adopted values, culture and above all tradition. Papaji was brought up the traditional way that would dictate how his family would be brought up. As head of the household he saw it as his duty to carry on this tradition. The power to wield patriarchal authority rested with him. He saw it as his duty to maintain traditions. He believed in upholding the tradition of his culture; its maintenance was akin to something ordained by The Almighty, he believed. Women had their place in society. He believed it was their duty to keep the order as he knew it and they all had a place within the hierarchical structure. Reputation of the family was equally of paramount importance, especially within their own community. Papaji worked at the local factory on the production line as a machinist making machine parts; he was the only family bread winner. Not surprisingly this brought power and status which he enjoyed immensely.

Papaji was a typical man. He failed to share his celebratory plans with his wife until the last minute on Friday night.

"My dear Begum I have invited many close friends from the local community on Sunday afternoon to celebrate the birth of Abdel. I have arranged for the circumcision in the morning on Saturday. Would you prepare the food for our guests on Sunday?" he said presumptuously.

Begum had become used to it and simply nodded her head without argument. She knew dissent was otiose.

Raazia on the other hand was seething when she learnt of this. She thought it to be patronising; she confronted her mother.

"Papaji always does this to us, Mother. Why do you let him do this to us? You have just given birth a few days ago. We end up doing all the hard work for his pleasure. I wanted to enjoy my half-term holidays, but it is all ruined. I know I will end up doing all the hard work," Raazia groaned at her mother, her tone raised.

"Hush, child, you will do your duty without any argument or saying '*oof*' to your parents. You know what the Koran says about disrespecting your parents, don't you?" Begum retorted sharply.

"Children have rights too, Mother. Why do you always side with him? I don't really understand. Look how he treats you. Making you have babies all the time, so he is satisfied that he has a boy. He treats us like slaves when we are not, Mother."

"You will not speak of your father in that manner, Raazia, I will not allow it," Begum said harshly.

"Oh, Mother. There is no point in arguing with you. *Is* there?"

Begum picked up a *chapal,* holding it up just slightly above her head as though she was going to strike her with it but stopped short of a strike.

"Oh, Mum, you always show me the slipper whenever I disagree, never miiiind."

"Do not 'oh, Mum' me. You should know better. We all have our place. You know yours and don't you forget it."

For the first time ever, she felt a touch of resentment towards her mother for failing to support her. Though she knew there would be no point in advancing the argument any further as the raised *chapal* was a sign of authority at its sharpest. She had heard the local *Imam* frequently talk about the duties of children towards their parents as stated in the *Koran.* Children who speak up oppose *Him.* Disrespect him. '*Oof*' was an ugly word. The old Victorian adage of 'children should be seen and not heard' was very much alive in the modern-day world, much to her annoyance. She knew the elevated status of parents over children quoted from the Holy book in which it is said those children who utter disagreement, commit sins, are not only not worthy children, but they will burn in the hell fire. Raazia was not convinced that the Book only spoke of parents' rights and not of the children. That seemed very strange to her that it would be 'one-sided'. She knew the men responsible for interpreting would have their interests at heart above everyone else's and expected nothing less as no doubt the interpreters were men.

"I do know what the Imam has taught us mum but I am not talking about the Koran, simply saying that Papaji expects far too much of us women and we cannot even say no to him. Hardly fair, is it?"

"That is enough, child. Go finish your chores now. I do not want to hear another word from you, understood?" Begum said sharply.

"Yes Mother," Raazia said reluctantly as she carried on with the chores, compelled to give in to the argument.

She stopped the chores suddenly and stood alone in one corner of the kitchen. As Raazia began to cry Allia came up to her. Seeing the tears rolling down her cheeks, she hugged her, offering comfort.

"Raazia don't worry, I am here. I will help you. We will get by somehow," said Allia, smiling, hugging her tightly. For Raazia a feeling of deep insecurity had set in. The seeds of doubt began to be planted firmly in her mind. Papaji's words describing the girls as 'his angels' began feeling decidedly hollow.

*

The week raced past like a flash. Abdel was to be circumcised by a priest in the morning. He cried a lot. Begum devoted time caring for him. Half-term break was nearly over with it being busy all week. Raazia hardly had time to enjoy the half-term school break. Daily chores looking after the family whilst Begum looked after Abdel ate away at the time. Papaji's planned celebration was only a day away. It was Saturday. He usually slept in, normally rising at about 11.00am. Not this Saturday. He was up early to greet the priest who had come to perform Abdel's snip. Raazia was in a rotten mood, having to wake up extra early to get everything done.

"Why Papaji could not have made the effort to get at least some items so we would not be burdened with heavy work I don't know," she muttered to herself loudly as Begum stepped into the kitchen. Raazia froze, seeing her mother there. Begum pretended she had not heard her remarks.

"Raazia I have the list for the food needed for the guests. Will you be alright in getting it? The list is in the dining room on the table," Begum said.

"Yes Mum, I have seen it and I shall ask Allia to help me."

"Good girl. Now is the milk ready for Abdel? He seems very hungry. I don't know if it is the cold weather or what but the boy drinks milk like a fish.

He wants milk every four hours."

"Fish drink water, Mum, I think, not milk," Raazia said as she sniggered.

They both laughed at the same time, breaking the tension from yesterday's contretemps between them. Begum hugged Raazia.

"I love you so much. You don't know how much I do Raazia, *betti*, do you?" reassuring her daughter.

Allia walked into the kitchen at that point, yawning and simultaneously rubbing her eyes vigorously. With her yawn still not finished she said something which neither of them of understood.

"Allia I did not understand a word you just said."

It made Begum laugh.

"Yes Mum, the milk is ready."

Begum took the bottle from her, gave Allia a hug and stepped out of the kitchen. It had been a long tiring week for Raazia, getting up at the crack of dawn every day to make sure everything was done on time.

"Mum was not going to listen to you, Raazia. I knew she would not. You were just whistling in the wind with her!"

"What does that mean, Allia, and where did you pick up that phrase from? I have not heard you use it before," she said, still feeling a little vexed about the issue with her mother.

"I heard my teacher use it at school one day. No one knew what it meant. This boy Kieran in my class put his hand up and said, 'Miss, what does that mean?' Miss said something like unsuccessfully trying to change something that could not be changed."

"Oh Allia, you are full of surprises. I have learnt something new today from no one other than my sister!"

"Raazia I do pay attention at school. I am not always playful you know, though most times people think I am dumb, but I am not."

"I know, take no notice of me. I am in a serious mood."

The cold February temperatures persisted. It was minus two degrees outside. From the frosty kitchen window, a layer of ice covering the rooftops could be seen. A cold, dark, grey morning it was. Raazia and Allia worked quickly to finish the regular morning chores together. Everything cleaned, tidied up, breakfast done, it was time to get ready for the shopping trip they both dreaded though there was no choice but to go out and get it done somehow. Begum was tending to Abdel when the two sisters went upstairs to get dressed.

As they got into the back garden, tiny rays of the sun were trying to break through the clouds. As they did, the ice glistened in the sun. Raazia was cold. She had donned several thick layers to keep warm. For Raazia it was a case of methodical planning. Allia on the other hand was busy staring at the list of things they had to buy.

"This is a long bloomin' list, sis. How we suppose to carry all this stuff home?" Allia asked.

Raazia opened the wooden outhouse door which made a creaky sound as she did, then she disappeared inside it for a few seconds. Allia stood there wondering what her sister was up to. Raazia pulled out a rickety old perambulator from the outhouse. It was dusty and covered in cobwebs.

"There! We will put it all in here, so we don't have to carry it!" said Raazia with a smile.

"Oh, pardon me with knobs on, sis, but who is going to push that thing down those icy pavements once it is full of groceries? Don't forget the slopes are steep too. I am not pushing that thing. Besides, people will laugh at us, Raazia," Allia said as she sniggered.

Raazia ignored her as she continued dusting the cobwebs off it. Allia stood there, arms folded, just staring at her.

"Are you just going to stand there gawking at me with that funny face of yours or you planning to help at all anytime today, Allia?"

"Erm... Do we have to buy all this stuff in one trip? It's not like a little amount that we can really manage in one go, sis, is it?" Allia said as she continued staring intensely at the long list.

Raazia did not respond. She ignored her sister's question and continued finishing cleaning the pram.

"There, *all* done," Raazia said.

"I am dreading wheeling that thing around, sis. We will not be able to control the flipping pram, Raazia. Just imagine what it will be like when it is fully loaded with things on it? Look at the bloody roads, they are all covered with ice."

"Allia, watch your language. Look, we will have to somehow manage, won't we? We don't have much choice here, Allia, do we?" Raazia responded sharply as by this time she was losing patience with her sister.

"I only said 'flipping'."

"Papaji does not like girls saying words like that or the word 'bloody' for that matter."

Raazia stood there staring at Allia with raised eyebrows. Arms folded waiting for a response from Allia who paused to think. There was a hushed silence for a few moments as neither spoke a word.

"Well okay, I suppose," Allia groaned, breaking the silence.

They went through the back gate, then via a passageway at the back of the houses heading towards the main street where the shops were. The cold frosty morning was unappealing. Pavements were as white as can be with a thin layer of ice making them slippery to walk on. The lack of brakes on the pram made its manoeuvrability difficult. Both of them had layers of warm clothing which though helped stave off the cold. It restricted the manoeuvring of the contraption, slipping at times on the icy pavements as they continued with their journey. Allia slowed down, gasping for air as she puffed out clouds of white air exhaled from her mouth. The rusty wheels squeaked as they pushed it. Almost out of breath, both nearly stopped but Raazia tried carrying on pushing. Heavy clouds of carbon dioxide expelled from their mouths repeatedly caused cloudy air veiling in front of their faces.

"Oh Raazia stop, stop, stop, it's no good, I can't go on. I am too cold," Allia said.

"Oh, Allia. C'mon girl, you can do it. I know you can. You can't quit on me now, please."

Raazia knew manoeuvring the rickety old pram through the icy streets was no easy task for the two teenagers as they were still about quarter of a mile away from Green Lane where they were headed. It had become a popular area for local businessmen who had set up shops catering for ethnic minority needs. Raazia was still trying to cajole Allia into mustering up energy to carry on as she was puffed out, though stopping to catch their breath helped. Whilst standing in one place Raazia thought to make use of the time to plan the logistics of the task that lay ahead. They agreed Allia would stop outside the shops holding the pram, whilst Raazia purchased the items when they got there.

Eventually they reached Green Lane. The plan worked very well. Raazia went into the shops, made the purchases, then asked an assistant to carry it over and place them inside the pram. Soon the street started filling up with people shopping as the time approached half-past ten. With many people milling around, the task of pushing the heavily loaded pram got harder. Both of them had to push hard every time more items were piled on. Raazia nearly tripped over outside one shop on an uneven pavement as they pushed the heavily loaded pram. As she tripped, she accidently bumped into a smallish, stout Asian man wearing the traditional *shalwar kameez and turban.*

"Mind how you go, girl, *batameez*," he bellowed in a harsh tone.

"I am sorry *sahib, maaf karna*," she said, walking away as the man continued to stare at her.

"Such nuisance these girls are, aren't they? Just look at them." Another stout Asian man going past made a passing comment too.

They ignored them as they walked on. A thin, scrawny, Asian lad came over to them.

"You young ladies look like you could do with a hand or two? Hahaha." He started laughing loudly.

He winked at Raazia. Unsure about his gaze, his real intentions, Raazia looked away. Allia on the other hand looked straight at him, grinning. She smiled at him.

"So you are our knight in shining armour then?" Allia asked.

"What?" the boy asked.

"Never mind," Allia responded swiftly.

"So what sort of motor is this then? I have never seen one like this before. You haven't got a baby in there as well have you?" he screamed with laughter.

"Are you out of you mind?" Allia said.

"Noh I am not, just having a laugh at your expense, ladies!"

"Oh *you must* be our knight in shining armour then?" Allia asked cheekily.

"A what?" the boy asked, shifting his woolly hat as he scratched the top of his head, looking decidedly quizzical.

"*Shukhria* but no, we can manage. My sister was just trying to be funny," Raazia replied, averting her gaze from his again.

"Well to be honest, ladies, it looks like you could do with some help, me thinks. What was that something in shining something you said?" he asked Allia.

"Oh, never mind."

"Well let me give you a hand anyways if that is alright with you, ladies?"

Allia looked at Raazia directly in her eyes, angelically holding the palms of her hands together and whispered, "Say yes, sis, please, please you know we could do with his help, Raazia. Please."

Malik Khan and Farzana's son Akeel was at the rescue. The Khans owned the local grocery store on Green Lane. Faizali was good friends with Malik. They had been acquainted from back home in Pakistan and had become close friends.

"Well all I can see is two young ladies desperately in need of a young handsome guy like me to help. Wouldn't you agree? Besides, it would not be right for me not to help, so go on, ladies what d'ya say? Don't take too long as the offer will expire soon. I will need to get back to the shop otherwise Dad will wonder where I am. The shop is getting busy and I will get told off for wasting time gassing with girls on't street. So, hurry up, girls, make up your mind quick! Okay, just wait here." Akeel went back towards the shops, poked his head inside the door of his dad's shop and shouted something. It wasn't audible. He returned shortly.

"Well stop gawking, ladies and c'mon. I take it the destination for all this nice stuff is your house aye?"

"Yes, home please," Allia responded.

"I am Akeel, and you are?" pretending not to know who they were.

The girls looked at each other and giggled. Raazia covered her head with her *dupatta.* feeling a little shy.

Allia kept up with Akeel, taking long strides, but Raazia purposely fell back a few steps behind them. He pushed the pram like a professional mother would do with a baby inside it, manoeuvring it past people but making sure the items stayed in the pram. Like a typical young teenage boy, the lad showed off his skill at controlling it with a quick burst of energy as he began pushing the pram faster as he went downhill using his feet as brakes. It squeaked all the way. Allia dropped back, her strides trailing way behind and Raazia was even further back from them.

"C'mon ladies, chop chop, walk faster?" Akeel said.

"Akeel be careful with those items, don't drop them as Papaji will get mad with us if they get ruined," said Allia.

Akeel slowed his pace by dragging both his feet, using them as brakes, pulling the pram towards him until he came to a halt to let the girls catch up with him.

"C'mon ladies, I have not got all day," he moaned.

Soon they were nearly home.

"So what's all this in aid of then? Are you having a party or somut, 'cos if you are hope you don't forget my invitation?" Akeel winked at them.

"Have you not heard the news then?" Allia asked.

"Noh, about what?"

"Well we have a little brother. Papaji has invited lots of people for celebrations on Sunday. Is Malikchacha not coming then?" Allia asked.

"Faizali Uncle has a son? Wow, that's cool."

"Yes, silly, everyone has heard. Papaji has literally told the whole wide world! Have you not heard then?"

"Well noh, not me I have not heard. I am too busy in the shop. I will be taking over the shop one day, you know."

Akeel was happy with the serendipitous invite. A chance to get to know Raazia and he for one was for sure not likely to miss the perfect opportunity. He smiled cunningly.

"Well I best be getting back to the shop before Dad sends out a search party. Can't stand here gassing all day with teenagers, I have work to do, you know?"

"Thank you for helping us, Akeel," said Allia as the girls disappeared through the creaky gate, into the back garden of their house. The gate door had been fixed with hinges that made it shut automatically.

"Bye Akeel!" Allia shouted from behind the gates as it slammed to shut position.

Papaji came into the back yard to see what the noise was about.

"Who was that?"

"No one special, Papaji, it was just a neighbour saying hello," Raazia said quickly before Allia could blurt his name out. Allia soon began taking credit for the idea as Papaji began to unload the items off the pram, congratulating them on a brilliant idea for transporting the items from the shop so diligently. Raazia went into the kitchen quickly to make *chai* for him. She made two sunny-side-up omelettes with *parathas* for his breakfast.

"Did the 'whatsit' go well, Papaji?" Raazia asked.

"Yes it did. Poor fellow, he just cried all the way through it. But he has settled down now and gone to sleep," he replied.

"Can't have been nice for him, Papaji, having his willy snipped like that, poor guy," Allia said.

"Allia it has to be done, you know that," he said sharply.

Begum popped in and out of the kitchen making sure all was well. Whilst Abdel slept, she spent time in the kitchen with Raazia and Allia. She helped the girls start preparing for the *pakoras*, chicken curry and *pilau* rice for the guests but later left to tend to Abdel when he woke up. As the cooking progressed the smell of fresh aromatic food wafted through the kitchen window through to the outside. People passing by the house sniffed, wondering what and where the delicious aromatic smell was coming from.

Darkness fell quickly. Preparation had taken up almost the whole day as time raced by. Raazia and Allia were completely exhausted at the end of cooking; so was Begum. Raazia commented later that her mother looked unwell to Allia and expressed she was worried about her. Allia seemed unconcerned as exhaustion was causing her to fall asleep.

Chapter 3

Sunday was a busy day for the Rehman family. It was around five o'clock in the afternoon guests started to arrive marking the start of the celebrations. Soon the house was packed with guests. As always tradition was observed; men were in one room, mainly the lounge, whilst the women gathered in the dining room. Gifts for Abdel piled up in the corner of the lounge. A whole bunch of unopened cards congratulating the couple were scattered on top of the pile of newspapers.

"*Salaam Alaiykum* and *janam Mubarak*." Several guests offered the couple congratulations as they came in through the front door followed by embraces. Papaji had a radiant glow all around him. You could see he was happy. The local *Imam,* Sheikh Ahmed soon arrived to offer his blessings to the family.

"*Mubarak ho Mubarak ho Bhaiji. May peace be upon you all and I praise Allah the all Mighty* for the wonderful gift of a son bestowed upon you. *He* is indeed the most generous one. *His* favour and the grant of *nehmat* is upon you today my *dhost* for which I cannot be more happier. *Insha'allah* (God willing) your family continues to thrive for many generations to come and I pray you all have long healthy lives," he said as he embraced Papaji.

"Ameen, ameen... *Maulana Shaahib,* a warm welcome. Please come in, come into our humble house. Have a seat," said Papaji.

Sheikh Ahmed began reciting verses from the *Koran.* The audience listened silently as the words of the Holy book enunciated in beautiful Arabic rhythm reverberated around the room and the house then proceeded to give a short sermon about Allah, about his *nehmat,(bounty),* his generosity finishing off by blessing the family, then ending with a request for all to recite the first *surah* of the Koran – *surah Al-Hamd* – to remember those who were no longer with us in this world but in the hereafter. There was a momentary silence in the room then the noisy, loud chatter followed.

"What a beautiful baby, *maa'sha'Allah,*" admiring Abdel as each woman held him for a few minutes then passed him around. He went from one woman to the next like a parcel, as in the 'pass the parcel' game. Abdel seemed to hate it soon started to cry. Raazia picked him up, making an excuse that it must be time for his next feed.

Akeel, when he arrived at first quietly sat with his father, Malik Khan. As he started to be a little more comfortable with the people around him, he began to fidget before getting up, moving around trying to spot Raazia. He weeded his way round through the crowd, making his way into the dining room. He smiled when he spotted her. Raazia was cradling Abdel. A perfect opportunity, he thought to himself as he could go see the baby. Akeel approached Raazia.

"Hello Raazia, you look nice in that dress. That must be your baby brother? He is cute."

Raazia nodded. Akeel's mother Farzana approached the couple.

"*Salaam alaiykum, chachiji*," Raazia greeted her politely.

"*Wa'alaiykum salaam, betti*," responded Farzana.

Akeel pretended to admire the baby, commenting how cute he was again, that he had striking features like his dad. Mother's instinct had kicked in immediately, telling Farzana her son had found the love of his life. She gazed at her son and could see that special glow about him.

"I must take him to Begum as he is probably hungry and needs feeding," Raazia said quickly, making an excuse to create some distance between them. Farzana knew at once. Akeel's nonchalant behaviour made it transparent that he liked her. The community gatherings were designed to give young people a chance to meet others from within the community which the elders encouraged. Straying to marry outside the community was risky for young people too. Often this would be testing, calling on the wrath of parents. Becoming a pariah and being excommunicated from the mosque discouraged them from marrying outsiders.

Raazia turned away, pulling herself a few paces away from Akeel and Farzana. Through the crowded room slowly she made her way over to Begum. The moment felt awkward for her. Akeel was on cloud nine, his heart missing a beat every time he had a glimpse of her. Allia had spotted Akeel speaking to Raazia and came over to speak to her.

"Raazia, did you know Aunty Farzana has gone looking for Begum? You don't think they are going to talk about you, do you?"

"Allia please don't you start again. I am feeling really stressed."

"Raazia I was only telling you what I saw, you know!"

"I know, sis, but you are right. Look, Aunty Farzana has gone over to talk to Mum. I know she will be talking about me."

"Ah yes, but they may be talking about anything. *You* know what these Asian biddies are like." Allia tried to comfort her sister.

Abundance of community gossip and good food whiled the cold evening hours away. People began leaving soon as it was getting late. Akeel and Farzana were the last to leave. Raazia started to tidy up. Akeel came over.

"Would you like some help cleaning? I am a good helper!" Akeel said.

"Thank you, that would be great."

Raazia was exhausted. All she could think about was collapsing her body on her lovely bed. It had been a long and tiring day for her; she was not about to decline such an appealing offer. The mess was chaotic – dirty plates, glasses, bowls, food, rubbish strewn everywhere. Akeel worked quickly, picking up the mess in no time. Farzana helped clear up too.

Within half an hour he had bagged up all the rubbish. He took a spray cleaner, a cloth and wiped of all the dirty areas, leaving them clean. It was an opportunity to show off his domestic skills, hoping it would appeal to her.

"Akeel is such a good boy, Raazia. Look how good he is with his hands. All that mess he cleared up in no time at all. Bless him, I don't know what we do without him. At weekends he spends all his time in the grocery shop helping his father. All the customers love him too."

"He has been good to us. Thank you, Akeel," Raazia acknowledged.

Farzana began extolling Akeel's virtues, going overboard. She knew most Asian women tended to do exactly that about their sons. Raazia knew why she was doing it too!

"*Auntyji* thank you for helping, and Akeel, you too. I really appreciate it," Raazia said.

"*Betti* it is my pleasure. Your mother would have done the same for me and we help each other out. That is what we are all about in our community."

"I shall bid you *auntyji* and Akeel goodnight. I have school in the morning."

"God bless you, my child. You help your mother so much at your age which is nice of you. Many girls these days don't. I bid you goodnight, my child," said Farzana.

*

Papaji and Begum, already retired, were upstairs in the bedroom.

"I am worried my daughter Raazia does too much work in the house. Her education will suffer, my dear husband. I want all the children to do well in their education. This country offers that facility and they should take full advantage, my dear," said Begum.

"Abdel I am sure will do well, *insha'Allah*. With girls I do not think it is so important. They will get married and will be homemakers so don't worry about them. Raazia can take care of most household chores from now on. It is not something to worry about as it is our traditions that matter. You just look after my – sorry dear – our son. He will carry the Rehman name after I have gone," Faizali said in a somewhat stern tone.

"I feel sorry for Raazia, having to burden all that responsibility on her shoulders at such a tender age. She is only a child still, you know."

"Fifteen years is old enough to be getting ready for marriage. She has to learn so it will help her. Talking of Raazia, I do hope Malik approaches us as his son seemed quite taken with Raazia I noticed. I had promised Malik many years ago when Raazia was born that if he had a son, I would be happy to seal the friendship into family ties."

"If it is meant to be, it will be. Akeel is a nice boy and he will make a good son-in-law," Begum acknowledged with a shade of reluctance in her tone of voice.

Faizali had dozed off to sleep; he could be heard snoring away. Begum tossed and turned for a while, unable to sleep. The cold night kept her awake, so too did secret arrangements that her husband had made with Malik about Raazia. It bothered her, but tired, eventually she fell asleep at around 2.00am.

It was 6:00am; Raazia's alarm rang. She turned sideways reached for the alarm clock to switch it off. The morning was cold, dark and dreary; staying in her warm bed curled up was an attractive proposition but Abdel was crying his lungs out. Everyone in the house was fast asleep. It was early Monday morning. Raazia prised herself out of bed half asleep, rubbing her eyes vigorously as she walked through the tiny hallway. She could hear Abdel crying. She entered her parents' room and picked him up from the middle of the bed. Both her parents were fast asleep. She covered him in a warm blanket, held him over her shoulders and went downstairs. She made the formula milk, tested it for temperature on her elbow before putting the bottle in his mouth. He gulped it down as fast as he could. Falling asleep in her arms, Abdel sucked the last drops of milk. Raazia then turned on the portable paraffin heater on in her room, then gently laid the boy on her bed next to Allia, covering him with a soft blanket. She went back downstairs turned the gas fire on then began getting breakfast ready. It was a school morning. Her sisters would be up in a couple of hours' time. Papaji would be up for 7.00am for work. Raazia got everyone ready for school. Allia walked her sisters to school. Raazia was the last to leave the house. Begum was fast asleep, so was Abdel.

*

It was 3.30pm; the girls returned home from school. They could hear Abdel crying loudly. Raazia thought him to be hungry, or needing a nappy change or both. She wondered why Begum had not seen to him. She went straight upstairs. Begum seemed asleep. Abdel was next to her blaring his head off. Raazia approached her mother quickly.

"Mother we are back from school. Abdel is crying..." Raazia shifted the blanket, Begum seemed cold.

"Oh my." She felt her face. It was cold. She immediately picked up Abdel from next to her, letting out a faint gasp, putting one hand to her face, the other holding the baby tightly. She knew. She tried to rouse Begum again but there was no response. Raazia hurried downstairs, told her sisters to stay downstairs, gave Abdel to Allia, whilst she put her coat on.

"Allia, just go feed Abdel. I will be back in a few minutes."

"Raazia where are you going? We are hungry," said Sara.

"Allia will make a sandwich for you. I will be back as soon as I can. Just stay downstairs."

"Raazia...!" screamed Sara.

Raazia ignored her sister, instead buttoned her coat up and headed on to Malik Khan's house to use his telephone to call for an ambulance. She returned back ten minutes later with Farzana to wait for the ambulance to arrive.

The ambulance crew attended to Begum. She was pronounced dead on arrival at the hospital by a doctor. Raazia went to the hospital with her mother in the ambulance whilst Allia went to Papaji's factory to fetch him whilst Farzana waited with the girls. Papaji dashed to the hospital in a taxi. He waited with

Raazia in the waiting area at the hospital. The minutes seemed eternal. A young English doctor wearing a white coat with a stethoscope hanging round his neck and shoulders came into the waiting area.

"Are you Mr Raaman?"

"Rehman is my name," correcting the doctor.

"Please can you come with me to the room over there and sit down, Mr Raaman. I am afraid I have some bad news for you. Your wife has passed away."

"What? That can't be. Are you sure?"

"Yes, I am sorry to say."

"What happened? She was fine this morning when I went to work. Are you telling me she has gone? How? I don't understand."

"Mr Raaman, unfortunately your wife, after giving birth to your son last week failed to have a placental expulsion done. Mrs Raaman's blood poisoned her body after the birth as the placenta remained in her womb for some time. I am afraid she died this morning. I am so sorry for your loss," the doctor said.

"I do not understand this, Doctor. How can this be? It cannot be possible. It can't be surely? This makes no sense to me, sir."

"I am very sorry for your loss. You may go see her. She is in the side ward there if you wish to see her." The doctor got up and left the room at this point. His brief was clinical. Papaji was in a daze, bewildered, not wanting to believe this terrible incomprehensible news. He muttered the words, "*Inna lilla hey wa inna ilaihey rajeoon.*" (To him we belong and to him we truly return).

A young English nurse in a blue uniform approached him. Raazia was standing by his side with her hands on his shoulders, comforting him.

"Papaji what shall we do?"

"I am so sorry for your loss," the nurse said. "Your wife is in that room over there if you wish to see her. I can tell you if it is of any comfort to you that she passed away peacefully. She is in a better place now."

They both entered the room where his wife and Raazia's mother lay still on a bed. She looked as though she was peacefully sleeping. The room was quiet but clinical, only punctuated by the horrid smell of hospital bleach. Both Faizali and Raazia sat with Begum, holding her hands, each side of the bed for a while. Tears flowed. The whole thing seemed surreal. One moment he was next to her in bed the night before and now his wife had left this world? He could not fathom the situation. "She is in the world hereafter," he kept muttering to himself.

Raazia was grief-stricken too though she seemed to hold her composure quite well. Faizali kissed Begum's forehead first then stood back in silence for a minute next to the bed, his head bowed where she lay. He bade his dear wife farewell for now. Raazia broke down and cried throughout the journey back home in the taxi. Faizali held his daughter tightly close to him. When the taxi driver enquired if all was well Faizali simply shook his head without replying.

They arrived home ten minutes after leaving the hospital to be met by his friend Malik who was waiting anxiously outside the house for news of

Begum. Malik knew from Raazia's distressed state it was not going to be good news.

"My dear friend Malik, Begum has gone," he said.

"What do you mean gone?" Malik asked.

"She has left this world, my friend. She passed away this morning. She was pronounced dead at the hospital, my dear friend."

They both embraced. Faizali was overcome with intense grief as tears began rolling down his cheeks. Malik tried to console his friend.

"*Sabar,* my friend, *sabar,*" (Patience) Malik said as he continued to comfort his friend in his embrace followed by the words, "*Inna lilla hey wa inna ilaihey rajeoon.*"

Both continued embracing each other. The next task for Faizali and Malik was to assemble the girls to speak with them about the tragic death of their mother.

"My dear children, I don't know what to say to you all, but your mother today departed from this world. She has left us. *Allah* today in his wisdom decided to take her in his arms. God bless her soul. I do not know what happened, but it must have been *Allah's* will to take her from us and you my children must now be very brave indeed. Raazia, *betti,* you are the eldest in the family and I am truly sorry to burden you but you must take charge in the place of your mother in looking after your sisters and your brother now."

Malik stood next to him with one hand resting on his shoulder as he spoke to his children. The girls began to cry and wail loudly. Papaji embraced them all at once.

"My dear friend Faizali, I will call the mosque and let Sheikh Ahmed know. You don't have to worry yourself about anything. I will take care of the funeral arrangements."

Chapter 4

Wednesday about 11.00am, a long black hearse pulled up a few hundred yards outside from the house. Pallbearers disembarked and stood still in line by the hearse. They waited outside the house for some minutes before the pallbearers began slowly pulling the coffin out. A crowd soon gathered outside the house, standing in silence to pay their respects. A sombre, poignant moment had gripped the street. Amongst the crowd a couple of elderly English gentlemen, both bespectacled with grey hair, stopped outside and stood still, heads bowed in silence. Their peaked capped hats held in their hands, the two stood side by side like on Armistice Day. It was a cold, windy morning. One old guy's tuft of hair blew to one side, exposing his bald patch in the middle of his head. He carefully grabbed it with his fingers, embarrassed, and a little slowly with the palm of his hand placed it back in place, returning his hand behind his back, holding his hat.

The pallbearers slowly pulled the coffin out of the hearse and brought it out carefully, carrying the coffin inside the house and laying it in the front room. The women inside the house began shrieking, wailing loudly with grief. The girls' cries were intense, filled with pain and sorrow at the loss of their mother. The coffin lay in the front room of the house for an hour with people walking past the coffin paying their respects to Begum. Then it was time for her final journey to her resting place to begin.

Faizali knelt by the coffin looking at the angelic face of his wife with tears streaming from his eyes down his cheeks as he said his final goodbye to his beloved Begum. Malik stood next to him with his hand on his shoulder. Sheikh Ahmed led a short prayer. As he finished the pallbearers then closed the coffin lid, slowly carried it out of the house then hoisted it up in the air upon their shoulders. Each bearer, side by side, locked their arms on the shoulder of the person on the opposite side, giving the coffin a firm, sturdy balance. They stood for two minutes before the slow march began. The mourners chanted '*Laillah ha illalallha Mohammed un Rasoolullah*'. The pallbearers continued on until they reached the rear of the hearse then slowly placed the coffin inside on the runners, sliding it into the hearse. The mourners continued chanting, followed the hearse as it proceeded down the street. They followed the car to the local mosque. The religious rites completed, the funeral cortege moved on to the next stage of the process with a ride to the cemetery. The crowd continued chanting '*Laillah ha illalallha Mohammed un Rasoolullah*' right to the end until the last grain of earth covered Begum's grave.

*

Spring of 1972 dragged for the family. Begum's untimely departure had left a gaping void in the Rehman household. Then the summer days seemed eternally long and blisteringly hot. Bright summer flowers were in full bloom. Trees were covered in fresh, thick, green foliage. The smell of fresh summer flowers permeated the air everywhere. Raazia's loss was as intense within her as the summer's days were hot. Abdel was growing up fast. Sara entertained her brother as he often played in his cot. She would wind the mobile. Abdel would kick his legs in the air and wave his hands about, making gurgling sounds as the mobile spun round overhead.

Raazia missed her mother most. She had missed many school days in the spring and summer terms since her mother's death. Begum's death had left all the girls with the feeling of emptiness and in a state of prolonged bereavement. Raazia, Allia, Sameena, Saleena and Sara were most times left to fend for themselves with Papaji coming home late most nights from work and prayers. Papaji lent no support to the girls, physical or emotional. Household chores took priority for Raazia. Approaching sixteen years of age, Raazia was compelled to take on the mantle of a full-time housewife looking after her four sisters and her baby brother Abdel, simply becoming mother to her siblings, including the baby, and slave to her father. It was not a life she had mapped out for herself. It became a life of drudgery at such a tender age for Raazia which Begum would not have wished for her first born, but became inevitable due to her untimely death. Raazia's thirst for education had to be bottled up. Her ambition to be a primary school teacher ruined. Her dream destroyed forever with her mother gone. A dream shattered by circumstances of events, trapping her like an animal caught up in the teeth of a metal trap. She knew it would not be long before Papaji would arrange marriage for her.

*

It was the last day of summer term. The girls arrived home happy and smiling for the first time in many months. Allia came over to Raazia who was asleep in the lounge. An open book rested on her chest. It was titled *Shattered Dreams*. She picked up the book, turned it over and read a passage from the page where the bookmark was placed. It read:

'My total life lay in ruins. My dreams of choosing a husband for myself, a life-long partner shattered in one blow when my father one day announced he had chosen a husband for me. I could not breathe. I cried upon hearing the dreadful news. My life was gone, I kept thinking aloud. How can I have lost control of my own destiny? I had hitherto loved my father. I had respected him. He, I thought, could do no wrong to me. I was after all his sweet cherub as he used to call me. Can it be true that he would do such an awful dastardly deed to me? Yes, to me? He was my idol. Someone I respected very much. I looked up to him as a role model in life. A man with impeccable manners, taste for freedom, but alas no more...'

Raazia woke up. Allia closed the book, making sure the bookmark stayed in place at the page where she had left the book open.

"You guys home already? What time is it?" she asked as she stretched her arms out.

"Three thirty in the afternoon. *Baji,* stay there. I will finish off whatever chores you have left," Allia said, smiling.

"I need to start making dinner," Raazia said, shooting up from the sofa.

"No you don't. Not today. We are going to give you a break from working so hard over the last few months, Raazia. You have just taken over from Mum. It's hardly fair. You have missed school and the CSEs," Allia said.

"Thank you, my dear sister. God knows how I need a break. I am so tired. These past months have been hard for me, taking Mum's place. I don't think schooling is something I need to worry about now! All the plans I had, and dreams have gone, Allia."

Raazia's eyes filled up with tears. Huge droplets started to roll down her cheeks. Allia took a hankie, wiped them off her cheeks. She embraced her sister.

"What about your dreams of becoming a schoolteacher, Raazia?"

"What do *you* think? There is no chance of that now, Allia. I am stuck. I don't blame Mum, but Papaji, *I do* blame. I almost hate him now for putting Mum through all this. He wanted a son. I hope he is satisfied as he has got one now but look at the price Mum paid. We lost our mother, Allia, for his selfishness. Look what's happened to us. Not only are we orphans but I have become a slave. Day and night, I curse him."

"Don't torture yourself, my dear *Baji.* It's not worth it. We will find a way. There must be a way. Nice book, by the way. Don't read it anymore please. It is a sad book."

"You have read it?"

"No, just a few lines of the page you had stopped at."

Raazia hid the book under a cushion.

"There is no other way. The next thing that will happen is Papaji will marry me off. I can see it."

"Like the girl in your book?"

"Yes, exactly like her! Whilst I do not want that to happen to me or any of you, I am afraid it will happen. It is our destiny. Forget about dreams. Whilst I crave *you,* all my sisters, do well to get educated, alas, it will not happen. This is why I work so hard here at home so you can all go to school. It's not easy for us girls, you know. Bloody traditions, I say," Raazia said for the first time ever using a swear word. Allia was taken aback.

"So you sacrifice yourself for us?" Allia said.

"Yes, don't you see it? Allia, each one of us will get married off to some Tom, Dick or Harry who comes along. Papaji will choose them for us, you will see. It will not be our choice, I can tell you."

"*Hai Allah*, you mean *gorah* lads? Array I prefer, Akeel, Shabbir and Moonaver myself." Allia laughed as she spoke.

"Huh, Allia don't joke. This is serious. We are trained to be domesticated deliberately so we look after our husbands and the in-laws. We are girls. We are expected to comply with our culture."

"*Hai ray Allah mein marjaoogi*. What a cruel world this is."

"Allia, don't joke. This is no time for that and don't ever say that," Raazia rebuked her sister sharply.

"C'mon, let's all go to the park today, *Baji*. It's a lovely day. It would be a real shame to waste it here in the house. Look how sad the house is. We all need a break anyway from this sadness and sorry state we are in. We can take Sameena, Saleena and Sara too. *Auntyji* can look after Abdel today."

Raazia agreed reluctantly, though it was a good idea. Allia was absolutely right. She packed some sandwiches, drinks and crisps to take with them to the park. The afternoon sun was high up in the sky. It was a hot, scorching afternoon, the sun beating down hard. Young kids rolled about in the park with their mothers watching them carefully as they played. A group of young teenagers played football, kicking the ball around, shouting to each other instructions as they did. The liveliness of the park cheered Raazia up. She smiled as she watched people looking happy as they lazed about in the beautiful summer's afternoon. It made her feel alive again. Life gradually crept back into her lethargic mind and body, hearing sounds of play and laughter all around her. A group of Asian teenage boys in another part of the park played cricket. Some people sat with their bare feet in the water cooling down in the heat, others simply enjoyed the slow, dry breeze in their faces as they rode along in their boats or catamarans.

"It must be around thirty degrees Celsius today, Allia. It is really hot," Raazia said.

"It must be. Let's put the mat down here in the shade. It looks like a nice spot to sit under this tree here. Let's just enjoy watching the world go around today."

Raazia smiled. She and Allia laid the mat on the ground for them to sit on.

"It is lovely to see you smile, Raazia. I have not seen that lovely face smile for months now," said Sameena.

Sameena, Saleena and Sara stood up and joined hands together. They held hands as they sang primary school songs.

"Look at them, Raazia. They look happy. We should do this more often. It is up to us to make life for us. I wish Begum, I mean Mum, was with us but sadly she is not. Life has to go on for us, Raazia. We have to cope without her, but you cannot do her job, Raazia. It's not right. You are not even sixteen yet. Let Papaji sort these things out. His family is not your problem."

"Allia I know but it is easier said than done. You are only ten and I do not think you understand how things work. It is such a beautiful day, Allia, let's not think about this right now. I just want to enjoy this lovely afternoon with us all being together here in the park."

Allia held Raazia's hand, looked at her and gripped it tightly. They both smiled. She then rested her head on Raazia's chest. Raazia ran her fingers through Allia's long, soft, black hair, continuing the strokes.

"Mum used to do that to me, Raazia," Allia said softly.

Raazia carried on running her fingers through her hair for a while, as both silently watched kids playing noisily, people strolling about slowly catching the hot sun. The place was alive, mostly young school kids celebrating the end of the school term, lazing around in the park looking forward to the long summer break. Some stretched out on the grass lazily. Tired of sitting in one place Raazia, Allia, Sameena, Saleena and Sara held hands as they walked around the park slowly just like others enjoying the afternoon sun. As they walked Sara spotted an ice cream van. A long queue of people patiently waited to buy ice cream. Ice cream cones seemed popular.

"*Baji* can we please have ice cream, please?" Sara asked in an angelic tone.

Raazia could hardly say no.

"Yes, of course you can, petal."

"Yay!" Sara said, delighted. Raazia had enough money on her to buy all her sisters an ice cream cone each. She spent her last twenty pence change left on an orange lollipop for herself. Allia knew there wasn't enough money so her sister settled for whatever she could afford.

"*Raazia* you have the ice cream cone; I will have the orange lolly," said Allia.

"No, dear sister, you enjoy it. I am happy with what I have. It tastes yummy."

The delicious sweet taste of ice cream simply melted in the mouth. Sara had ice cream all over her face which made them all laugh. The ice cream was loaded with sugar. It helped release endorphins in the brain. A nice moment of euphoric happiness pervaded them much to Raazia's delight. She had forgotten what it was like to feel happy, to be a child again, a nice feeling which made her forget the drab life at home.

Papaji was already home, much to Raazia's surprise, when the girls returned from the park. Raazia was unsure why Papaji was home early. Suddenly she was filled with a horrible feeling of dread inside her. Fear gripped her. She began feeling regret.

"The decision to go to the park was a mistake, Allia. I had a feeling, almost a premonition, telling me not to go. Allia, Papaji is at home," she whispered. "What do we do now? I have not cooked for him. He will get mad with me," Raazia said in a frantic tone.

"Raazia don't worry, just tell him the truth. What can he do to you?"

"Raazia, *betti,* can you come here? I need to speak with you." He summoned her sternly.

Raazia put a *dupatta* from around her neck onto her head, covering it partially. She approached Papaji slowly with trepidation. He asked her to sit beside him. Her stomach churned with fear. She clutched her tummy as she sat down next to her father. Papaji stood up from the seat, closed the door to the dining room, came back and sat down beside his daughter. The girls gathered in the dining room by the door in a bunch like rugby players in a scrum, pushing forward trying to listen behind the door. Allia was the strongest and closer to the door, pinning her ear to it, trying hard to listen to the conversation.

"I wish I could be a fly on the wall right now," Allia whispered.

"Papaji it is such a nice day. It was the last day at school for Allia, Sameena, Saleena and Sara. I thought it would be nice to take them to the park. I can cook now. It will not take too long. It will be ready very soon. I did not expect you home early today."

He put one hand on her shoulder. With the other

he put his flat palm out towards her like a stop sign, shaking his head simultaneously. Raazia fell silent. Papaji's posture was enough signals for her to say nothing more. She could see the lines on his forehead surface. A moment Raazia dreaded. A deafening silence had descended in the room for some seconds which seemed like as long as the summer's hot day. Raazia waited anxiously for the punishment about to be meted out. She was almost on the edge of her seat waiting for the pronouncement of the sanction.

"*Betti* I have been thinking these past few months about our situation. How hard you have been working to keep us all going." He paused for a moment.

Raazia could hardly believe what she just heard. She looked incredulous, finding it hard to believe that he had recognised her hard work over the months. He continued.

"You will, *insha'Allah,* get married soon. I need to think about the family, especially Abdel and who will care for him."

Raazia looked at him quizzically as he eased up on the aggressive posture, relaxing a little in demeanour. Raazia was almost expecting a rebuke from him about going to the park.

"Erm..." he continued. "This is not easy for me. I mean, what I am trying to say is that family back home in Pakistan have found someone for me to marry. This will help our situation here. No one, I can tell you, will replace your mother, I promise you that, as *Allah* knows I loved my dear departed Begum completely, but I have to make hard decisions about what is the best for the family now she has gone."

Raazia's stomach muscles almost instantly relaxed at hearing the subject of his conversation with her. She stopped clutching her stomach as Papaji stumbled for the right words to convey the full message. The feeling of fear suddenly ebbed away. She exhaled air slowly from her mouth, covering it so as not to show her relief.

"You are flying out to Pakistan?"

"Yes."

"When?"

"Tomorrow."

"As soon as that, Papaji?"

"Yes. I need you to pack some things for me as I shall be away for three weeks. I have booked a holiday at work. My employers were good about it."

"Yes, Papaji. I will see to it straightaway. What about Abdel?"

"I have made arrangements with Malik and Farzana. They will be looking after him and you girls whilst I am away. Farzana aunty has agreed to look after him as well as keeping an eye on all of you girls too. If you need anything just ask her. Malik's family has been good to us. I am very much indebted to him for helping us over the months during our difficult times. I am on my way out as I have lots to do. I shall eat at Malik's house tonight as I have a *dawaat* to eat there. Here, get some fish and chips from the local chippy tonight for you all. Just make sure the packing is done for me."

"Yes, Papaji," she said as Raazia took a £1 note from him.

Raazia's stomach muscles completely relaxed; she called out to Allia and her sisters. They rushed out of the room like a torrent of water gushing out of a broken pipe.

"Raazia, I thought he was going to be angry with you about going out today for not having the food ready for him. What a relief, Raazia," Allia said.

"You guys have been eavesdropping? Shame on you. Anyway I thought so too, Allia. I was shitting myself thinking I was in trouble. But imagine my relief when I knew he was not angry! My heart was racing at one point. I could feel my heart pounding away in my chest as I waited to see what he wanted to see me about."

"Raazia just think, he is away for three whole weeks. It will be like a holiday for us."

"What about when he gets back, Allia? There will be a stranger here in the house. *Sowtelli Maa, boothoo*, a stepmother here living with us in this very house and taking Mum's place. Have you thought about that? She will be telling us what to do and what not to. I will hate whoever it is for taking the place of our mother," Raazia said.

"Look, let us worry about that later, Raazia. For now, can we not enjoy the time we have without him being here? Besides, who knows? She may be nice," Allia said philosophically!

"You, my sister, are a truly an optimist, an odd one at that, funny at times I have to say, but I love you for who you are, Allia," Raazia said.

Chapter 5

What a glorious three weeks the girls had whilst Papaji was away. They spent most of the time lazing around during the summer of 1972. It was virtual freedom. There were no restrictions apart from when Farzana visited. Household chores were left undone an hour before Farzana visited which was usually around three in the afternoon. There was no pressure on them, no one to tell the girls off, or if the chores remained undone it did not matter to anyone. Daily routine was out of the window and it was the most enjoyable time ever. The only time good behaviour was necessary was when Farzana popped in to check in on them. She brought Abdel with her when she visited. Any other time was time to let their hair down. It was a fantastic time for them.

"I wish we could live like this forever," Allia said.

Time had rolled on and Papaji's return was dangerously imminent. It was a Sunday evening in August, a taxi pulled up outside the house. Papaji disembarked from it with a woman stepping out of the car next after him. Papaji had opened the door for her. The woman was in her late thirties, dressed in traditional Pakistani clothes adorned with gold jewellery. Papaji came into the house with his new bride.

"*Salaams,* my girls, Papaji is home," he announced.

He had both his arms up in the air like he was waving at someone.

"Papaji is home," he declared again. "Come and give me a big hug, my lovely angels. I have brought gifts for all from back home. Let me first introduce you to my dear wife and your new *Amii,* Fauzia. She is now your mother and you must all treat her as our own. Do you hear?"

"Yes Papaji," all but Allia replied.

Papaji did not require an endorsement from the girls, but the position was asserted from the very start. "Come girls, introduce yourselves to your mother. I want you to make her feel at home as this is her home now."

The tone used almost felt like a stern instruction. The girls responded apart from Allia. They took it in turns making their introductions with *Amii* starting with Raazia.

The words '*I want you to make her feel at home as this is her home now*' irked Allia. Here was a total stranger in *their* house taking *their* mother's place. Allia for one would try and resist. Her refusal to come forward was dissent not looked upon favourably. Allia protested in her own way. She would not accept it. The mood turned icy. Raazia feared Allia's dissention would not go down well with Papaji who asked her again, this time in a slightly sterner tone, but Allia remained resolute in her refusal. The atmosphere tensed up even more. There was silence in the room. Raazia did not know where to look. A sudden pain in her head gripped her. The veins in her temple started pulsating. They began throbbing as Allia continued to refuse or acknowledge her stepmother's presence.

"Raazia my dear, are you okay? You look a bit off colour, *betti*," Papaji asked, breaking the minute-long silence.

"Oh I am fine, Papaji. I just have a headache. It has been hot this summer. I have not been sleeping well as I was worried about you."

"Oh *betti,* you know your old dad. You don't have to worry about me. We should be okay now as we are a complete family again."

The words irritated Allia even more. She was not her mother. Allia simply sat on the sofa arms folded with a glum face.

"Allia, *betti,* you need to come and introduce yourself to *Amii*," Papaji said softly this time.

"I am not introducing myself to *her*. She is a stranger in this house as she is not my mother."

"Get up off the sofa and come here. You have been taught manners, haven't you? Get up and do the right thing Allia!"

"Oh Faizali dear, don't worry about that now. I am sure she will come around soon. I know she will just give her time. *Bachay hai naa?* Where is the baby?" Fauzia enquired.

"Do you mean our brother Abdel?" Allia asked sharply.

Raazia elbowed Allia on her left side which Fauzia pretended not to notice.

"Yes, my dear. Who else is a baby in the house?" Fauzia responded with a smile.

"Well Sara is a baby in the house!"

"I am not a baby, Allia!" Sara shouted back at her sister.

"Come, come, girls that will be enough of that. Allia I shall speak to you later. I shall go and fetch Abdel from my friend Malik's house. His *bibi* has been very kind enough to look after him whilst I was over in Pakistan," said Papaji.

"*I* will be going up to my room now and I would like you to bring my bags up for me, girls. Allia you can carry the large one, dear."

As she disappeared into the stairwell area Allia imitated her catwalk-style walk, letting the long *dupatta* on her shoulders trail behind her.

"Allia you are going to get us all in trouble. Stop this tomfoolery at once. Please be serious about these things. Papaji catches you doing that he will have your guts for garters," Raazia whispered.

"I can't help it. Besides, I don't care. Have you seen her *chal*? Oh my god, she looks so bloody pretentious. A bitch if you ask me."

"Allia shush, you are not helping yourself. This is not a joke, you know Papaji will not be happy with you. He has already said he will speak to you later. If he ever hears you say things like that, he will skin you alive," Sameena said.

"Where are my bags, girls? Did I not say to bring

them up?" Fauzia shouted from the top of the stairs. Raazia and Sameena quickly got hold of the bags and the two of them dragged the luggage up.

"Can't she do it herself, the cow?" Allia muttered.

Some minutes later Papaji returned home with Abdel in his arms. Abdel was screaming his head off.

"Where is *Amii*?" he asked.

"Upstairs," Allia responded, pointing her finger up towards the ceiling.

At which point Fauzia appeared through the door.

"*Salaam alaiykum,* my dear, here is the boy Abdel. Isn't he the most handsome boy you have ever seen?" he said proudly, showing off his boy to her.

There was a long pause from Fauzia.

"I knew you would be speechless when you saw him. Handsome chap, isn't he?" said Papaji.

Allia rolled her eyes. Apart from Abdel still crying loudly, the awkwardness of the situation was evident. The girls knew Fauzia would not by choice want to look after someone else's children, but by marrying Papaji she had been left with little choice. She may loathe her husband's children as unwanted 'baggage' but she had inherited them by virtue of marriage. Abdel at least was hers to care for whether she liked it or not.

"Oh my dear husband." Breaking the awkward silence, she continued, "The flight was so long. The journey was so tiring. Besides, I cannot stop thinking about those hideous customs people wanting to check my entire luggage, can you believe? Oh, it was a real nuisance," Fauzia said, changing the subject as she sat down wearily on the sofa with one hand on her forehead, the other on her chest, pretending to look decidedly troubled.

"Yes dear, I was going to object to the shocking treatment but sometimes it is best to exercise some caution with these officials as you never know with them, how they will react. They seemed the type very much that you stay silent as it is the best way, and you cross the street to the other side when you see them coming towards you, never mind a dark alley," Papaji said.

Allia could not contain herself listening to the two of them engaged in what seemed to her a hideously funny conversation. She knew Fauzia was putting on an act. She burst out laughing loudly. Papaji turned around and looked at her sternly.

"Oh, did you not see? I had to open all my bags. I could have died of embarrassment. The cheek, I say. Seeing those *gorah* men going through my lovely clothes, touching them with their vile filthy hands was unbearable. I could have fainted. It was such an embarrassingly unpleasant experience for me. *Chee chee chee* it was horrible to see them touching my beautiful clothes. I simply nearly died when they were going through them! I ask you, do I look like a drug smuggler to you?" she said rhetorically.

Papaji was shaking his head sympathetically, acknowledging the complaint.

"What a cheek treating me like a common criminal when I was new to this country. Anyhow I am here now. Here to stay too for my sins!" letting out a false laugh, "I am sure the girls will look after me. Won't you, girls? It will be lovely having five girls all fussing round me. I have never had that luxury before, I have to say," she said sarcastically.

She paused for a second and turned her head to the side with a bobble, glancing straight at Allia who had her eyebrows raised in total disdain at the comedy acting she had just witnessed. Fauzia looked at her with piercing eyes then turned her head back, looking at Abdel before sitting down again.

"I am fine now that I am here with all you lovely people, especially your lovely charming children you have *maa'sha'Allah*. The boy seems to be an adorable treasure, my dear, looks just like you. He has your eyes. He surely takes after you, Faizali dear."

"That sounds like a wolf in a red dress," muttered Allia with one hand on her mouth.

Then she almost puked. Her tummy churned seeing Fauzia's obviously false acting. Allia could not stomach any more of the pretentious garbage spewing out of Fauzia's mouth. She got up in disgust, walking out of the room. Raazia's fear was her sister's behaviour had not gone unnoticed, though unchallenged for now. She knew she needed time to adjust but Allia had gone about it the wrong way, Raazia thought. Her obvious belligerence towards her stepmother was not the right thing to do. She feared Allia was taking fate in her hands.

"I am so sorry my dear, but you know we are in a foreign country. We have to abide by the laws here. I am sure my girls will look after you well," Faizali said.

Raazia reserved her feelings to herself as did the others, apart from Allia, learning fast the art of diplomacy. Raazia thought about the possible positives of having a stepmother. This woman she felt might not just take the pressure off her daily tasks but relieve her from the daily drudgery so she could get back to her education she craved for. Allia was different. She was direct. Her instinct told her this woman would turn out to be despicable, making their lives a total misery not to mention unbearable. This did not bode well for them.

Chapter 6

The seasons changed fast; summer months melted into autumn then winter. The dark nights were endlessly long, cold and dreary. Papaji was happy with his new wife. In fact, he was fonder of his second wife than Begum. His display of affection towards Fauzia was more obvious. Some days when he arrived home after work or evening prayers, he would bring with him a bunch of flowers, nicely wrapped too. Gave her boxes of chocolate which she would not share with anyone, but she just took them to her room. Often, he would bring two boxes of *mithai* sweets, one for her and the other for the family. Fauzia did not share her gifts with the girls. Allia thought he was fattening her up for another boy. "She has had two boys, I bet that's why Papaji is doing it. She is obviously fertile for carrying boys," Allia muttered a few times in a joking fashion.

Raazia could not ever remember him displaying such romantic affection towards Begum and if he ever did Raazia never noticed. It was not even random but Faizali made sure it was at least once a week. She knew how to please him. Looking after his only son was something, she gained brownie points for from him. She occasionally cooked special food for him. She made sure he knew it was especially for him as it was made with her own fair hands. Allia was a precautious eleven-year-old commenting to Raazia, "Well *sis* you know what they say – the old adage, 'the way to a man's heart is through his belly'. I think definitely works a treat for her."

She knew how to control him. Fauzia's relationship with the girls was one of ambivalence. She pretended to like them when Papaji was around, but she hated them, especially Allia. Allia did not let up. Fauzia found her behaviour challengingly unruly. She was not used to such impertinence. Back in Pakistan she would have used corporal punishment to bring her in line. Slowly Fauzia was getting a grip on the girls as she became more confident of her husband's trust. She was cunning enough to show affection for the girls when Faizali was around the house, showing him her caring side, but when he was not there the reality was different, she mistreated them. Conflict between Fauzia and Allia continued every single day unabated. Fauzia had a perfidiously dark side to her.

Fauzia did not do housework as a rule. She would only do a bare minimum to show her husband she was domesticated and a good wife. Most times she made the girls do the household chores. Cleaning and cooking chores had to take priority over school homework too. Allia was often vexed as Fauzia took credit for the work the girls had done, telling Papaji when he returned home how busy she had been all day keeping the house clean and taking care of the children. The dynamics of the Rehman family had changed completely since Fauzia had taken Begum's place. It was like the scales were slowly tilting in Fauzia's favour.

Another dark side was that Fauzia harboured grudges. Vicious treatment was beginning to be meted out sometimes. One afternoon Raazia was in the kitchen cooking food as normal with Allia giving her a helping hand. Raazia was making chapattis. Allia watched her sister as she rolled them into shape, making them as perfect a round shape as she could with relative ease. She had perfected the art of making *rotis*. She used a thin wooden rolling pin to shape them. She continued making them at some speed. She rolled each one then with her flat palm she flung it on a hot *taava*, using a cloth to press them as hot air filled up inside. They puffed up every time much to the amazement of Allia. She made it look so easy. The art of using a rolling pin to shape the flat bread on a board had come naturally to Raazia. In no time she would have a stack of about twenty-five to thirty *rotis* placed in a neat pile in a steel container.

"*Baji* how do you get them shaped so perfectly round, the same size too and so quickly?" asked Allia.

"There is some dough left over. Why don't you try?" Raazia asked.

"Okay, let me try then."

Allia took the dough in her hand; using the palms of her hand she rolled it into a ball then placed it on the wooden board. Then using her fingers, pressed it flat. She sprinkled flour all over it. Using the rolling pin she began to roll it but it turned out long and shapeless.

They both giggled looking at it on the board.

"Allia that looks like the shape of Africa to me, you know. You are meant to make them round, not like that!"

At that very moment Fauzia happened to walk into the kitchen, discovering Allia's weakness. It delighted her. Finally, she discovered her *Achilles heel* that she could exploit to her advantage.

"Come on Allia, let me see you make that *roti*. C'mon, don't make me wait and ask you again," Fauzia taunted her.

"I will finish off here, *Amii*," said Raazia, taking the rolling pin off Allia.

"No, I did not ask you, did I Raazia? I want to see Allia finish the last *roti*."

Allia tried but it did not shape up. Fauzia grabbed the rolling pin of her hand. She struck Allia three times on the back of her legs with it.

"You *Kootee* (bitch)! How can you not know how to roll *rotis* at your age? I learnt how to make perfect round *rotis* when I was only eight years old. And you had the audacity to make fun of me when I arrived here. Well who is laughing now, huh? Don't think I don't know you have been imitating me either! You are a disrespectful little bitch. You will learn how to behave properly, my girl. I will see to it that you do now."

Raazia intervened. Her desire was naturally to protect her sister but as soon as she did Fauzia pushed her away. The jolt caused Raazia to fall to the ground, banging her head against the cooker. Allia was screaming with pain and continued crying loudly. Fauzia dropped the wooden pin on the floor, walking out of the kitchen muttering words in Urdu.

"And wash that bloody rolling pin before you finish making the *rotis*!" she hollered at them.

Raazia got up off the floor, pressing the top of her head gently with her left hand, nursing the bruise on her head. By this time Sameena and Saleena had come into the kitchen, hearing the commotion. Raazia had tears rolling down her cheeks, trying to ease the pain by slowly massaging her head. Allia stopped crying. She took a bag of frozen peas out of the freezer and put it on her sister's head. The four sisters sat on the cold linoleum floor hugging each other.

"Do you remember that hot summer's day you came home from school on the last day of term, Allia, and we all went to the park?"

"Of course, Raazia, I do. I can never forget that day."

"You forced me to go to the park. All of us went that day," Raazia said, wiping the tears off her eyes then Allia's.

"I do. Wasn't that a perfect day, sis?"

"Yes it was, Allia. Perfect. Too perfect, in fact, I knew it would not last. What a shame we have come to this now. Why do such horrible tragic things happen to us? Is God punishing us for something? Why has this happened to us, Allia? What have we done? We are only children."

"Shsssh... dear sis. God is Merciful. Sheikh Ahmed has told us many times. We can tell Papaji about the mistreatment we suffer at the hands of this bitch, Raazia, can't we? I just cannot bear it anymore. Day after day she makes us do housework which she is supposed to do. She really treats us like slaves. I hate her. She is such a pretentious cow; sweet in front of Papaji but an evil bitch when he is not here."

"Oh my dear Allia, she will hear you, keep your voice down as she will exact revenge. She has obviously not forgotten that first day when she came to the house with Papaji. You had the guts to challenge her. None of us did apart from you. Maybe we should have. I don't know anymore. In any case there is no point in telling him. Fauzia has already worked her magic on him to the point she has blinded him. It would be pointless telling him now. He will only side with her. We need to be careful. We are going to have to put up with this tyrannical bitch."

"Raazia it's not fair, is it? I feel like Cinderella cooped up inside the house all the time working my fingers to the bone."

"Allia you are always dramatic with your words. I know. Please be patient. I pray to Allah the Almighty each day to help us. Come, let us finish off those dreaded *rotis* before she comes back."

They all smiled. Raazia gently held Allia's cheeks and squeezed them.

"You gorgeous little numpty. C'mon, let's practice on those *rotis* and finish off, shall we? Show that witch the Rehman girls are made of sterner stuff."

Chapter 7

December of that year came and went by like a flash. Christmas for the family was not a celebration time as it was not a Muslim religious event. Papaji certainly would not allow it to be celebrated. Raazia could not figure out her father's hypocrisy. He had gone out especially on Christmas Eve to buy Fauzia a bottle of perfume as a gift for her which Raazia had to wrap for him. The girls wanted to get into the festive mood as schools were shut for Christmas holidays. It was exciting time for them as good films were on the TV and they wanted to watch. Raazia had bought the 'Radio Times' which had a two-week programme schedule. They all sat around the table looking through, marking it, circling the programmes each preferred to watch. It was something they were looking forward to, staying up late and having popcorn whilst watching TV, but Papaji did not allow it. The Rehman household had to keep to the routine; daily prayers, reading the Koran before going to bed he kept saying was far more spiritually beneficial than watching 'Shaytan' as he called the television. Papaji was obsessed with religion to the point it was crazy, but he had double standards. It was alright with him that Fauzia often stayed up well into the early hours watching television. The girls began to question their father's ethics, fairness and his belief, if they were true or fake.

February 1973 was special for Faizali. Abdel was a year old and celebrating his first birthday was all he could think about despite the first anniversary of Begum's death approaching, being days away. Abdel was his pride and joy, after Fauzia of course! Faizali organised Abdel's birthday party. He gurgled with laughter when Papaji held him up in the air with his arms. He loved blowing the candle out on the cake; he shrieked with laughter when the camera flash went off again and again as guests took pictures of the toddler. Raazia had made a Yogi Bear shaped cake with one candle in the middle. She got lots of compliments from women who admired the cake. It was shaped like Yogi Bear with a white collar, a black nose made of marzipan and icing sugar. It tasted so delicious that most of it was gobbled up in no time. Abdel's face was a pretty sight. It was all covered with cake and mostly icing sugar. He looked a real picture. It was a memorable birthday for the Rehman family.

Raazia, Allia, Sameena, Saleena and Sara enjoyed the day too but for them it was tinged with sadness as Begum was not there to see it. For the girls the day's merriment was momentarily a happy one. It made them forget the harsh days which had become part of their daily lives.

7th February 1973 was Begum's first anniversary and surprisingly Faizali did have a memorial service in her memory at the local mosque. The day began with the family visiting the cemetery where Begum was buried. Fauzia did not come. Raazia laid flowers on the grave. Allia recited a poem. Sameena, Saleena and Sara arranged some red carnations in the pot by the headstone. Faizali stood at the grave and recited a *surah* from the Koran.

20th February 1973 was Raazia's sixteenth birthday. No formal birthday celebrations were planned for her, unlike Abdel's day. Papaji had not believed in ever having birthday celebrations for the girls. He would say it was *'fazool kharch'*, lavish and unnecessary. Raazia could not figure out quite why but that day she had an odd feeling all day long. It was something she could not quite understand but a premonition of something that would happen to her that would change her journey in life. Sure enough, she was right. That evening, there was an unexpected gathering at the house. Raazia felt a momentary elation that Papaji had arranged a surprise birthday celebration party for her. A surprise birthday cake would be arriving for her. Papaji was dressed in his new clothes, looked preened and well presented with his new *Shalwaar Kurta.* So was Fauzia. When Malik, Farzana, Akeel accompanied by his two younger brothers, Bilal and Amjjad, arrived the premonition became a reality. They all sat in the lounge. Papaji for a change had turned the heating up on the gas fire to warm the room, making it comfortable for the guests.

As always it was a cold, dreary February evening. Raazia was in the kitchen with her sisters making tea for the guests. Papaji walked into the kitchen. It was her birthday. He wished her *Janam Mubarak* first, then asked her to go get dressed in the new clothes he had bought for her which he had put in her room. Raazia obliged. She looked radiant in her new red outfit.

"Raazia, *betti,* come into the lounge *when* you are ready."

"Yes Papaji, I will be there shortly, just give me a couple of minutes please."

Raazia went over hugged Allia first, then Sameena, Saleena and lastly little Sara. All the sisters came into the room together holding hands. Fauzia pulled a face and sniffed with her nose but Papaji smiled when he saw Raazia dressed up looking beautiful. Akeel's family sat on one side of the room on the long red sofa, Papaji and Fauzia on the chairs on the other side of the room. Abdel was on the floor playing with his toys. Papaji stood up as Raazia walked into the room pretending to wipe a tear from his eyes with a clean white hankie. He motioned Raazia to come closer to him. She obliged. He held his daughter's hand as he made his announcement speech.

"Raazia, *betti,* come sit here with me. You all know it is our tradition that we make promises when our children are born. That way we keep our traditions alive. They are as strong today as they were long ago. The promise we make to family or friends are our children's *rishta*, which weave the fabric of our community and most importantly our way of life, setting us apart from others. I made a promise to my *dear* friend Malik when Raazia was born. I am so happy to say I can fulfil that promise today made to him sixteen years ago. I promised him that if he had a son that my first-born child's hand in marriage would be given to his son. Malik accepted that promise. Your *rishta* was sealed then and I gladly discharge that promise today. We cement our friendship, not just family ties by bringing Malik's family to our family, creating strong bonds by marriage, but keeping our traditions alive. Raazia will, I am sure, be a wonderful daughter-in-law for his family. She will be a good wife to his son Akeel too."

Everyone in the room cheered hearing the speech. Allia sneered and walked into the kitchen.

"*Mubarak ho, aap ko, Mubarak ho.*" People in the room shouted congratulations. Abdel sat up and clapped his hands, mimicking people clapping. It was a rare spontaneous baby moment that was so funny it caused a roar of laughter in the room. Akeel could not keep his eyes off Raazia; at the same time he had that quaint grin on his face. He made contact once as Raazia glanced at him. He looked into her eyes and smiled. She smiled back with half a smile but then immediately looked away. Akeel was tall, slim but gangly. He had quite a few well-ripped red spots on his face which made him look like a teenager and geekish. He had short black hair and wore gold-rimmed spectacles. Not physically unattractive though. Raazia displayed little emotion towards her future husband.

"The wedding will take place in two months' time," announced Malik. He placed his right hand on her head and said, "I am a proud father today. I cannot tell you how happy I feel that you have agreed to be my daughter-in-law, *betti*. You are a wonderful girl. The Malik family welcome you as our own daughter into the family. I might add I am as happy as the day Faizali came to me a year ago to share the news of the birth of his son."

Raazia had not herself agreed to anything, least of all marriage at the age of sixteen, but it was not a surprise to her. Her mother had been married at the age of fifteen. "It is tradition," Begum used to say. "Girls marry at a young age so they can have babies early." Malik embraced Faizali as they congratulated each other. They sat down together on the sofa indulging in traditional 'horseplay', feeding each mouthful of *mithai,* trying to get as much in the opponent's mouth as possible as Akeel's brother Bilal took pictures of them on his Canon A-1 camera. The families chatted as they celebrated the engagement of Raazia to Akeel. Farzana had come bearing engagement gifts for her new *bahoo,* daughter-in-law. She brought with her a heavily embroidered *shalwar kameez* dress suit with a twenty-two-carat gold bracelet and matching gold bangles for Raazia. She went over, sat next to her, embraced her first before handing them to her.

"Here, my *beautiful bahoo,* these are for you. You have made me so happy today. I say that as very proud mother too."

"Thank you, *auntyji,*" Raazia responded quietly, nodding at the same time in acknowledgement her appreciation for the lovely gifts. She pretended in her head they were birthday presents, as she never had any given to her. This made her sad, having to pretend. More poignant was Begum's absence at her momentous occasion which caused Raazia to sob loudly. How she would have loved her mother to be there to see this celebration even if for her it was premature and not something she wanted. Nevertheless she would dearly have loved to have Begum there.

"*Array betti oodaas naa ho, aaj khushi kaa din hay. Begum tow firdos may hey haaj. Ooper sey dekhti hongi. Bahot khush hongi naa betti? Inkee laal Raazia kaa beeiah honaywala hey. Aajaaw mere pass duaa kurty hoon inkaylia or sub kaylia jo naa ho eesee dunya sey chayley geeyay ho.*" (Don't be sad, your mother Begum (God bless her soul) is in the highest heaven today looking down on you, smiling, very pleased to see her daughter going to get married soon. She will be so happy for you. Come here, let us pray for those who have left us from this world.)

Farzana's emotive words, apart from Fauzia, Akeel, Sara and the baby, had left not one single dry eye in the room. Farzana beckoned Raazia to come over to sit closely next to her. She placed her hand on Raazia's head and said.

"You have always been like a daughter to me. Bless you, my child, you *will* truly be my daughter now. I look forward to that very much. Akeel is my *laal* and *putter*. I am sure he will make you happy. You can call me *Amaaji* if that is okay with you, *betti*?"

Raazia nodded.

From the other side of the room in the far corner where Allia sat on the floor playing with Abdel, she glanced across at Fauzia who was throwing daggers at her but with a grin on her face. Allia's giving everyone a hug except Fauzia in front of her guests was the ultimate rudeness. Allia had done it deliberately. She knew Fauzia was planning something for Allia when Raazia was out of the way. From the look Fauzia gave her Allia knew troubled times lay ahead for her.

Later that night the girls were huddled together upstairs. Allia was in a bit of a mood, not with Raazia, but Papaji for giving her sister and best friend away so soon. She sat on the bed quietly which was highly unusual for her.

"What is the matter with you, Allia?" Raazia asked.

"This is not fair, Raazia, Papaji should at least have asked you if you were happy to accept Akeel's proposal of marriage. I know I was messing around that day when Akeel helped us with getting the things home, but you are only a child like me still. He has taken it for granted that you will be happy with all this," said Allia sharply.

"My dear sisters, believe me I have no choice in the matter. You heard him. My *rishta* was sealed when I was born. I dare say when the time comes neither will any of you have a say. It will just happen like it did to me today. He will do exactly what he has done to me. If you fight against it, he will only blame you as this will bring dishonour to the family. They will protect this honour with their lives. Dishonour is a curse," Raazia responded.

"I will run away, and no one will find me if he does this to me," said Saleena.

"Oh Saleena, I wish I could tell you different. You are the gentlest, most graceful and beautiful of us all. I don't mean to be unkind to Allia, Sameena or Sara. But it is true. You only have to see how people look at you when they see you. I do hope very much you will be able to pick a husband of your own choice. I hope it happens for you, dearest Saleena. Don't dishonour your parents as otherwise you will pay dearly."

The girls sat holding hands for a while in complete silence until they fell asleep.

Chapter 8

It was spring of 1973. The trees came alive after a bitter cold winter for the second year running. It was a beautiful sunny morning that greeted Raazia as she drew back the curtains on her wedding day. She had struggled to get out of bed as her hands, arms and feet were covered in henna. Most of it had dried, peeling off her skin – flakes of henna were scattered everywhere. Raazia smelt lovely though. The fragrance from the henna permeated all around her body as well as her room also. Her sisters woke up one by one as the sunlight flooded into the bedroom, each one rubbing their eyes vigorously.

"The room smells nice. Raazia you look very beautiful," Sara said, continuing to smell and sniff at the same time as she absorbed the fragrance of it in her nose.

"Thank you, little sis, you want to see my *mehndi*?" Raazia asked.

"Yes please," they all said in unison, now fully awake by this time.

"Aaaaa... it looks lovely. I want it too," said Sara.

"You will have this when it's your turn, baby, but don't be in a hurry to grow up," said Raazia.

Raazia had bright orange henna patterns painted on her hands, arms and feet. She looked beautiful, truly like an Indian bride. She wore a long white dress at the civil ceremony which was at the local registry office in Leicester, attended by the bride and groom's families with a few select invited family friends. Later on at the *nikah* ceremony (the vows) in the evening at the local mosque, she wore a red and green *garrara* with a gold-coloured top adorned by heavy pieces of gold. As part of the bride's ensemble she wore gold bangles, a heavy necklace, earrings that dangled, a *Matya Tikka* which she found awkward as it swung from side to side as she moved her head, and gold anklets with bells which jangled as she walked. The henna patterns on her hands, arms and feet completed her as a bride. Akeel wore traditional clothes expected of a Pakistani bridegroom picked by his mother. He wore a long, shiny *Shervani, Kurta*, bottoms which seemed to be uncomfortable for him on account of them being tight fitting, too snuggly for his liking, and to complete, as part of a groom's ensemble a turban which had a veil made of fresh flowers, draped over his face. The *nikah* ceremony was a brief one performed by Sheikh Ahmad, the local Imam at the mosque.

Raazia's departure from home the next day was heart-wrenching not just for her but especially for her sisters. She was leaving home for good, a home that she had known for all her life, and now she was saying goodbye to it. It was a profoundly tearful, intense moment for her sisters. They clung tightly to each other in an embrace. She would no longer be there to protect them. It was a final poignant moment for her at what had been her home for some years. Raazia was separating from her family for good. Her family gathered outside the house, as did the people from the local community, to see her off. They sang traditional songs in Urdu, serenading the bride's departure. Allia and Sara clung on to Raazia as tightly as they could. They did not want to let go. Papaji had to literally peel them off her.

With Raazia's departure, the status quo in the Rehman household was about to change, a moment Fauzia had been waiting for. It had arrived sooner than Allia expected it would. Worn out from the previous day, Allia pulled the duvet over her head the next morning, closed her eyes as she was snug in her bed. There was no school on account of Whitsun break. Suddenly the duvet was pulled off her. A cold burst of air surrounded her waking her up.

"Get yourself out of bed, you little bitch. Raazia is here no longer for you to laze around in bed anymore. The chores your sister did still need to be done. It is your job from now on to take care of them. No time to waste. Now get on with it!" Fauzia yelled at Allia.

Allia was trying to get out of bed. Her sisters looked on silently as Fauzia, arms folded, stood menacingly by the bed waiting for her to get out. Allia just about managed to prise herself out of bed.

"This is not fair…" Allia began protesting.

"No? I will show you what is fair. You are a lazy cow. For protesting, the rest of you girls can get out of bed too. Go downstairs and learn from Allia as your turn will come too. Make the beds first before you go downstairs!" Fauzia hollered.

Sameena, Saleena and Sara quietly made the beds before they made their way out of the room.

"And no bitching, might I add, about me either, when you get downstairs, as I can hear what you girls say about me."

Like a slave, Fauzia made sure Allia did all the household chores. Housework was hard work which was bad enough. She now knew how Raazia felt as she too was made to miss school most days. The days she was at school she dozed off in class from sheer tiredness. Her schoolteacher, Miss Jones, attempted to speak to Papaji on the telephone a few times about Allia's education being critically damaged if she continued to miss school, complaining to him that when she was there she usually fell asleep at her desk. Papaji listened, appearing to be sympathetic, nodding his head in agreement. But his agreement seemed perfunctory only. Just before retiring for the night the same day Papaji spoke about it to his wife.

"Fauzia this afternoon Allia's teacher telephoned me. She said she was missing school a lot and when she was there, she was falling asleep at her desk. It was not acceptable. Do you know why?"

"Dear I do not know why that girl pretends she is so tired all the time. I have been keeping Allia home some days to help around the house as I simply cannot manage by myself. Abdel is growing up fast. He is hard work to look after by myself as well as doing all the housework. I need her to help."

Papaji agreed as it was important. Abdel's needs were priority; the subject was closed.

The chores seem unending. Allia got up around seven every morning. She attended to Abdel's needs first, changing his nappy, clothes, then feeding him followed by getting Papaji's breakfast and his packed lunch ready. Then breakfast for Sameena, Saleena and Sara before they left for school. Fauzia had a habit of rising from bed around ten thirty every morning. Her daily breakfast comprised of fried eggs and freshly made *parathas*. If her breakfast was cold, she would chuck it in the bin. Allia's patience with her stepmother was about to run out when one morning Fauzia opened the dustbin lid and threw the contents of the plate away.

"Make some more fresh breakfast for me as I am not eating it cold," Fauzia said sternly.

"That took ages to make, it was perfectly fine. Why can't you like normal people just warm it up? It's not hard. Besides, why do you waste all the food?" Allia protested sharply.

"You have never liked me from the moment I stepped into this house, Allia. Well I do not like you either and so, now we have got that straight, you have your place, don't you?" she retorted sarcastically.

Though arguments between them were frequent, Fauzia's bellicose nature was unrelenting. Allia stood resolute. She consistently refused to call Fauzia *Amii* but '*Sowtelli* bitch' much to Fauzia's annoyance. Allia hated Fauzia intensely. She used to be a funny and jovial child but lately her development had been restrained, perhaps transformed into an angry child.

Four years dragged. For Allia it seemed like a life sentence as time moved on so slowly for her. Then she approached her sixteenth birthday. She remembered her sister's words about being married off at sixteen and a husband being chosen for them. She cared not one iota about that as the only thing she could think about was getting away from her parents. One night she happened to be on her way to her room. She stopped, being drawn by some loud chatter, almost sounded like an argument, coming from Papaji's room. Her natural curiosity made her stop. She crept up to the door to Papaji and Fauzia's room. She gently pressed her ear against the door.

"Fauzia dear, Allia is almost sixteen and we need to think about getting her married."

"Oh she is still not ready to marry, my dear husband. She can't even make proper *rotis* yet. Give her time. I will teach her, and she will get a good husband in time I am sure."

Allia whispered, "Bitch," and muttered to herself.

"Tradition is tradition, my dear. The girls always get married at sixteen. Any older, the chaps tend to shy away," Faizali said raising his voice.

"Very well, dear, as you wish, but I tell you that girl is not ready. You should see the shape of her *rotis*. They are absolutely shocking."

Allia smiled as she walked to her room. "*Yes,*" whispered to herself as she closed the door behind her.

"What was that, Allia, did you say something?" asked Sameena.

"No, just talking to myself as usual, you know

what I am like. Go to sleep now," Allia responded. Allia was not a religious girl. She certainly did not believe in praying. Her predicament of mistreatment had ebbed away her faith. That night was different. She prayed hard to Allah. She raised her hands, knelt on her knees and whispered.

"Please Allah, I know you know I am not a fan of yours. I am sorry about that. Sheikh Ahmad said one day that he believed that you were merciful. You have a big heart, and I do in my way think you are there. But not only are you there, you also listen to your subjects. I am sorry, I meant believers. You are just when you decide upon the sanctions or mercy you shower upon us, I have been taught by Sheikh Ahmad. So please let Papaji have his way and let him find me a husband quickly. Thank you, Allah."

Allia slept like a log that night. She did not have to wait long to find out if her prayers had been answered. She was married to Sajjid Abbas, a man eight years older than her, within two months of that conversation taking place between her parents, in a very simple wedding ceremony with a handful of guests. There was no resistance from her to the arranged marriage, contrary to her previous belief of wanting a choice in the matter. Marriage cannot be any worse, she thought to herself, than being a slave at home. Getting away from Fauzia was priority. It was the best thing ever. In particular the last four years of hardship endured by Allia was unbearable to her. Her husband Sajjid was not someone particularly of good looks. But he was a tall, simple caring man, sharing many of her jovial qualities with a pretty good sense of humour. She was sixteen, her husband twenty-four, but to her the age difference did not really matter. Allia's married life in fact turned out to be a blessing for her. Marriage for her was surprisingly freedom, a blessing and a form of escape she had longed for since Raazia's marriage. Unlike Raazia, Allia broke all ties with Fauzia and Papaji once married immediately. The scars of abuse suffered as a child over many years were raw to the extent that they were hurtful. This was a moment primed to her advantage. She would cut the apron strings with brutal force if necessary, to show her disgust with them, for they were scars and memories not easily removed, forgotten or erased. She thought to her own self that she would rather be estranged from them than be pretentious. She remained bitter with her parents, refusing any attempts at reconciliation no matter how hard Sajjid tried. To her it was the future that mattered, not the past which she preferred to forget.

Sameena stepped into Allia's shoes for a short while until she married Faraz Khan in 1979. Sameena's marriage, like her sisters' before her, was an arranged marriage at the age of sixteen. Unlike Allia, Sameena's good nature and understanding of complex family relationships helped as she remained in touch with the family. Sameen's husband Faraz was twenty years old. Rather a handsome man. Her day was completely perfect. Even Fauzia seemingly enjoyed Sameena's wedding. She had a tear in her eye as Sameena departed from home. Allia attended her sister's wedding but did not speak to Papaji or Fauzia.

Saleena celebrated her sixteenth birthday on 1st December 1980. She turned out to be the beauty of the family of all five sisters. Her nature matched her beauty too. She was kind, considerate, compassionate and most generous. Whilst Fauzia had shown at times extreme jealousy of her beauty, Saleena did not allow herself to project her beauty overtly. Her modesty was the key to her existence. She dressed in simple clothes, hardly ever wore make-up, often donating her meagre pocket money to charitable causes rather than using it on herself, often ensuring she complimented Fauzia, *Amii* as she called her step-mum, on having a flare for nice clothes which suited her. Such compliments made sure she enjoyed a relatively harmonious relationship with her stepmother. Fauzia enjoyed being showered with compliments especially from someone as beautiful as Saleena.

From about the age of ten Saleena involved herself in raising money for different charitable organisations. Her favourite was Help the Aged. After school she would visit elderly folk nearby, keeping them company and helping out with small household tasks, particularly at Christmas time. At fourteen she would attend a local soup kitchen at the local Christian St Barnabas Church nearby. In winter months she helped serve bread and soup to the homeless and hungry which she found immensely fulfilling spiritually. At school she took the lead on charitable events, raising money for a number of different charities.

Papaji almost daily received phone calls from parents of sons who wished to have her hand in marriage. Saleena had hoped the variety of interest may just allow her a choice in picking her husband. It did not. The decade may have been the 1980s, but traditions were timeless, they could not be eroded for Papaji. Timeless traditions were quintessential. They had to be maintained. As was expected of him Papaji chose the man for her. He picked Nawaz Khan for her who was twenty-eight years old. He was a six foot four inches tall man with a slight pot belly, supposedly a businessman from Manchester. Papaji had aspired to be a businessman himself but never had the courage to take risks in life to do it. Saleena found Nawaz to be repulsive when she first saw him on the first day, he and his family arrived to meet her at the house. To Papaji Nawaz was a businessman which would elevate his status in the community. People would look up to him, he thought, and so *he* was a perfect match for his daughter.

Saleena's wedding day was a bleak, cold Sunday in January 1981. It rained all day, completely ruining the day. It was evening as she was about to leave for her *nikah* ceremony at the mosque, but the weather was unkind to her. Whilst Saleena looked beautiful and elegant Indian bride the rain ruined her red and white *sari* dress.

Nawaz was a self-employed taxi-driver making just about enough money to get by though he projected an image of a rich businessman. He was a perfidious man who had pretended to be wealthy only supplementing his income from nefarious activities dealing in heroin. He was rather a big man physically. Nawaz had three brothers, all younger than him – Bilal, Adam and Azad. Azad was the same age as Saleena. The first night was rough for Saleena. She had not expected Nawaz would be like an animal in his carnal desires. As the days went by, she discovered Nawaz had a real unhealthy and voracious sexual appetite. For her it was painful and distasteful. After a few months of marriage, she began the habit, once he was done, of leaving the bedroom and showering before sleeping in the spare room. Nawaz hardly noticed her absence next to her in bed. He neither cared nor expressed any opinion or disapproval for that matter.

His family appeared supportive on the surface but Saleena had detected early on in her marriage that they kept their distance from Nawaz. His brothers were friendly towards her, respecting her as their sister-in-law. At times Azad expressed feeling sorry for Saleena, warning her to be careful, to remain guarded of his brother as he was not what he had made himself out to be. She did not explore the nature of this warning further as she had not known him or the family long enough to trust him. Azad once expressed hate for his brother, calling him a 'buffoon', 'a fucking drug dealer who was a waste of space'. Nawaz went over and whacked him hard on his head, punching him in the stomach. It was clear Azad intensely disliked Nawaz. He clearly knew about Nawaz drinking alcohol and dealing in drugs, information he must have shared with his mother. Azad did not converse much with Nawaz after that incident.

Amaaji had shared her thoughts with Saleena one day whilst in the kitchen cooking that once Nawaz got married, he may settle down, grow up and change his bad ways. *Amaaji* could not do much as she was crippled with osteoarthritis which had caused her to give up work at the age of forty. *Abbaji* had retired. His passion was cricket. *Amaaji* called him a cricket fanatic. All he ever did, rather annoyingly, was talk about cricket. Unlike Papaji, he was not a religious man, certainly did not go to the mosque every day, nor pray. His passion in life was cricket.

Amaaji at first came to see Saleena every day during the first few weeks of marriage. She lived within walking distance of the house. *Amaaji* was a short, five-foot-tall but dowdy woman, in her mid-fifties. She had a few black hairs but greys almost covered her head. Her hair was often not brushed. She wore traditional clothes which often looked shabby. Small gold-rimmed spectacles sat firmly perched on the bridge of her nose. She spoke very softly. Conversations between *Amaaji* and Saleena were mostly about cooking food. One day *Amaaji* revealed she had an unhappy life herself. She had married at a very young age. Bore four boys during marriage, worked in a factory making socks from the age of sixteen, then at twenty years of age discovered she had osteoarthritis which as time went by became debilitating, finally forcing her to give up work at the age of forty. She revealed she took indomethacin tablets for the condition. She shared with Saleena that the drug had become ineffective. Her body had become immune to the drug as it had stopped responding to her condition. She complained the drug had ruined her digestive system, causing her to have eating problems. *Amaaji* stayed with Saleena a few hours a day at a time. Though *Amaaji* taught Saleena some of her cooking methods, Nawaz was not keen on eating *rotis*, rice and *shabzi* which Saleena liked very much. Nawaz often ate fast food, burgers from McDonalds even though they were not *halal*. Sometimes he would bring food home, turn on the TV, eat then fell asleep leaving the television on all night. The rubbish would be left strewn in the lounge for Saleena to clear up the next morning.

Saleena, since her childhood days, always had a habit to retire early at night. About 9.00pm was her ideal time. She looked forward to reading her favourite Mills & Boon romance novels before falling asleep. It became routine for her. Nawaz often started his day late every morning then preferred to be out late most nights, usually returning around midnight. By the time he returned home Saleena would have long been asleep. He took things for granted. Often, he would simply walk into Saleena's room wake her up to have sex, claiming it to be his 'right', a wife's obligation. He was a man. He had a God-given right, being superior to her. She hated this horrid and disgusting habit of his. She hated also the fact he ate *haram* food, drank alcohol, smoked weed in the house. She hated his ideology of being superior over women. She was not his property.

On many occasions he had some of his friends round the house, much to her annoyance, who did much the same, smoked weed and consumed large quantities of alcohol in the lounge. The next morning the house would be in a mess, empty beer cans and takeaway food wrappers strewn everywhere. Saleena used to try and clean up before *Amaaji* arrived at the house. Despite opening all the windows one morning the stale strong smell of takeaway food and alcohol lingered on in the house. *Amaaji* could smell it when she arrived. She made 'sniffing' sounds with her nose like a dog. She would cover part of her face with her *dupata,* trying to avoid the smell of it. The smell was rather pungent but *Amaaji* said nothing to her son about his habits, much to Saleena's annoyance. She just helped Saleena clean up if Saleena had not finished by the time *Amaaji* got there.

After a couple of months *Amaaji* started to come less and less, then one day she suddenly stopped coming. Her arthritis had got worse. One morning she telephoned Saleena sounding tearful.

"*Salaam alaiykum betti*, it is *Amaaji* here."

"*Waa alaiykum salaam, Amaaji.* Are you okay, *Amaaji*?"

"I am unwell. My arthritis has been playing up. I was up all night last night in excruciating pain. Today I just cannot bend my knees. I am so sorry *betti,* I cannot make it to you anymore. My pain is getting worse. I am finding it difficult to cope with everything I have to do so I am so sorry."

"*Amaaji* it is perfectly alright. You don't have to apologise. It was good to have your company. Look, don't worry, I will be fine. You need to look after yourself. I shall come over to help you. *Khudda hafeez, Amaaji.*"

Saleena got dressed as quickly as she could and went over to see *Amaaji*. The house was in a mess. The front room was littered with items everywhere. Cups and dishes were piled up high in the kitchen sink. The furniture had that distinct acrid smell of Chinese takeaway food. Empty crisp wrappers left everywhere, particularly behind the sofa. Apart from the mess everywhere the house was decently decorated. There were lots of pictures of some players of the national Pakistani cricket team which were hung everywhere in the lounge. She recognised two of the players, Imran Khan, an all-rounder, and Abdul

Quadir who was a leg spin bowler famously renowned for his wrist-spin 'googly' bowling action.

Amaaji was lying down downstairs in a foetal position on the lounge sofa massaging her knees when Saleena got there.

"Salaams, *Amaaji.* I was so worried about you when you called me. How are you feeling?"

"It is very cold today and my pain is bad. I cannot move at all. I am so sorry I could not come," she said.

"*Amaaji* it is quite alright. You don't have to trouble yourself to come over every day. Don't worry yourself unnecessarily as I am fine. Would you like a cup of nice *chai*? Have you had your tablets today?" Saleena asked.

"I have but it's no good. They don't work anymore."

"Why don't you go see your doctor, *Amaaji,* and ask if you can have a change in medication or something stronger?"

"I have been a hundred times, *betti,* it is no good. He does not have any solutions. Just says I can go to hospital for injections. I have had the injections before. They work for a few days but afterwards my joints go very stiff once the effect has worn off. It is just putting up with the pain until it is my time to go. I cannot wait for my eyes to close permanently. I have had enough of this pain."

Saleena did not know how to respond to that, though she felt sorry for her. *Amaaji* looked so sad. Saleena sat next to her on the edge of the sofa slowly pressing and massaging *Amaaji's* hands, legs and knees. The gentle massage helped ease the pain a little. She closed her eyes and fell asleep. Saleena gently threw a blanket over her to let her rest. Then she tiptoed into the kitchen. As she began tidying up the mess her father-in-law walked into the kitchen, greeting Saleena. He was a tall, thin man. Leathery skin hanging off his neck, a short grey beard which was cleanly cut and shaved round it.

"*Salaams, betti,* thank you for coming and helping today. *Amaaji* has not been well. It is a great thing that you are here to help."

"I will try to help, *Abbaji,* if I can. Now, would you like some *chai* and breakfast?"

"That would be nice. I shall have some *roti* and *shabzi* that was left over from last night if you could just warm it up for me please, with a very strong cup of *chai* with two sugars. I shall take it in the dining room."

Saleena then heard the small television come on but could not quite make out what was on as the volume was low and inaudible. He closed the door between the dining room and the lounge as *Amaaji* was still sleeping.

"Will there be anything else, *Abbaji*? I shall make some food before I go."

"No, *betti,* this is fine, you carry on."

Some hours later *Amaaji* woke up. Saleena sat with her, chatting whilst *Amaaji* had some freshly made *rotis* and *shabzi*. The conversation was dry. She talked about her pain all over her body, how she was fed up of it and craved relief from it. Saleena sat next to her quietly listening as *Amaaji* described in detail how debilitating her condition was, that she was progressively getting worse and wanted to die.

"*Amaaji* how about if I took you swimming say two days a week? I know water can be really therapeutic."

"No, no, that is not for me. I feel shy having to go in public like those women on TV on the beach do. It is not me."

"*Amaaji* you don't have to dress like them, we can get some decent swimwear outfits for you," Saleena said laughing.

"No thank you, *betti*. That is for *goreyhs,* not for me. We have to keep our bodies covered, you know."

"*Amaaji* at least think about it, please? It will help with the pain."

She nodded reluctantly. Saleena left the house at around midday. As she walked home, she thought about her mother-in-law, the pain she was in and the hard life she had as an Asian woman. Saleena was in good health. She quietly thanked Allah for being blessed with health if nothing else. She showered first when she got home then sat down on the sofa in the lounge pondering about how difficult life was for women. Poor *Amaaji,* she thought. A woman who has had a hard life having to work for much of it, bringing up a family at the same time, now her arthritic condition has made her virtually immobile. The worry of it all must have aged her faster than she deserved. A son like Nawaz did not help either. He was a real brute, a painful burden and a worry for any parent turning out the way he had. Saleena felt it couldn't have been easy for *Amaaji*. It couldn't have been easy for her worrying about him. Someone so ungrateful that hardly deserved any sympathy at all from anyone, least of all from his own mother. She became depressed thinking about it all. The future for women looked bleak. She thought about her own mother Begum. Her life was tragically cut short. All she did was housework and rear babies. She picked up the phone dialled Raazia's number. Raazia was not at home so she dialled Allia's number.

"Allia, it's me, how are you?"

"I know it's you, Saleena. I am doing well, sis, and it's lovely to hear from you. How are you?"

"I just came back from *Amaaji's*. She is not doing well at all. I will have to go help her every day, I think. I don't of course mind, but it looks like I am going to be used by the family. I hate to say as it sounds so horrible, you know I am not like that, but you know what I mean, don't you?"

"Yes, I know. If I said it, Saleena, you know I would mean it, but you are so nice. I don't know how you do it, Sal."

"Don't get me wrong, helping *Amaaji* is charitable and all that as she is a nice lady, but the family should really get a helper for her. She deserves it. That is the least they can do, now that she cannot manage. She has had a hard life and it isn't her fault she is ill. I have just been dwelling on how life is for women. For us lot, you know, Asian women. All we do is stay at home and bring up children. Some turn out to be idiots like my husband."

"Speaking of which, Sal, how are things with you?"

"Allia, don't even ask. I honestly feel trapped here with that monster. All we women do is, we spend our younger days as maids for the families. Then by the time we can enjoy ourselves, it is often too late as we get old by then. Oh, sis, what shall I do?"

"Oh my god, Saleena you know what my advice is? Get out of there, leave now before it is too late. I mean it."

"How is Sajjid by the way?" Saleena changed the subject.

"Do you know, I wish you had a bloke like my Sajj. The guy dotes on me. Sajj has made my life so happy. I was so glad to get away from the wicked witch from the east."

"Allia, I am so happy for you. You got your sense of humour back too then, I see? It's lovely to have my old Allia back. I remember how tough life was at home for you with *Amii* on your back all the time. You truly deserve to be happy after what you have been through with *Amii* at home."

"Saleena don't even mention that bitch's name to me. It makes my blood boil when I think about her. How cruel she was to me. Sajj is wonderful. We are going on a world cruise in the summer. When he told me last night, I nearly peed in my pants, I was that excited."

They both giggled and laughed.

"That is just lovely, sis. I am glad to have my old sister back. I mean it. It is really good to hear you so lively again. Don't worry about me, sis, I am sure things will turn out fine in the long run. How is Sara? I have not heard from her for a while."

"Sara is not happy. Papaji is planning a trip to Pakistan. He is taking *Amii* and Sara with him. Sara thinks they have a bloke lined up for her over there. It may be one of *Amii's* sons. It's all hush-hush, no one is supposed to know about it."

"What? You are not serious, are you? Sara is only thirteen!"

"Yes she cannot marry here but *Nikah* in Pakistan would be easy. Besides, when has age ever stopped them, Saleena?"

"I bet it will be to get a right to come here for *Amii's* son?"

"Yes you guessed it, BP."

"BP?"

"British Passport, idiot," Allia said.

"That is dreadful. I am lost for words, Allia. I don't know what to say any more about the family. Sara will need to stay in Pakistan for three years before her husband will be allowed to come here then. This has to stop someday," said Saleena.

"Sara is livid. She said she will not go but I know that bitch is going to have her way," Allia responded.

The two chatted for over two hours. It made Saleena elated to hear Allia was happy though extremely sad to hear what her parents were planning for Sara. Time ticked on that afternoon. It was nearly three o'clock as Saleena glanced at the clock. After hanging up the phone she got dressed. In a strange way hearing of Allia's happiness invigorated life in her, which seemed gloomy especially after speaking to *Amaaji* that morning. Re-energised, she picked up courage to venture into the city by herself. It would be her first trip by herself on public transport into

Manchester city centre. It seemed daunting, especially since the town centre of Manchester was a place she had only been to once before in the car with Nawaz.

Her ride on the bus into the city took her through some of the depressed areas of Manchester. She took a bus from Eccles New Road, through Salford into town. It was dry but cloudy. She kept looking through the window trying to log some landmarks in her mind to help her remember the bus route when getting back home later that day. She peered through the bus window feeling terribly sad seeing some of the run-down areas of Salford. Many of the council estates looked ready to be pulled down. The poverty and the state of the near dilapidated houses was a depressing sight. The bus route took her past Salford University then onto Chapel Street, eventually into the town centre. She got off the bus in town and had a good walk around.

Manchester was a big sprawling city compared to Leicester. Tall skyscrapers firmly visible to the eye everywhere she looked, with plenty of shops all round town. It was an awesome sight though traffic congestion seemed everywhere, with impatient drivers honking their horns at other drivers or pedestrians eager to dodge cars as they hurriedly crossed busy roads. She walked around looking at the tall buildings, eventually ending up in Arndale shopping centre. Through Wades Furniture at Withy Grove she made her way into the new shopping centre, overwhelmed by its size. The new building had been started in the late seventies; completion of the huge structure was finished in 1980. The shopping centre was a huge, amazingly attractive place for shoppers, unlike anything Saleena had seen before. The centre housed superstores everywhere, Woolworths, Argos C&A and many more. Saleena loved window shopping, looking at the beautiful clothes displayed in the windows of some shops which caught her eye. "Wow, shopping would be fun here, I bet," she muttered to herself. The floors were gleaming everywhere.

Feeling weary walking around, she ended up at Arndale's epicurean delights area where she stopped at Fozzie's Café. It was a busy place. She bought coffee with a slice of chocolate cake then found an empty seat across from the café, sat down on a bench and sipped her coffee. It was a lively, vibrant place with people milling around. She sat back sipping her coffee, watching the world simply go by. She closed her eyes for a moment, casting her mind back to that hot summer's day she and her sisters had gone to the park in 1972 when school had finished for summer. It was a glorious day. Thinking about it made her feel happy. She finished drinking her coffee, and then she wandered around from one shop to another, window shopping, looking at beautiful variety of things displayed in shops. She did not have much money, but window shopping was exhilarating enough for her. Exiting back onto Withy Grove, she walked past a young man who looked to be in his early twenties.

"Please Miss, could you spare some change?" the man asked.

Saleena looked at him for a moment, not exactly staring but looked at him with pity. The man had covered himself up to his chest with a dirty torn sleeping bag. He was wearing a green parka-type overcoat with its hood covering part of his head keeping it warm. He was rubbing his hands together to keep them warm from the bitterly cold winter chill. Saleena went over to the café, bought a coffee and a sandwich. She went over to him and handed them to the guy with a fifty pence coin which she tossed into his hand.

"Thank you Miss, and God bless you," the man said.

Saleena walked a few steps on turned back to look. The man had nearly gobbled up half the sandwich in no time. Saleena smiled, feeling good about the random act of charitable kindness as she made her way back home.

Chapter 9

Some days later in the morning Nawaz was sat at the dining table reading the Daily Echo eating breakfast, fried eggs and parathas which Saleena had cooked for him.

"*Amaaji* did not look right, Nawaz, when I visited her the other day. I am really worried about her. Can you not take her to the doctors?" Saleena asked.

"What am I, my mother's keeper or something stupid? Why don't you take her if you are so concerned?" he responded sharply.

Saleena was taken aback by the harsh words, thinking for a moment that he might take pity on the old woman given her condition was desperate. She bit her lip, turned away and went back into the kitchen, wanting to avoid an argument with him. Nawaz had a habit of turning nasty if challenged. She had thought he might have feelings for his mother but from his aggressive reactive tone she was clearly wrong. Next thing she heard was the front door slam shut. She breathed a sigh of relief hearing the door shut as the last thing she wanted was a confrontation with him over the subject.

It was still early in the morning. Saleena sat on the sofa in the lounge for a while on her own trying to collect her thoughts, as she did most days. Suddenly a terrible feeling of loneliness gripped her. She refused to accept her loneliness for it was too depressing. She got dressed to go see her in-laws. She got the cooking done in no time as *Amaaji* was asleep. Then on her way back home she took a detour, taking a short walk into the local park. The openness, fresh air, people walking in the park, some with dogs, cheered her up. Allia's happiness had uplifted her spirit too. There was an old lady sitting on the park bench feeding a flock of very hungry ducks. Every single time the lady threw a small piece of bread into the water, a flock of ducks raced to it, fighting to grab the morsel of bread. It was always the fittest one winning the prize, leaving the weak ones with the hope that the next one would be theirs. It made Saleena smile.

"Hello dear," she said.

"Hello. Those ducks love you, don't they? Look how they are all looking at you vying to get the next morsel of food," said Saleena.

"Oh, it fills my time. I buy bread for ducks mostly as being on my own I can hardly get through the whole loaf of bread by meself. Are you from round here as I have not seen you here before?"

"I got married a while back, moved from my home town of Leicester to here."

"Oh my, it must be awful for you with different surroundings, it must seem like a very strange place to you."

"It is not too bad, I guess. As time goes on I shall, I am sure, get used to Manchester. It does seem a lot colder up here then the Midlands."

"Us Northerners are traditionally very hardy people and so we don't feel the cold that much you know," she laughed as she said it.

"Oh, give over," Saleena said.

"Here, help me feed the ducks so I can go put the kettle on at home as I am parched. I could do with a nice cup of tea. You can come and join me if you like. I am Doris."

"Doris, I am Saleena, I am pleased to make your acquaintance, darling," Saleena said.

"Likewise, I am sure. You have a beautiful Indian name," said Doris.

"Thank you, Doris. Do your family live around here?"

"My Albert, bless him, he passed away, been ten years now. I do miss him sometimes. My daughter Carol comes over every weekend. Comes to see if her old maa is okay."

"That must be nice for you."

"It is, it is lovely. I have another daughter Emily, she lives in Australia now. We just write to each other."

"C'mon, let's go have that brew," said Saleena.

The house she lived in was a large 1930s-style semi-detached property with four bedrooms. It was an old house which Doris complained was always cold in the winter, made her bones ache though she was grateful that she was able to manage on her own at the age of seventy. They had tea and homemade Victoria sponge cake. The two of them were worlds apart in age, culture and tradition, but the commonness of loneliness, their gregarious nature had brought them together that day. They chatted away for an hour as they sipped tea and ate some cake. Saleena enjoyed Doris's company. She was sorry to leave her on her own but loved time spent with Doris.

Saleena got back home later that afternoon and opened the front door. A Yellow Pages booklet dropped on the floor behind it. As she opened the door wider the Yellow Pages came into her view from underneath. She picked it up, curious as she had not seen one before. She ripped open the plastic cover as she closed the front door, walked to the kitchen, discarded the plastic wrapper in the kitchen dustbin and put the heavy book on the worktop. She began to flick through it, slowing down as she got to the pages under the charity section, soon spotting an advertisement which caught her eye. It simply read:

'Do you have spare time you can put to use for a worthy cause helping the less fortunate? We are a charity helping local people in need of your help. Please call Nadine Nugent on 0161 555 3088.'

Delighted at the perfect possible opportunity, she picked up the telephone handset and dialled the number.

"Hello, may I speak to Ms Nugent Please?"

"One moment – your name was?"

"Saleena."

The line went quiet for a few minutes.

"Hello this is Nadine speaking, how may I help?" a posh voice answered.

"Oh yes, hello there Ms Nugent."

"Please, it is Nadine, call me Nadine," she said.

"Okay Nadine, thank you for taking my call. I was looking through the Yellow Pages today and noticed you had advertised looking for volunteers. Is that right?"

"Yes Saleena, we most certainly are. We could always do with help around here as we are so very busy."

"I have lots of experience helping people and I am very interested," Saleena said.

"Good, can you come and see me tomorrow at 2.00pm?"

"Yes I can. I shall see you tomorrow," said Saleena.

"Good. Do you have a pen and paper handy? You will need to write down the address."

Chapter 10

Sara turned out to be stronger than her sisters had thought. She threatened to report Papaji to the police if he compelled her forcibly to go to Pakistan to marry one of Fauzia's sons. One afternoon she was at home as Papaji was going on and on about the trip to Pakistan.

"Papaji I do not want to go to Pakistan, how many times am I to tell you? I am only thirteen. It is against the law in this country."

"*Betti* it is our tradition and I have made all the arrangements. Think about how embarrassing it will be in front of all our relatives in Pakistan. What would they think? Have you thought about the family honour?"

"No Papaji, I am not going."

"Yes you will. I have said," he stated sharply.

Sara picked up the phone and dialled 999. That was enough to scare him, backing off only momentarily though. He knew she would succumb at some point. A brush with the law was the last thing he wanted so agreed to postpone the trip.

Sara was doing well at school. She dreaded the thought of turning sixteen as she knew it would be her time for marriage just like her sisters before her. Though the tables had turned in Papaji's favour. He regained control of the situation. The trip had not been postponed. *Amii* had packed her bag. Papaji lied to Sara. When Sara discovered the secret plot she refused to be manipulated like her sisters before her. One night Sara packed some few belongings in plastic carriers and slipped out in the silent dead of night. She had left a note behind in a sealed envelope for Papaji. When Papaji read it, he screwed it up and threw it away in the bin in sheer anger.

*

It was summer of 1989. Abdel had turned seventeen in February of that year. Papaji and *Amii* were in Pakistan. It was a Saturday afternoon, a hot, humid day. Abdel was bored on his own at home, so he wandered onto Green Street and lazily walked around looking at the shops and eyeing up local talent. A smartly dressed young woman passed by and smiled at him. He smiled back. It was taboo and unacceptable for a young woman and a man of their tender age to be seen talking of all places on Green Street without a chaperone. This would have been frowned upon by people of his community. He walked on, so did she; apart from a smile no words were exchanged. He popped into the local Express shop to buy some essential items – bread, milk, a newspaper and some chocolate. A tall, thin, Asian gentleman was at the checkout till. He looked tired, almost haggard. He rang up the items one at a time in a lazy manner on the till. His tiredness was palpably obvious. The look on his face, slowly ringing up each item on the till, was noticeable, kind of funny in a way as he lethargically ran each item up. Abdel initially restrained himself from making an observation. The man then took out a plain white carrier bag and placed the items in it, handing the bag over to Abdel.

"That will be £2.95, please. Do you want the newspaper in the carrier bag too?"

"Yes, thanks. That will be good. Sir, you look tired if I may say so. I hope you don't mind me saying," Abdel asked unable to stop himself from observing.

"Do I look tired, boy? I have been up since 4.00am. I have to. I have no choice as the newspapers arrive very early in the morning. I have to sort them out then display them on the rack which takes time. The shop is open all day and it's busy throughout the day. What do you expect?" he said with a harsh tone in his voice.

"Sorry, I was only asking. I did not mean anything by it, truly."

"No, no, you got me wrong. I did not mean to sound harsh. I am, I mean, glad you asked. Would you be interested to help me in the shop some days, as school must be closed for the summer? I will pay you cash. I really could do with some help. I don't have any children and no one to help except my wife but she is expecting a baby so I have to do all the work myself."

"Erm... can I think about it?"

"Sure but don't take too long. I could really do with your help soon. I do the national lottery too which means I have to keep it open until at least 7.30pm at night so plenty of hours there for the taking."

Abdel then glanced at the notice by the lottery machine which read:

'Rollover Jackpot tonight 6.6 Million – could it be you?'

"I bet you could do with that money, couldn't you?" Abdel said to him.

"Oh yes, who wouldn't? If I won that lot, I would pack up my bags straightaway, go back to India tomorrow."

"It's a tidy sum, isn't it?"

"You bet it is! I could live like a *raja* over in India! Fancy having a go? Mind, you have to be over sixteen to buy the lottery though," the shopkeeper said.

"I am seventeen. Okay, I guess no harm in it but I have never played before," Abdel said.

"Here, I will give you three lucky dip lines, is that okay?"

"I guess so."

"Sure," the shopkeeper said.

He pressed some buttons on the lottery machine which produced a pink-coloured ticket which he handed to Abdel.

"Thank you, how much do I owe you?"

"It will be £5.95 please with the shopping items and your lottery. Well good luck then, and if you win don't forget who sold the lucky ticket to you," the shopkeeper said with a smile.

Abdel smiled as he walked out of the store having

safely tucked away his lottery ticket inside his wallet. He walked past a bus stop shelter on his way back home. A young shabby-looking English lad, looked about Abdel's age, was begging for money. Abdel took a fifty pence coin out of his pocket and flicked it over into the boy's hand.

"Thanks mister," he said with a smile on his face.

Abdel got home feeling happy. He sat down on the red sofa in the lounge after turning the television on. A light breeze blew the net curtains in through the open window. Abdel closed his eyes thinking about how nice it would be to have plenty of money. He dozed off to sleep dreaming about being rich. A few hours later a sudden loud bang woke him up. It sounded like a car collision outside. He darted across the room to get a better view through the open window. He could not see much except a crowd of people gathered around the incident. He went outside to have a better look. The crowd began to swell. Abdel stood on the tips of his toes stretching his neck out like a crane, but the view was still obscured by the thickness of the crowd. He waded in through the crowd to get closer to the incident. As he did, he could see a car in the middle of the road with a cracked windscreen. He tried to get even closer, weaving through the crowd. As the road collision came into his full view, he discovered something horrifying right in front of him, not a pleasant sight. An old woman was on the ground, her body partially underneath the car. A man was crouched down by the victim. Someone handed him a blanket which he gently slid under her.

"Don't move her, she may have hurt her neck or

back!" someone shouted from the crowd.

The man held her hand, comforting her. There was no movement from her. She lay there completely still. The ambulance arrived soon. The crew went over to examine her but it was too late for her. The ambulance crew lifted the woman onto a gurney, covered her with some sheets, and placed her into the ambulance. A police car arrived shortly after. Two young officers came over to make enquiries. They began cordoning off the area first with blue and white tape before speaking to witnesses.

Abdel stood for a while watching the police at work but standing watching in the heat was tiring work. He felt hungry as he'd only had a cheese and tomato sandwich earlier on in the day. He walked to the local chip shop. As it was Saturday it was exceptionally busy. There was a long queue of people waiting to be served. Abdel waited in the queue patiently, listening to the chatter about the unfortunate accident earlier on. Mostly people spoke in Urdu. He paid very little notice as hunger pangs dictated a pressing problem on *his* mind.

"A piece of your best cod with a portion of chips, please."

He ordered from the man behind the counter as he reached it.

"All our cod is best," the man in a white coat and hat retorted in a terse tone. "You want salt and vinegar?"

"Yes please," Abdel said.

It was sweltering in the shop even though the double glass doors were wide open. On the other side of the counter he could see a middle-aged man with a whitish beard holding a plastic bucket with freshly cut chips in it. He opened the lid and threw the whole contents of the bucket into the fryer. The wet chips made a fierce sizzling sound, throwing out a cloud of steam from the fryer into the air. To avoid the hot oil splash on him the man quickly stepped back.

"How is Uncleji, Abdel?" someone asked.

Abdel tried to see who was asking as the plume of cloud rose up, clearing the view.

"Is he back from his trip to Pakistan yet?" the man serving him asked. "Your dad is a really cool guy. He is funny. Makes us laugh at the mosque sometimes with his jokes."

"No, he will be back in two weeks' time," Abdel responded once he could see who was asking about his father.

"He is one lucky man being away on holiday in this heat. I wish I was. I would love to win that lottery tonight." He chuckled as he finished serving Abdel. The man then shouted, "Next!"

Abdel stepped out of the takeaway holding his bag of fish and chips with both hands. Hunger pangs intensified. He couldn't resist tearing the paper open from the top. He took out a couple of piping hot chips, popping them into his mouth. He opened it as wide as he could to blow air out to cool the hot chips before masticating then swallowing. They were far too hot to eat but tasted delicious. Abdel tried to cool his mouth by fanning it with his hand as the heat from the chips had slightly burnt the roof of his mouth. He waited a little before eating more.

He reached home and sat down in the front room after turning the television on. Blankety Blank was on a BBC channel. He tried not to think about the incident in the street earlier, but it preyed on his mind. He had not seen anyone die so tragically and violently before. He was restless.

It was a warm Saturday evening. The heat was stifling. The breeze had died away. He finished eating the chips first then the cod pieces last, scraping the fish batter off the paper, popping it in his mouth before it cooled completely. He licked his salty fingers, screwed up the wrapper and threw it in the dustbin in the kitchen. Abdel walked to the front door, opened it to let some fresh air in, but it was too dry. He decided to stand at the frame of the door, holding the sides, pretending to be swinging in and out, creating a breeze. Two of his school friends, Billy and Adnan came by, stopping to chat mainly about girls. The three then walked to the local park, stopping on the way at a takeaway to buy cans of ice-cold Coke. The place was vibrant with people milling around as it was too hot to stay inside. As they walked Billy and Adnan admired a group of the Asian girls walking past. They were all about their age. The girls, wearing traditional light summer wear with *dupatas* hanging off their shoulders, some quite pretty, walked past them, giggling. One in particular gazed at the boys with interest, looking at Abdel mostly as he was the most handsome from the trio.

"Hey Abdel, bet that tall one with a cute smile fancied you," Adnan said.

"Yeh I think so too," he responded.

"No, bro, did you not see how she looked at me

and smiled before she walked on?" Billy commented.

"Cute, lads. Very, very cute. C'mon, let's go," Abdel said.

Abdel returned home at around 10.00pm. Just in time for Saturday night BBC news. He turned the TV on, got a can of Pepsi from the fridge and sat down on the sofa. The news headlines were about protests in East Germany. The Communist-dominated government had resigned following a massive exodus of 30,000 East Germans from the country to the west. The protestors' focal point was the Berlin Wall which was being torn down bit by bit. He waited eagerly to find out the lottery results, which finally came after the weather. He jotted down the numbers quickly on a scrap piece of paper. Moments later he fished out his ticket from his wallet. As he checked his numbers against the ones on the scrap paper one of the three lines matched all the numbers. He checked and rechecked the numbers again and again. Abdel felt numb. He could not move as he sat there, incredulous in disbelief.

*

Saleena got bored watching television by herself that same night. The humidity was stifling downstairs. She was on her own so had decided not to open windows downstairs except the kitchen window which she left slightly ajar. She opened the window to her room upstairs as wide as she could to see if it brought in air. She read her book a little to help her sleep but couldn't. She tossed and turned until about midnight. She must have just dozed when she heard the front door slam closed. Nawaz made his way up slowly, finally stopping outside her door. The door was locked from inside. She could see the handle turn. He tried the door but could not open it. Suddenly he started banging hard on it, threatening to break it down if she did not open it. Saleena, concerned, not wanting to disturb the quietness of the neighbourhood, stupidly unlocked the door. He charged in like a bull but stumbled as he was worse for wear, falling on the floor with a thud. He reeked of alcohol.

"Why are you making such a noise, *baba*? The neighbours will hear," she said.

"I don't fucking care, bitch!" Nawaz roared at her.

He struggled to get back on his feet, falling to the floor a few times before he managed to lift his body up. As soon as he did he went for her, grabbing hold of Saleena's neck, then he flung her on the bed, forcing himself on her.

Saleena ran into the bathroom as soon as he was done. She sat on the toilet for near enough ten minutes trying to get rid of all the semen from her body in her wee. She felt unclean. She could feel him crawling under her skin, and then she stood up, turned the shower on. She turned the tap to cold and stood under it for a good few minutes. She grabbed a bathrobe, wiped her body down with it then wrapped it round her body. She let the water from her long jet-black hair drip onto the floor. The shower helped cool her body from the intensity of the humid night. She went back into her room, locked the door behind her and sat on the bed crying. She wiped the tears, holding back more, picked up her paperback book and attempted to read from where she left off last to get her mind diverted. The book was *Shabanu: Daughter of the Wind* a fictional story by Suzanne Fisher

Staples. She loved the book. Narrated by a young girl, it was a story about a heroine, Shabanu, growing up in Cholistan desert, Pakistan. She was content with her life herding camels but as she was a girl marriage would be on the cards as she neared an age. She would naturally be expected to marry even though still a teenager. Saleena read a good few pages before finally dozing off with the book resting on her chest.

It was 6.00am Sunday morning, her alarm buzzed. Saleena stretched her body as the sun rays poured in through the gaps of the floral curtains which were blowing slightly now with the gentle morning breeze. Her window was still wide open, letting in the gentle breeze. It was a day of tight schedule to keep. Although upset from last night she had the fortitude to carry on. Undeterred, she prised herself out of bed to plod on with her schedule. 7.00am to 10.00am she was at Elmwood Church. The church was on Eccles Old Road. Every Sunday she helped the volunteers feed the hungry and homeless as well as looking after collections for the food bank.

Nadine Nugent loved Saleena the minute she saw her. Her enthusiasm was unchallenged. She liked her very much, not least her determination caring for the less fortunate, but the girl was unequivocally dedicated to helping the less fortunate. She also worked four days a week at the Red Cross store in Manchester town centre. One day a week she visited her friend Doris from the park. She saved enough money and passed her driving test without Nawaz knowing, buying herself an Austin Mini car to get mobile.

As she turned her car into the centre's car park, she could see a long queue of people stretching about a quarter of a mile. Sad to see so many people not being able to manage, she thought. The economy was in a bad state. Jobs were hard to find. People were being squeezed for money in every direction. Saleena could see some mothers standing patiently waiting with their little ones in tow waiting to be fed. It was a busy morning at the centre, labour intensive getting through nearly a thousand people that morning, feeding them and handing over bags of food but completely satisfying for Saleena as a lot of hungry mouths had been fed that morning.

As she drove to the local Co-op supermarket, she glanced at her silver wristwatch. It was 11.30am. She was right on schedule. She hurried round the aisles filling up the trolley with groceries and sundry items for her in-laws. Why *Abbaji* could not help getting the weekly shopping done, only God knew, she thought to herself as she whizzed through the narrow aisles. It was Sunday morning and seemed like all the locals had come to do their shopping all at the same time too as the supermarket was very busy. *Abbaji* was after all retired, had a car and could easily have got it done on any morning. It was a man's pride not to do menial tasks or even be seen to be doing them, which was typical of Asian men. 'It was a woman's job' he said to Saleena once when she suggested he do the weekly shop. It was far too much trouble for Saleena engaging someone when they were clearly not going to listen. She just got on with it.

Amaaji's health deteriorated to the point where she was almost bed-bound. She had to be helped up to go to the bathroom which was a real struggle for *Amaaji*. She kept saying all the while that she eagerly awaited the day her eyes closed permanently.

Eight years putting up with abuse from her husband was enough to age Saleena. She spotted a few grey hairs one morning as she was getting ready for the day. Being lumbered with looking after her in-laws was an additional burden which she could have done without. One small mercy was that *Amaaji* did have a carer coming in every morning except Saturdays, who looked after her hygiene needs. At least that was something for *Amaaji* as well as Saleena. Clarissa came daily to see to *Amaaji*'s personal care needs; hygiene, bathing and so on. Clarissa was a charming, middle-aged, bubbly and very chatty person of West Indian origin. She had mostly black wavy hair with a few greys showing here and there. When she walked, she shuffled everywhere, making an odd sound with her feet as she dragged them on the floor. She needed Clarissa's help. Adam helped on Clarissa's day off which was usually Saturdays.

Abbaji was too immersed in cricket to be bothered about his wife's needs, never mind that she had spent many years of her life not just looking after him, his needs, but brought up his four children. She had worked in a factory on industrial machines for many years. She had, after marriage to him, looked after *Abbaji* too and now that she could not manage, he was not prepared to return the favour or honour his vows 'in sickness and in health'. She had slavishly shown her husband loyalty, duty and cared for him over the many years as she was tied to him by marriage.

All the three brothers were at home when Saleena got there. They greeted Saleena, expressing their gratitude for helping the family out. *Abbaji* and the boys seemed engaged in a lively conversation about cricket that morning. Pakistan had been playing. Saleena paid little attention to the idle talk but cooked *parathas* and scrambled eggs which she served with *masaala chai.* The boys helped Saleena clear up after they had finished breakfast. She prepared lamb *shabzi* and rice for them for later on before saying goodbye to *Amaaji* and the boys.

It was nearly 2.00pm when Saleena got home. She dashed upstairs and had a quick peek into Nawaz's room to see if he was there. He was still asleep, snoring away like a hog which made her giggle. Saleena showered, got dressed, got some things together, got into her little mini car and took off to the road. It was a beautiful day. She drove down the M6 motorway south through the A50, then onto the M1 to Leicester. She arrived at Raazia's house at around 5.30pm.

Raazia was surprised but thrilled to see her sister. She could not believe her eyes when she saw Saleena standing at her front door. She grabbed her arms, dragging her in from the front door and hugged her tightly. It made Saleena feel good.

"Oh my god, you should have said you were coming over, Sal. I would have made something nice and special for you to eat," said Raazia, still embracing her tightly.

"No, don't worry sis, sorry about the impromptu visit. I really came over just to see you guys. I am off work for a couple of days. I thought I'd come stay the night with you, you know, surprise you all! Take a break as well, is that okay?"

"Oh Sal, don't be silly my sweet. Yes, of course it's

okay. You are welcome here anytime, you know that."

"Where are those two little darling nieces of mine?" Saleena asked. "*Salaam Alaiykum* Akeel. How are you?" Saleena asked as she passed by him on the stairs.

"Oh, you know me, Sal, as good as ever. Your sister takes far too much care of me. I am putting on some weight finally!"

Raazia rolled her eyes and made a *t'sk* sound with her tongue. Saleena smiled and spotted Meesha and Sakeela playing on the lounge floor. She went over, picked up the four-year-old twins and hugged them both. They did not recognise their Aunt Saleena straightaway but seemed comfortable when picked up. She put them back on the floor then sat down and played with them for a while.

"My, *my*, sis, haven't they grown since I last saw them? *Masha'Allah*. They are beautiful."

She hugged them tightly. They responded back equally with loving hugs, making Saleena feel wanted and loved which she longed for.

A few minutes later Raazia and Saleena disappeared into the kitchen, Raazia insisting on cooking something special for her unexpected guest. Later that evening Akeel took the twins upstairs and off to bed. Saleena and Raazia sat down on the sofa to chat. They sat until 3.00am that morning chatting, not realising the lateness of the hour as they whiled away the time catching up on the family. Raazia was in absolute tears hearing how sad Saleena's life was. She did not know what to do except hold her sister tightly to her. For Saleena seeing her sister, Akeel and the twins helped her momentarily forget Manchester.

Offloading her troubles, pouring her heart out to her sister actually made her feel ten times better. It really just felt good telling her story of a young Asian woman's tragic situation which her forced marriage had compelled her into, making her life totally miserable. Raazia's eyes had filled up with tears which soon began rolling down her cheeks. Seeing Raazia upset was upsetting for Saleena too. She wanted the time spent together to be a happy one.

"Raazia have you heard from Sara?" Saleena asked, changing the subject quickly. Seeing her sister in a distressed state was quite upsetting for her.

"No I have not, but I have a pretty good idea where she is."

"Do you?"

"Yes I do. The information comes from a reliable source."

"Wow, you seem well connected. I don't suppose you know how she is. It can't be easy for her. What I admire about Sara is that I never expected her to have the guts to do what she did. Well bully for her, I say! I must confess I wish I had done the same, but I was too scared," said Saleena.

"Not scared, Sal, too nice. Papaji was livid when Sara went missing. You know how he is. His reputation was tarnished as a result. 'What will our community say?' he kept complaining," said Raazia, mimicking her father. "Why he is so bothered about the honour business in this day and age I really do not know."

"C'mon, we need to get to bed now," Saleena said.

Chapter 11

The dilemma facing Abdel was enormously heavy. Although he was buzzing with excitement, he dare not get overly excited just in case the decision was not to claim the money. He was brought up as a Muslim, the money was technically *haram*, prohibited for him, so what was he to do? The weekend dragged for him as he immersed himself in worrying about the predicament he had unexpectedly found himself in. It was as though time had stood still for him. The excitement was unbearable, the nervousness unnerving to the point that he needed to visit the toilet so often to relieve his bladder, he got tired of it as he was not used to going so often. He kept checking the jackpot numbers over and over as the reality of his win had not completely sunk in. Each time he saw the complete line of numbers in front of his eyes the reality got a bit more tangible, though it did not feel real. The real dilemma for him was whether he should claim the money. Should he then keep it? Or should he give some or all to charities? Should he not claim it at all? Chuck the ticket away? He knew he would regret it if he took the latter option. It was hell. He felt utterly traumatised.

Raazia had loved having her sister there for the whole of the weekend. Schools were closed for summer. Being pampered by Raazia's family was lovely for Saleena. The weekend was relaxing which made a change from the tense and dreary home life in Manchester. She relished every moment of it.

"Sis, I must make tracks get back home to Manchester as it is getting late. It would be nice to get back to Manchester before dark. I shall pop my head in at Dad's and say hello to our baby brother before leaving Leicester. See what he is up to."

She seemed lively, cheered up, in a good mood. Being with Raazia was just the right kind of therapy she needed. Raazia's instinct somehow made her feel uneasy about something she could not pinpoint. The feeling about Saleena had been a bit eerie she couldn't quite figure out why. She kept the thought firmly to herself. She simply kept hugging Saleena tightly.

"Sal, you can stay here you know. You are welcome here anytime, day or night," Raazia whispered in her ear as Saleena was about to get into her car.

"I know that, *Baji*. Thank you, sis, it means a lot to me," Saleena smiled.

Akeel loaded her bags into the car along with some food Raazia had packed for her.

"Thanks, brother-in-law Akeel. The weekend was nice too," said Saleena.

"Come back soon and drive carefully, sis-in-law Sal," Akeel said.

"I will, don't worry."

"As soon as you get home give me a quick ring to say you have reached home safely," Raazia said.

"I will, don't worry about me, I will be fine."

Saleena stopped over for a few minutes at the house to see Abdel.

"Is Papaji still away, Abdel?"

"Yes Saleena. Be back next Sunday. So how are you doing and how is Manchester?"

"Manchester is okay. Big city with lots of people, congested with traffic everywhere, but I have got used to it. It's just another place. Maybe you might come to Manchester or Salford Uni if you get the grades, ay?" she said, winking at him.

Abdel stared at her.

"So what are you up to these days, little bro? Anything exciting happen to you lately?"

"Err..." Abdel simply paused and stood there in absolute silence, not knowing what to say.

"Abdel, what is the matter? You look like you have seen a ghost or something. I only asked like if you were seeing a girl or something, you know?"

"Oh, oh that... err.. no."

"Abdel you are acting very strangely, I have to say. *Amii* has not worked her special magic on you as well has she?"

"No, I don't think so Saleena, I just have things on my mind that's all."

"What sort of things? You are not in trouble with the law, are you?"

"No I am not."

"How did your A Level exams go?"

"All right, I guess. I won't know the results till mid-August."

"Have you applied for uni places?"

"Yeh."

"What do you want to do and where have you applied?"

"Birmingham, Leicester, Manchester, Wolverhampton, and I want to do law."

"Oh, who's a clever boy then? Well, a lawyer in the family, well I never. Papaji will be pleased if you become a lawyer. He will be proud. He will buy *mithai* for the whole wide world, you know! Well are you going to just stand there gawping at me or give your sister a nice big hug then before I go?"

"Oh yeh, come here, sorry sis," Abdel said.

He gave her a nice warm hug with a peck on her cheek which was unusual, as he had never done that before even when she got married. It made her smile so she reciprocated.

"Well little brother, I need to get to Manchester so I will make tracks otherwise I'll get into trouble if I am late."

"What kind of trouble?"

"Oh never mind that, it's nothing really. As long as you are okay, that is the main thing. *Bhaijaan,* let me know your results when they come through, okay? I hope you get to come to Manchester. It would be lovely having my baby brother near me for a while."

Abdel walked with her to the car. They hugged again before Saleena climbed into her car. The drive up the M6 back to Manchester was as pleasant as was the lovely bright summer's evening. She put the radio on to get some company while driving back on the long journey home. First, Queen – I Want It All, then Cliff Richard – The Best of Me, Donna Summer – I Don't Wanna Get Hurt, Ten City – That's the Way Love Is, Rick Astley – Hold Me In Your Arms, Bananarama – Cruel Summer.

Having spent the weekend with family, seeing Raazia, the twins, Abdel's unexpected peck on the cheek, which she was not going to easily forget, had lifted her spirit immeasurably. A good time spent with family. The music was soothing as well as relaxing. She reached junction 19 on the M6 before she knew it. Suddenly a feeling of tight cramp in her stomach struck her. It was dreadful. She knew why though. As she drove down the A556 her stomach began to churn.

It was nearly 9.30pm. The sun was ebbing away in the distance. The sky had turned bright red. What a beautiful sight the sunset was but she did not enjoy it as the knots in her stomach became tighter, dreading Nawaz being at home. She reached home and pulled her car onto the drive, breathing a huge sigh of relief. Nawaz was not at home. She unloaded the car bit at a time, piling the stuff by the front door. As she opened the front door a horrid smell of cannabis, booze and stale food hit her in the face. Saleena covered her nose and mouth with her *dupata* as she slowly made her way into the hallway, then the kitchen to store the food Raazia had given her in the fridge. The kitchen was in a complete mess. She opened the lounge door unsurprisingly to find the place was strewn with empty booze bottles, food wrappers and cigarette butt ends with ash everywhere.

"Oh *my*," she said to herself loudly. "This place looks like a bombsite. *Yaa Allah*."

She now knew why she had that awful feeling of dread. She was annoyed finding the place as though it was a rubbish tip. Her stress levels increased tenfold as she could almost feel her blood pressure rising. The rancid smell of alcohol caused her head to spin. She sat on the sofa for five minutes but could not take it anymore. *Why should I be a bloody slave to him*? she thought to herself. She closed the door, leaving the mess behind, and went upstairs to her room, bolting the door from inside. She picked up her book, opened the page where the bookmark was, and began to read. Tiredness from her long journey caused her to fall asleep. A sudden loud noise downstairs disturbed her sleep a few hours later. The front door had been slammed shut. She had a quick glance at her alarm clock. It was 1.30am. Saleena sat up on the bed, the duvet pulled up towards her neck. Heavy footsteps approached, the loose floorboard on the landing creaked. Fear gripped her as her heart began to pound stronger.

"Please, please God let him go to his bedroom," she whispered repeatedly to herself. Her prayers unanswered, she saw the door handle turn. Nawaz attempted to open the door only to be prevented by the bolt holding it tight.

"Saleena let me in or I will break the bloody door down, you fucking bitch," he threatened. Saleena sat still, frozen like an iceberg, tightly staying in bed. He continued to bang on the door and the banging got louder each time. Saleena ignored him, hoping he would go away. Suddenly the door flung open. The force applied split the wooden door in half. With his hand he opened the bolt, pushing the door inwards as half the door fell onto the floor, debris flying everywhere, the other half held by the metal hinges with jagged edges protruding, flapping in and out like a saloon bar. Saleena cowered behind her duvet.

"Nawaz what the bloody hell do you think you are doing? You are drunk, just go away and leave me alone. What will the neighbours say?"

"Fuck the neighbours. You beg as much as you want, bitch, but you have been neglecting your husband while you gallivant about meeting your boyfriends. Going off somewhere without asking me, huh bitch! Been to see a man, have you? You whore," he shouted, speech slurred. He raised his open palm up, extending his hand in the air, gesticulating. Then he swung it about to slap her. Saleena moved away as he missed contact with her, striking the headrest then falling onto the bed then the floor, as Saleena quickly moved away from him.

"Nawaz for God's sake I am not your slave. I went to see my sister Raazia, call her if you don't believe me."

"You should've asked my permission first before you went. I don't take kindly to you going off without telling me."

"I don't need your permission. You don't own me, you know, now just go. You are drunk. Just go away, will you?"

He managed to get up off the floor and stood there. His silhouette on the ceiling against the dim light of the room made him look like a gorilla in a rage.

"There will not be a next time, bitch. What about every day you disappear in your car, huh? I don't know what you get up to, do I?"

"You mean my charity work?"

"What fucking charity?"

"I help the homeless people at the Elmwood Church centre."

She picked up a leaflet from her side table to show him.

"Here."

"I am not looking at no fucking leaflet, bitch. You whores are all the same."

He snatched the leaflet from her hand and chucked it back at Saleena, making contact with her head. She began trembling. He grabbed hold of her neck next with his right hand and squeezed it tight with his fingers. She could not breathe. She gasped for air trying to fight back. He let go of her neck then got hold of both her arms and twisted them behind her back. Saleena began to cry as the twist of the arm behind her back became excruciatingly painful. He let go of it and pushed her on the bed, getting on top of her. With his left-hand fist, he struck a hard punch to Saleena's face. Her nose began to bleed. Holding his grip tightly with one hand he unzipped his trousers then tore Saleena's top off her with force. He forced himself upon her, raping her. She was still gasping for air, breathing heavily, making strong rasping sounds.

When he finished, she felt bruised all over.

"Shut up, you bitch. I am going to show you who is the master of my house."

He managed to get himself off the bed and staggered out of the room with his trousers round his legs. Saleena stayed still for a few minutes waiting for the pain to subside. A while later she went into the bathroom heading straight for the toilet as she relieved her bladder hoping to get rid of as much semen as she could. Then with her night clothes on she stood under a cold shower for about fifteen minutes. The cold water cascading down her body soothed her pain. Taking her night clothes off she just stood in the shower for countless minutes, then scrubbed soap all over her body vigorously trying to get clean. She could feel him crawling under her skin, a feeling she loathed. She turned the shower off, grabbing her bath towel, wrapping it round her body. A glance in the mirror revealed the extent of bruising on her face. She could feel throbbing pain returning. She pressed her fingers gently against the nose. It felt tender. Saleena opened the bathroom cabinet door wide open, reached for the bottle of paracetamol, unscrewed the bottle, and took two out into the palm of her hand. She rushed downstairs to the kitchen, opened the fridge door and reached for a bottle of cold Evian water. Swallowing the tablets was painful as her neck felt sore. She managed to get them down her throat with a gulp of water. She went back up past the broken door and lay down on her bed, eventually falling asleep.

*

Monday morning sun had risen. It was a bright sunny day. Saleena slept through to midday. A sharp, intense pain to her face broke her sleep. She gently pressed her nose with her fingers. It felt quite tender, broken possibly, she was unsure. She picked up the clock and looked at the time. She had missed her morning session at the centre. The front doorbell rang. She ignored it at first but whoever it was persisted. Saleena put a bathrobe on and went downstairs to see who it was. She opened the door.

"Saleena I have been worried sick about you. I have been calling you all morning. There was no... Oh my god, what on earth, sweetheart, has happened to you? Lovee your face is all black and blue."

She grabbed Saleena's hand and put her arm around her shoulder, motioning her into the lounge. The state of the lounge was atrocious. It was littered with beer cans, dried chips on the sofa and empty KFC boxes strewn everywhere. Nadine surveyed the mess.

"It looks like someone has been having a party here, Saleena?" she said with half a smile.

"Err... I am sorry about the mess, Nadine. I meant to clean it up. I am so sorry about this morning too."

"Lovee you don't have to apologise. The mess can be cleaned up in a minute. Now where is your kitchen? You could do with a nice cup of tea, I think."

Nadine made her way into the hallway past the staircase then into the kitchen, filled the kettle and turned it on. She returned with a black bin liner and started to collect the rubbish off the sofa. She could hear the kettle whistle as she returned into the kitchen, soon emerging with two mugs of tea, one in each hand. She sat next to Saleena looking at her face. She knew exactly what had happened here.

"I have seen it before many times, my love. You need to do something soon. If you don't, he will kill you. Don't underestimate the seriousness of it. Most women put up with abuse and domestic violence for years. It will not stop until you put a stop to it yourself. He will say sorry countless times, but the next time soon comes around when he bashes you again. 'A leopard never changes its spots', as they say. You must put a stop to it, love. No woman has to suffer this degrading treatment at the hands of a man," Nadine asserted.

Saleena tried to defend her husband but Nadine just shook her head in disbelief.

"Saleena look, don't defend him. You are the victim here. He is a violent man. Let us face it, this should not be happening nor should it be allowed to happen. Let me tell you about my friend Grace. She and I were real chums from school days. We used to go out every Friday night when we were young. Thick as thieves, we were, as my mother used to say. Saturday would be our shopping day. We spent all day in town spending our hard-earned money buying clothes. Afterwards we would get back home, dress up into our new clothes and head into Manchester town centre. We used to have fun. We would ring each other up all the time, share lots of things about life, some very private."

Nadine paused.

"Grace... Where is she now?" Saleena asked.

"Sadly she is not with us anymore, Saleena. Grace met this guy, Steve. Oh, you should have seen her. She was head over heels in love with him. They married, had two lovely girls, Rosie and Ellie. Grace shared all her secrets with me, well, almost all, but not all as it transpired. I did not know Steve had been bashing her about. This was mostly after he came home inebriated. One night Grace fought back as he hit one of the girls, Rosie. Grace would not have that. She would do anything to protect her angels. They were in the hallway by the stairs when it happened. Apparently, she threw a shoe at him which caused him to go into a rage. He pushed her down the stairs and killed her. He argued provocation in court, the swine."

"Oh my god," Saleena said.

Saleena put her legs on the sofa and brought them towards her body in a tucked position. She folded her arms across her chest tightly. She began shivering as she heard the chilling tale of someone, a stranger she never knew, but recognised the stranger's predicament as hers.

"Nadine how do you know all the details?"

"I sat through a gruelling two-week trial at Manchester Crown Court. Steve was charged with murder, but eventually the jury returned a verdict of manslaughter and he got eight years in prison."

"Is that all?"

"Yes. I was devastated. I could not believe it. Grace's family were completely destroyed. She was her father's pride and joy. He had a complete mental breakdown after her death. I lost my best friend. That horrible monster got away with killing her. You know what the worst part of it was?"

"No."

Nadine looked straight into Saleena's eyes with a strange expression, her eyes completely filled up with tears.

"She never let on about him being a wife beater. She kept that side of her life private, a very well-guarded secret which hurt as I thought we shared everything with each other. I never suspected it either as she never had any obvious bruises I could see, nor displayed any signs for me to pick up. Not like you have, my dear. Her bruises were hidden."

Nadine was a medium build, well-groomed, nicely presented, middle-aged lady. She wore a pleated tartan skirt with black shoes all the time Saleena had known her. She had lovely shoulder-length light brown hair. Not a single hair was out of place. Not one single grey hair either, always looked as though she had freshly come out of a salon having had her hair done up. It was that perfect.

"What happened to him and the girls?"

"They went to live with their grandmother, Isobel. I see the girls once a week. Ellie the youngest is now fourteen but reminds me so much of Grace as she is a spitting image of her mother. Grace's mother has never got over the loss. She still always talks about Grace and every time without fail her eyes completely fill up when we talk about her. I think *she* only lived for her two granddaughters otherwise I believe she would have died of a broken heart, truly."

"What a sad tale, Nadine," Saleena said as she wiped the tears from her eyes.

"Exactly, my dear, you don't want to end up like Grace, do you? You must sort this out one way or another soon, even if you have to leave him. You *must* and I mean it. If you have to leave that is what you *must* do. You have heard of the expression 'never the twain shall meet'?"

Saleena nodded.

"Well that is how life turns out sometimes, but always remember sometimes you only have one chance at it. Only one, so take my advice. Fix this before it *is* too late."

She took Saleena's hand and squeezed it tight.

"Tell me about your family, dear."

The two sat for a long time talking about her family which whiled away the hours of a beautiful summer's day.

Chapter 12

A full week went by, but Abdel had still not made a decision though he was still buzzing with excitement. "*I could give most of it to charity and no one would know.*" He began talking to himself. "*But then I will never be in a position like this, ever. I know God takes care of us all, but I could not ever make this much money in a whole lifetime. God, please help me make the right decision here. It must have been written for me. Allah must have wanted me to win. Yes, that is it. He wanted me to win. I am convinced of that now. It was luck for me. It only happens to a select few. Why would he bring me all this luck now if he did not want me to have the money?*"

Abdel talked to himself as he began to rationalise a tough decision for a seventeen-year-old Muslim lad. He continued having endless dialogue with himself. His mind was troubled. He lay down on the sofa one afternoon; his brain had become weary from all that thinking he had to do. He fell into deep sleep.

Billy and Adnan were sat next to him. Abdel's slumber was disturbed by beautiful sounds of gentle music playing on a harpsichord coming from a distance. All he could see was white clouds everywhere. His two friends Billy and Adnan were in the guise of angels. Wings firmly tucked behind them, masculine ripping biceps with angelic features dressed like mythical Greek gods.

"Abdel are you awake?" Adan asked.

"Where am I? Addy is that you?" Abdel asked, rubbing his eyes.

"You boy, and my friend, are amongst the chosen few."

"Am I dead?"

"No, not yet." Billy laughed.

"Well where the hell am I?"

"You are not quite in hell, my friend. I can assure you of that. Well not yet anyway!" Adnan said, grinning at Abdel.

"Are those wings tucked behind you? Why are you guys dressed as angels, what's happening?"

"Like Adnan said, you my friend are amongst the chosen few," Billy stated.

Abdel sat with his legs tucked towards his body. He surveyed the surroundings. Clouds and angels flying around in the distance is what he could see. The gentle angelic music continued to play in the distance.

"Why am I here?" he asked.

"You are a fortunate boy. The gods smile upon you today, my boy. You have peace and blessings from all of them."

They both suddenly stood up, their wings at full stretch, and then flapped their white feather wings, scaring Abdel, then vertically took off. Abdel flinched as the two flapped their wings...

Abdel woke up. "What the... where am I? Oh boy. I must have fallen asleep." He ran his fingers through his jet-black hair. His scalp was sweaty. He could feel the sweat collected in his hands from his scalp. "Oh boy, it was a dream," he murmured. It took him some minutes to get himself together to try to make sense of his dream. "Money is not the root of all evil. I think it's religious zealots who are hypocritical. I shall go for it and worry about them later," he said to himself. Decision made and matter settled.

Abdel picked up the phone before he changed his mind and dialled the numbers from the rear of the ticket. He was shaking like a leaf as he did. He pulled the cable of the telephone towards him and sat down on the sofa.

"Good afternoon, Jessie speaking at Famelot, may I help you?"

"Erm... I have the winning numbers in last Saturday's Lotto draw. I wish to make a claim for the dosh, I mean jackpot."

"You have, sir?"

"Yes I do."

"Well congratulations. That is wonderful. I shall need to take you through some questions, is that okay?"

"Yes it is," he said, still shaking.

"May I have your full name, address, where you purchased your ticket from and the ticket number please?"

Abdel gave the details in chronological order until he got to the numbers question.

"Do you mean the winning numbers?"

"No. You will see there is a strip at the bottom of the ticket where there is a row of numbers there. Could you read them out to me please?"

Abdel read the numbers out. A long pause followed. It felt like an eerie silence which made Abdel feel even more nervous than he was already.

"Sorry sir, the computer is taking a little bit longer for which I apologise but I am just waiting for it to confirm your ticket numbers."

A momentary silence followed, making him feel terribly uneasy. Abdel's breathing got a little louder.

"Yes sir, all confirmed. A very big congratulation to you. Of course we need you to send the ticket over to us please. Here are the instructions to do that."

The operator proceeded to issue the instructions to him. He wrote them down word for word.

"An invitation to the Dorchester hotel in London where the presentation of your cheque will take place will be coming out to you once the ticket is with us and verified. In the meantime, one of our advisors will be in touch with you to look after you. Is that okay?"

"Yes of course, thank you."

"You are most welcome, sir."

An invitation and itinerary were delivered by special delivery the next day. Abdel sat on the sofa staring at the envelope for a long time before he opened it. The thought of travelling first-class for the first time in his life to London was exhilarating enough. He ran upstairs to the toilet to empty his bladder. He had never travelled first-class before. He looked forward to travelling like a VIP in style and comfort. The next day he was up early. He boarded the train for London at Leicester station. His seat had been reserved for him. It made him feel important. *I could get used to this life*, he thought to himself. This was his first trip to London too.

When he got off the carriage at St. Pancras station, he walked slowly down the platform following the hordes of people who had just disembarked from the same train. London station was a congested place, busy, buzzing with the hustle and bustle of a large sprawling city with loud noises of train engines roaring, motor cars speeding along outside, bus engines running. You could hear the sounds maybe miles away. There were hundreds of people rushing around going about their business. As he exited into the foyer of the station he spotted a man dressed in a chauffeur's uniform holding a placard with the name 'ABDEL REHMAN' written in capitals. He made contact with the chap by holding up his hand.

"Good afternoon, sir, I am Alex. I trust you had a pleasant journey?"

"Yes, it was pleasant. Thank you, Alex."

"Good to hear, sir. If you would please follow me, I will take you to the limousine."

Abdel almost went, "Wow," but restrained himself when he saw the size of the black limo. The chauffeur held the door open for him as Abdel hopped into the back of the car. A fresh scent of roses greeted him. There was a bottle of champagne in a bucket of ice in the middle console. The back of the car was roomy to say the least. He felt it was bigger than the size of his sitting room. He grinned to himself sat back and relaxed.

"Please help yourself to the complimentary drinks, sir. There are some Cuban cigars if you smoke in the middle console although I must say you look rather young, sir, to be smoking, let alone cigars. May I enquire how old you are?"

"Yes, I am seventeen."

"A lucky young man too, sir, if I may say so? I trust the ride will be comfortable. I shall try and get you to the hotel as quickly as possible, but the traffic in London can be very trying some days."

"It's perfectly okay, Alex, take your time. I am not in a hurry. I would love the journey to last as long as possible if I'm honest. I have never sat in a limo before and I have always wanted to visit London. Of course, I have heard a lot about landmarks like Bucks Palace, the Tower of London and other places. Can you take me round please?"

"Oh absolutely, sir, it would be my pleasure. In fact, sir, it will be my very great pleasure, no, an honour, sir, as I am here to please my guests who travel with me."

"Thank you so much, Alex, where you from?"

"London. Born and bred here, sir. It is a wonderful place. I have lived here all my life. Tourists come from all over the world to see the sites here. I love meeting different people of all nationalities. It is great."

"You love your job then?" Abdel enquired somewhat sarcastically.

"I would not give it up for all the tea in China, sir,"

the driver said wittily.

Abdel opened the mini fridge. He surveyed the selection of beverages then picked out a can of Coke. He sat far back into the limo's leather seat, stretching his legs as far as he could. The driver took him through The Mall then onto Constitution Hill past Buckingham Palace. As the palace came into view Abdel moved forward onto the edge of his seat to take a better view.

"Wow, that is a beautiful sight. Look at that building."

"Isn't it marvellous, sir?" the driver said.

"Driver, I mean Alex, is that Bucks Palace?"

"Yes sir, it is Buckingham Palace, the residence of the current reigning Monarch, Her Majesty Queen Elizabeth II."

"Wow, I have never seen such a beautiful building, I mean palace, before." He sat back in his comfortable seat again, turned his head round ninety, then one hundred and eighty degrees still looking at the Palace through the rear window as the driver went past it. Abdel could not contain his excitement at seeing the beautiful palace at the same time as being driven in a limousine. He had always dreamt of visiting London one day and having a tour in an open-top red bus was his dream but he never imagined he would do it in such style.

"Are visitors allowed inside the palace?"

"I don't believe so," the driver said.

"What a shame, I would love to have a look inside the palace. The architecture must be amazing."

The limo soon pulled up in Mayfair outside the Dorchester hotel on Park Lane. The driver got out, opened the car door for Abdel to disembark. Overawed by the size of the place – he could not believe how big it was – he surveyed the elegant surroundings. A hotel concierge greeted him then showed him the way into the hotel, opening the wide glass double doors for him. The hotel foyer was sumptuous with its opulent theatrical-style decor. He had never seen anything like it before. Abdel had to pinch himself to believe that he was actually inside one of the most prestigious and expensive hotels in London. It was breath-taking for him. He looked all around. The lovely fresh smell of bright red roses greeted him in the long foyer as Abdel looked around with awe walking towards the reception. Expensive chandeliers hung from the high ceilings above. Sparkling bright lights from them illuminated the beauty and grace of the hotel. Shiny polished marble floors ran from the entrance to the reception desk. Guests wearing smart, expensive designer clothes seemed busy milling about the hotel, some relaxing with hotel staff getting on with serving their guests, pampering them. Bellhops were busy taking care of their guests' luggage, pampering them with a friendly service no doubt for favours of supplementing their meagre salaries hoping for tips from the rich guests. Now he was one of them being pampered. The VIP treatment was exquisite. A young English man in his early twenties, dressed impeccably wearing a smart, grey-coloured, tailor-made designer suit, white shirt, perfectly starched collars, a pink tie, gold Gucci cufflinks, and tanned shiny shoes introduced himself as Philip Benson. The suit hung on him perfectly, Abdel noticed. Comparatively Abdel felt completely out of place with his denim jeans and polo neck T-shirt.

"Mr Rehman I presume?" Abdel nodded. "I trust you had a pleasant journey from Leicester," he said, shaking Abdel's hand. The guy had a warm, tight grip as he continued shaking his hand.

"Yes I did, thank you, and it's Abdel, please."

"That is wonderful. Congratulations, Mr Rehman. Erm... I mean Abdel. I believe you are the youngest winner in the history of the lottery so far. That is something for us to celebrate as this has never happened before. Famelot would like, with your permission of course, to celebrate this event in a grand fashion. Now if you would follow me, we can check you in at the front desk first." Philip led the way to the front desk. Abdel followed.

"I like your suit. It's very nice," Abdel said, paying Philip an impromptu compliment as they walked.

"Thank you. It is a Savile Row suit made to measure. I shall show you the one I use later. They are great. I do have a schedule for you. Here, it's all there," he said, handing a booklet to Abdel which had the lottery logo on the front with a heavy printed schedule on the reverse side of it. He turned it over to have a quick glance at it.

"It is my job to take care of all your requirements today. All the arrangements are complimentary courtesy of Famelot. You will also find a few new suits hanging up in your room. I had to guess the size, but a couple should fit nicely. I am quite confident that one or two will be a perfect fit on you. I shall come back in two hours to get you. You can freshen up in the room. A suite has also been booked for you for an overnight stay should you wish to do that. I shall accompany you at the cheque presentation ceremony later on. Is there anything else I can assist you with?"

"No thanks, I will be fine. Sorry, I am ever so clumsy with remembering names, what did you say your name was again?"

"Philip Benson."

They took the lift up to the eighth floor. Abdel was unsure what sort of conversation he should have. Philip seemed to be very posh, spoke the Queen's English. He had no particular accent which could be easily recognised, not that Abdel was an expert in the accent department. The two stood in the lift quietly. Abdel could smell the strong cologne Philip was wearing which pervaded the quietness in the lift. It mingled with a residual lingering smell of ladies' perfume. The lift pinged, stopped at level eight as the doors opened. They walked up the corridor to room 808.

"Here you are," he said opening the room door for Abdel.

"Oh I say," Abdel said, surprised, not expecting the room to be elegantly sumptuous.

"I thought you would like this room. Most guests do! Now I shall, unless there is anything you need, see you later. Enjoy the stay."

The room was beautiful. Abdel could not believe all this was real. He looked around the luxurious room. Like a little kid discovering adventure he began by opening all the closets, drawers and cupboard doors. He parted the lace curtains covering the window in the middle to look at the view from his room. The view was simply breath-taking. He could see Hyde Park a mere distance away as he surveyed the view in the distance. There were tall London skyscrapers. He stood there for a while admiring the majestic view of the capital.

He ran the bath as he continued looking around, discovering the room. Bath filled, he turned the taps off; bath robe off, he immersed his body, head just above water, in the luxurious foam which hugged his body. It felt like being in heaven. The jasmine aroma of the bath foam together with the grand surroundings of his room made Abdel feel good. He lazed in the bath for nearly an hour dreaming about the good things to come. He felt convinced he had made the right decision. The water had turned cold when he got out of the bath. He wrapped himself with a huge, soft, white bath towel which he lifted off the silver rail above the bath, then walked into the room. He jumped on the grand four-poster bed, bouncing on it a few times like a little child. He got off the bed, opened the fridge door and took out a bowl of strawberries, poured some fresh cream on them then sat back on the bed to enjoy. A knock on the door interrupted his enjoyment.

"May I come in?" asked Philip.

"Yes, yes, come in. I had not realised the time. Sorry. I will get dressed now. My god, has two hours just flown past?" Abdel asked.

"I see you have been having fun. Would you like me to assist you to get dressed?"

Abdel did not expect to be asked that as he had never been asked such a question by another man before. Abdel looked at Philip with a quizzical look.

"No thanks, I think I should be able to manage," Abdel retorted.

"I don't know if you have watched any period dramas or TV programmes say like 'Upstairs Downstairs'. You see, the valets help their gentry employers get dressed. I can be your valet today as it is all part of the service," Philip stated as he smiled.

Phillip's invitation to help him dress was unexpected as Abdel could only recall Raazia, *Amii* or his other sisters ever dressing him when he was young, but not Papaji. Help getting dressed from a stranger seemed even more bizarre to him.

"What help me get dressed you mean? Thanks, but no. I can do it myself."

"That is fine," said Philip as he sat down on the bed watching Abdel get dressed.

Eyes pinned on him, looking at him, staring whilst he got dressed, made him really nervous. He held on to his towel firmly then Abdel went into the bathroom, returning into the room with his underpants on. Philip looked at him and smiled. He reciprocated, and then he picked up a pair of trousers from the wardrobe and put them on quickly, followed by a striped blue shirt, but did not button up. Then he began drying his hair with a hairdryer, brushing it all back with his fingers as he dried it one section at a time. Philip watched him dry his hair. Abdel stood in front of the mirror, once he finished drying his hair. He continued to stand in front of the mirror admiring his jet black hair, brushing it back with his hairbrush, then with his fingers a few times.

"What do you think?"

"Yes, looks presentable. Can I suggest, if I may, I do think the grey tie; the one with the pink dots will go very nicely with the shirt you have on," Philip said as he got off the bed, came over to where Abdel was standing, reached for the tie and held it against Abdel's shirt from his neck down.

"Do you like that?" Philip asked.

"Yes I do. It looks nice. Matches well with the dark blue suit I want to wear. Well you are good, Philip. Look at you. You are dressed so nicely," Abdel said.

"Impeccably, you mean to say, or just simply an example of sartorial elegance?" Philip asked rhetorically.

"I know what some of them big words mean, you know!" Abdel retorted.

"Good, it looks nice. Do you want help with the knot?"

"Yes, as I have never worn a tie before and I do not think I can tie it, never mind get it straight, so yes thanks," said Abdel.

Philip stood directly in front of Abdel who surprisingly acquiesced to the offer of help this time around. He fed the tie round his neck then looped it into a knot before tying it. He adjusted it a couple times, straightening it. Philip had blue eyes. Abdel could not avoid looking directly into his luminous eyes. Philip reciprocated then took his gaze away. Abdel averted his gaze too.

"There, how does that look?"

"It looks great, Philip, you are a star," Abdel said, making a three hundred sixty degree turn to look in the mirror.

"You are welcome, Abdel." Philip smiled. "You look like proper gentry now."

"I *do*?" Abdel asked.

"Yes, you can afford to employ a valet too!" Philip said.

They both laughed simultaneously. Abdel for some odd reason found himself relaxed with Philip, helping him dress. Next item was the cufflinks, then the grey jacket. Philip brushed his palms on both shoulders and ran them down the length of the jacket then the sleeves, removing any residual fluff and creases.

"There! You look exquisite, my boy. Now c'mon, get your shoes on as we need to go otherwise we will be late and I will get into trouble, so hurry."

Philip led the way. Taking the elevator down to the foyer through the long corridor, they made their way to the lobby then across from the foyer into another long corridor they entered a large conference room. The room was crowded which took Abdel by surprise as he had not expected so many people to be there. Cameras flashed in quick succession, a standing ovation as he stepped into the room. The glitzy razzmatazz of the occasion overwhelmed him. It dawned on him, *he was* the VIP today. A famous BBC personality, Nick Knolls, presented him with a cheque for £6.6 million.

"Congratulations, young man," shaking his hand.

"Use it wisely," he said, offering prudent advice. Bottles of champagne were popped open by the hotel staff. Trays full of champagne were passed around as the occasion was to celebrate Abdel's win. Abdel declined the alcoholic beverage and instead chose a Britvic orange with lemonade and ice. Paparazzi seemed to be happily clicking their cameras away in succession, taking myriads of pictures as this *was* a big story. A seventeen-year-old, the youngest lottery winner from an ethnic background, was worthy of a national story. Reporters fired questions at him in quick succession. Suddenly the glare from unending flashes from cameras, all those questions being fired at him from all angles by journalists, became oppressive for Abdel. A sudden migraine gripped him. He signalled Philip to take him out of the room.

*

Around 8.30pm that evening Abdel woke up. The afternoon was but a blur. His immediate priority was dealing with a thumping headache. He picked up the telephone by his bedside, dialled room service ordered some paracetamol with a glass of warm milk to be sent up to his room. The sheer number of people at the cheque presentation ceremony in the afternoon coupled with the incessant flash photography had given Abdel a nasty headache. There was a knock on the door five minutes later.

"Room service," he declared.

Abdel rolled out of bed, went up to the door and opened it. A young man in uniform stood there with a glass of milk on a tray with two white tablets.

"You ordered room service?"

"Yes I did, thank you."

He tipped the waiter, closed the door, picked up the tablets from the tray, and popped them in his mouth one by one, washing them down with the glass of milk, then hopped into the shower. Soon he felt hungry.

"Hi Philip, it is Abdel here. I was wondering if you could tell me where I could go to get a bite to eat as I am absolutely starving. I don't know my way round here. To be honest I am really feeling a bit lost."

"Of course, I will come over, give me twenty minutes."

"Sorry, am I intruding?" asked Abdel.

"Not at all, it is all part of the service so it is no trouble at all. See you anon."

His headache had subsided. Feeling better, he got dressed. It was nearly 9.15 in the evening when there was a knock on the door.

Abdel jumped off the bed to answer the door.

Philip walked in. He was wearing casual clothes this time.

"It is a warm night so hope you don't mind the casual wear."

"No, not at all, feel free to be comfortable. I had a thumping headache so got room service to get me some tablets. It's better now but I am starving. "

Philip drove him to an Indian restaurant in Central London where some celebrities and famous people ate. The restaurant was packed as it was Saturday night. Philip worked his charm with the head waiter he knew so he had no trouble getting a table for two after a twenty-minute wait. The food was great and the evening seemed to go fast as Abdel enjoyed the food with splendid company. Philip talked endlessly about his work, the places he had been to on holiday and his ambitions in life to be a pilot one day as he would love to fly planes. Abdel talked sparingly about his family life in Leicester as it did not seem as interesting as his host's. He talked more about his plans for the future now he had a bob or two to spend freely as he pleased. After the meal they both walked for a little distance as they carried on talking. It was a warm night. The sky was clear with hundreds of stars glittering far away high in the galaxy, probably millions of miles away, as the two enjoyed the stroll.

"I had a great time, Philip, thanks to you."

"It was my pleasure. I am glad you had a good time. I will get my bag and leave you to it. Hope you have a good sleep. I shall see you in the morning around 10.00am for checking you out."

"Okay."

Philip turned around to bid Abdel goodbye but could not help noticing there was something troubling Abdel as he sat quietly on the bed. Philip put his bag down on the floor.

"Abdel are you okay?"

"Can we talk? I need to talk about something," Abdel replied.

"What is it?" Philip asked as he came back into the room, closing the door.

"I am in deep shit."

"What do you mean? You haven't done anything illegal have you?"

"No, no, nothing like that, but could be seen to be equally as bad."

"Really, what do you mean? You are talking in riddles!"

"The publicity about me winning the jackpot is going to be sensational and all over the papers soon if it isn't out there already. My family, my friends, my community will disown me."

"Why? Will they not be happy for you?"

"All this money I have won is gambling money, Philip. As a Muslim I am not allowed to gamble. I will get crucified. I will not be able to go back to my old life now, I don't think. What will I do?"

"Oh, kiddo, surely it's not that bad? Do you really want to go back to your old life anyway? With the money you can start afresh. You must be the envy of every single person in the country!"

"Err... sorry but you don't know what it is like to be brought up like I have been. It's different to yours."

"All I know is you are young, seventeen years old, lad, no experience in life but it will all be okay, you'll see. Besides, you are one handsome young guy. You will be a real catch for some nice girl out there." Abdel gave out a little smile but lapsed back into looking glum. Philip put his hand on Abdel's shoulder to offer some comfort.

"I am pretty sure you have heard of the old cliché 'money is the root of all evil'. This, believe me, will be a massive thing with my family. I cannot help but feel forlorn as it will lead to my ruin. I should have just thrown the ticket away," Abdel said sullenly.

"Hey, c'mon now. I truly believe life is what you make of it. God has truly smiled on you. Look at the luck you have had. Your first lottery ticket turned out to be a winner. What are the chances of that? Millions to one, I would say. You, my boy, must make life what you want it to be now. This is a big break for you. Fuck the rest."

Abdel smiled. He knew Philip could not possibly begin to understand the enormity of his predicament but was grateful for the kind words, above all for the empathy shown. Philip sensed the deep feeling of sadness for this young man was so overwhelming for him. He knew Abdel felt dejected to the point that he had descended to thc lowest ebb mentally, perhaps. No matter what he said to him it seemed to make no difference. Philip placed one hand on Abdel's shoulder blade, gave it a squeeze. Abdel sat head bowed, almost to the point of being in tears. He did not react at first to Philip's physical contact with him as he continued to comfort him.

"C'mon man, chin up. Let's see that smile you had on this afternoon at the presentation ceremony. Besides, life ain't that bad. "

Abdel unexpectedly rested his head on Philip's shoulder; his jet-black hair almost covered Philip's face, the smell of his hair alluringly charming. As Abdel lifted his head, their lips met. Unexpectedly, they kissed.

Philip stood up, walked over to the fridge, opened

the door and took out a couple of chilled Coke cans. He flicked one over to Abdel who caught it. Philip returned to exactly where he was sat before and opened the can of Coke, taking a huge sip from it.

"Boy, you must be thirsty?" Abdel asked.

"Yes I am. That move was unexpected for me."

"I am sorry. I did not think I would do that myself. I really am sorry," Abdel said as he looked into Philip's blue eyes directly.

"No, it is okay, really. You are not so bad yourself."

Abdel looked away but knew he was attracted to his host. He moved his hand onto Phillip's thigh and rested it there. It was unfamiliar territory for him. He was not sure what to do next. Abdel had not been in any similar physical situation with a man before but knew he felt deep attraction to Philip. Phillip reciprocated. He moved his lips closer to Abdel's and they kissed passionately.

Chapter 13

Saleena was staying at Nadine's house at her insistence. The prospect of leaving Saleena with the same fate as her dear friend Grace was, to her, unthinkable given her state of mind had been so fragile. Saleena came downstairs after getting dressed. Nadine's house was spotlessly clean with a lovely homely feel to it. Saleena looked through the kitchen window; spotting Nadine in the back garden she walked over to where she was sat seemingly enjoying breakfast al fresco in her lovely garden. Her head was buried behind a newspaper she seemed engrossed in. A dark green parasol shaded the garden furniture. It was a bright sunny day. A mug of tea rested on a coaster on the glass top of the garden table. There were four cane chairs with cushions on them which were tied around the back of the chairs. The chairs were all neatly placed around the table. The lawn was lush green, despite the summer's heat wave; it stretched for about a hundred yards. Right at the very far end of the garden Saleena could just about see an apple orchard. Fruit hanging off the trees – damson trees, pear trees. They all looked in full bloom with fruit hanging on the branches of the trees. The lawn borders had a plethora of mixed colour flowers, roses, carnations, amaryllis, bells of Ireland, chrysanthemum, dahlias, heliconia, pear blossoms, all in full bloom. The array of bright colours mingled with the scent from the flowers was completely indescribable.

"Isn't it a lovely day Nadine?"

"Oh, gorgeous day my dear. Come sit down. I am normally up very early as I don't like to waste a beautiful day especially if I am in my lovely garden. I make the most of it too before heading out to Elmwood."

"Your garden is so gorgeous, Nadine, where do you find the time to attend to it with your busy schedule?"

"Stan, my husband, loves gardening. That's his baby. He will spend hours out there in the garden. He is a perfectionist too, you know. He will tend to the garden, nurturing it all day long without getting tired. He amazes me. This year he is hoping to enter the Chelsea flower show!"

"Oh my word, he is serious about this then? Is there anything interesting in the paper today Nadine?" Saleena asked, changing the subject.

"Well the front cover story is about a seventeen-year-old boy from Leicester winning the jackpot of £6.6 million in Saturday's lottery draw. The papers say he is the youngest lottery winner so far. I wouldn't mind a bit of that, I have to say. Just think what you could do with all that money. Never mind 6.6 million, a mere million would do it for me!"

"Oh, a dream. That would do it for me nicely too, Nadine. I would get away from my husband for starters. So many things you could do with that kind of money. I would go to Africa to help those poor people out there."

"Would you really? That is very laudable, Saleena. You truly are a philanthropist."

"I am sure you would do too," said Saleena.

"Well it would I suppose be spiritually fulfilling."

Nadine then held the newspaper up to show Saleena the front-page picture of the young winner. Saleena immediately put both the flat palms of her hands on her mouth on top of each other. She stood up, stood as still as she could, as though she had seen a ghost. She had an incredulous look on her face. She looked pale.

"Saleena, what is the matter dear? You look as though you have seen a ghost!"

"Oh *my* god, it's my brother Abdel," she said loudly.

"What is wrong with him?" Nadine enquired.

"No... I mean Abdel is the lad on the front page."

"What, your younger brother Abdel has won all that money?"

"Yes!" Saleena said, still looking incredulous.

Saleena was trying to make sense out of this incredible revelation.

"Saleena dear, come sit down. You are obviously in shock. But think about it, dear, it could be a blessing in disguise for *you*. He can maybe now help you get away from that monster of a husband of yours, Saleena. Think positively."

"Dad is going to murder him. It is *haram*, to gamble err... I mean a Muslim is not permitted to play the lottery as it is gambling."

"What do you think he will do?" Nadine asked.

"He will get crucified, I tell you. And not only that, he will have all the vultures descending on him for a slice of the cake. I saw him last Sunday. He was acting very strangely. I now know why he was acting like that. All peculiar, you know. I asked him how he did in his exams, but he did not seem too bothered."

"I would not be too quick to judge him, my dear. It may all be fine. These things have a way of sorting themselves out. You'll see they will, so don't fret yourself, Saleena."

"I know what Papaji is like."

"Tell me about your family, dear."

Saleena returned home later that day. Surprisingly her door had been fixed but Nawaz was not at home. The rest of the house as usual was in a complete mess. Tidying the mess took hours. Once she had finished, she picked up the phone and spoke to Raazia about Abdel. Neither could believe what he had done. Raazia seemed annoyed, expressing her desire to strangle that brother of theirs who was going to cause a lot of grief to the family. Saleena paced anxiously whilst talking on the phone.

"Papaji will kill him, Raazia. Oh my god what are we going to do?"

"Nothing, sis, as it is not our problem. Let him sort it out."

"What? He is our little baby brother, Raazia, you can't just say that!"

"Listen sis, you and I have got other things to worry about. Let Abdel deal with this one by himself, I say. He got himself into it, let him get out of this himself. No one told him to gamble, did they? Maybe Papaji will be okay about it, I don't know?"

"Okay Raazia, maybe you are right. I shall speak to you soon, bye."

"Okay, bye sweetie. Look after yourself. God bless and *Khodda Hafeez*."

Saleena forgot about Abdel, turning her focus onto the unpredictability of Nawaz's mood when he returned later. *I wonder what he will be like when he comes home,* she thought to herself. *What will he do?* Minutes and hours went by as the clock ticked away. Saleena remained in an agitated state; her tension grew worse with every minute that went by. As the minutes folded into hours her heart palpitations grew even stronger. Eventually, tired of worrying her fragile mind about Nawaz, she decided to head for bed and try to sleep.

She heard Nawaz come home as he slammed the front door closed. She glanced at her bedside clock. It was dead on midnight. The tense feeling she had, had grown stronger. She could feel her heart pounding inside her chest which grew stronger as the sounds of his footsteps got closer to her bedroom. A loose floorboard on the stairs made a creaking sound. Nawaz was a big man with heavy steps as he walked. The doorknob turned, making a squeaky sound. She suddenly remembered she had forgotten to bolt the door. The door was soon wide open. His large figure silhouetted in the light from the hallway as he stood in the door frame. He flicked the light switch on in the room as he walked in with heavy steps. Saleena shielded her eyes from the sudden burst of bright light in her room. He looked haggard, unshaven and dishevelled.

"So where were you then for the last week?" he asked. "I thought you had left, gone for good."

"I went to Nadine's house over in Parrs Wood in Didsbury. She had come over that day found me in a terrible state when you attacked me. She saw the bruising all over my face. She insisted I go with her."

"Oh that *Goree* from church you mean?"

"Yes, she is a nice caring Christian lady."

A plausible explanation seemed to calm Nawaz. He sat on the edge of the bed. For a change he seemed different, even may be remorseful about what he had done, and then stood up, leaving the room much to Saleena's surprise. As he left, he even flicked the light switch off before closing the door behind him. Saleena could not believe what had just happened. She had to pinch herself. "What's he up to?" She spoke aloud to herself. She had relaxed and was calm, though extremely perplexed. Saleena jumped out of bed, seizing the opportunity to lock the door just in case he decided to come back into her room. She was glad the door to the spare room had been fixed whilst she had been away the past week. Her anxiety receded, soon she fell asleep.

Next morning Nawaz was already up early for a change. He was seated at the dining table when

Saleena came downstairs.

"Anything for me to eat?" he asked in a relatively calm voice.

"I can make you some eggs and some *parathas*, if you'd like?"

"Thank you, that would be good."

The conversation dried up as Saleena quietly disappeared into the kitchen to make his breakfast. Saleena remained guarded. She wondered why he was so calm that morning. She avoided conversation with him in case his Jekyll and Hyde personality surfaced all of a sudden. She preferred him like that. Civil. He ate breakfast quietly, leaving without saying goodbye to her. Saleena did not dwell much on this but preferred to get on with her day.

Papaji and *Amii* returned back from Pakistan a few days later to find their only son had made front-page headlines in the national newspapers. Papaji was furious. As he arrived home a crowd of people from the local community had congregated outside his house. Some even knocked on the door to speak to him but Papaji, guessing by the hostile mood of some of the people gathered outside which had the appearance of a mob and seemed to scare him, resisted the temptation of opening the door even simply to tell them to go away. They were chanting in a loud voice – "Abdel is *beysharram*." Abdel has no shame. This unnerved Papaji, as it was turning ugly much to his annoyance, but surprisingly *Amii* seemed very calm.

"Just close the curtains and ignore them, I say," she said to him.

"You don't understand, do you? These people *are* from our community. They are *our* people. Listen to the anger. The mood they are in out there shouting like they are. I commanded respect in our community. That has been lost. How can I face them? Why has that boy done this to us? He has brought shame on me. Why does he have to gamble? He knows it is *haram*. Oh dear, what are we to do? And where is that *naalaiak* boy? I will kill him when I lay my hands on him. Just listen to them outside. How can I hold my head up high in the community now? *Bapray* I am crucified now."

"Calm yourself down, my dear husband. He is a boy, *baacha hey, chorr do naa*. Besides, you know what young ones are like nowadays as it is all different, not like it used to be in the old days when you would lift your *chapal* they would be scared and fall in line. Times have indeed changed. They don't listen to their parents anymore. If you want my advice, ignore them outside. It is a storm in a teacup, I tell you. It will blow over soon."

Papaji could not believe how calm *Amii* was. For him the situation was dire, even desperate, to the extent he was really concerned, yet his wife seemed absolutely calm. Papaji spent time on the phone for hours speaking to people from the community, apologising for his son's actions which he put down to his immaturity, trying to limit as much damage to his reputation as he could. He called Raazia, then Sameena and lastly Saleena.

Chapter 14

Abdel's confused state of mind continued to bug him. Philip tried to help with his wise counsel, but Abdel's agitated state of mind grew stronger day by day. Deep-seated anxiousness had firmly set in as Abdel randomly began to rant about how it was against the principles of his religion to gamble. How he should have thrown the ticket away. Philip felt some exasperation but seemed to have endless patience with Abdel. Philip was young himself and not used to counselling someone so young. Though not a duty, he felt dealing with whatever was causing Abdel to be in a state of mental torment to be a challenge for him. He invited Abdel to stay at his apartment. This helped keep the paparazzi at bay from him at least. For a seventeen-year-old teenager discovering his sexuality could not have come at a worse time too, with his agitated mental state. The matter was serious enough. It was bad enough winning the lottery, but his attraction to his host was confusing to him. The wretched dilemmas about how wrong it was to gamble was something he could perhaps just about cope with, but to discover he was attracted to men was unfathomable. He knew isolation may be an inevitable result but painfully unbearable. Neither he nor his family would be able to cope with that. To bring shame upon the family was a bad thing.

Philip suggested Abdel go abroad for a while, have a break and let the dust settle completely, an idea which to Abdel was very appealing. He loved the idea. Philip saw to the flight arrangements out of the country. After a comfortable flight, travelling first-class on a British Airways 747 jet, Abdel arrived at Grantley Adams International Airport on the Caribbean island of Barbados at 7.40am. He took a taxi to his hotel in Bridgetown. Abdel had not travelled abroad before, let alone first-class on an aeroplane. Discovering the beautiful island occupied his mind. It was an ideal distraction from his worries. He loved the tropical sunny island which unlike England was surrounded by blue skies and the appealing Atlantic Ocean. The first few days he spent lazing around on the white sandy beaches of the island, relaxing with speedboat rides on the sea on most days. As days went by the novelty, the excitement of a tropical country was wearing thin as loneliness began to set in, especially at night. The only thing he could do was to sit on his own, read a book or watch television. Not much fun being on his own when he had been used to people around him all the time. He was beginning to miss home terribly, craving for familiar food, especially *Amii's* curries and *rotis*. Philip spoke to Abdel every night, making sure his little protégé was okay. Abdel talked endlessly about what he did that day to Philip.

It was around 4.00am when Abdel was woken up by a sound of a door closing hard in the hotel corridor. He could not get to sleep after that. After emptying his bladder, he turned the television on. Some quiz programme was on, but he did not pay much attention to it. He paced around the room for a while. He drank a bottle of milk out of the hotel fridge hoping it would help him get back to sleep. He tried to get back to sleep but he could not. He picked up the phone and dialled Philip's number.

"Hi, it's me, sorry to trouble you, not sure what time it is over there, but it is about 4.30am over here and I just cannot get to sleep. Philip. How are you?"

"Hi Abdel, I am good thanks. Don't worry about the time, it's perfectly okay. It is 9.30am over here. I was about to leave for work. What are you doing up at that hour? Go back to sleep, I would."

"That's just it, I can't sleep. I am so bored. I am feeling really lonely out here. I want to get back home unless I can tempt you over to come see me for a few days. It would be nice having some company. Please?"

"Let me have a think as I have a few things to complete at work. I will also need authorisation from work. So, let me get back to you later on tomorrow. Is that okay?"

"Sure. So, Philip what's happening over there, anything exciting going on?"

"No, not really Abdel, it's just the same ol' everyday stuff. You know. The news people have reported your disappearance though."

"Really, is that good?"

"Newspapers, you know, they will print anything to sell papers! Don't worry about it. Just try keeping a low profile as you are still a news item worthy of reporting, especially the disappearance."

"Okay, I hope you will say yes though. I will pay for your flight across first-class. By the way has my Swiss account been set up? I need to get access to my funds."

"It's all been done. The bank stuff will be with you hopefully tomorrow. I despatched it by special courier yesterday. You should soon have the cards for accessing the funds."

"Thanks Philip. Call me tonight with your decision please."

"I will. Bye for now."

Nawaz got home at around 8.00pm that evening. When his car pulled into the drive Saleena got up to have a peep from behind the curtains through the front room bay window; she had just finished watching Coronation Street. She returned to her seat on the sofa. Nawaz walked in, mumbled 'hello' and went straight upstairs. He showered, got changed before coming back downstairs. He was still seemingly calm, not his usual nature. She was unsure of this odd calm behaviour he was displaying. She could only remember he was nice in the first couple of weeks after they married.

"I am going out to eat with some friends of mine. Don't wait up for me as I will be home late."

Saleena spent the next few hours on the phone speaking to Raazia then Allia and then Sameena. The conversation was mostly about Abdel and his sudden disappearance. Raazia said some *gorah* guy called Philip had called her, said he was fine and not to worry about Abdel. "Sal, please don't tell Papaji though. I do not want him to know. Papaji *kaa deemach toh kharaab ho geeya hai naa*. Papaji has gone completely mental. He rants and raves all day about Abdel. He shouts at *Amii* all the time," Raazia said.

"She deserves it, dare I say, after how she treated us all. Let her taste a bit of that medicine herself," Saleena said.

"He rants about his good reputation in the community being ruined. He wants to die as a result of the shame brought on him. Papaji can be such a drama queen. The thing is he will not let go. I think he has turned bipolar without realising it. He is being such a drama queen about it!" said Raazia.

"Knowing how Dad is with his outdated traditions, Abdel should have done it quietly and not have all that publicity. I ask you, why go public like that? I don't understand it," Saleena retorted.

"Saleena he is still a *bacha hey naa?* He is a baby still and I don't think he gave it much thought. Being an only boy he was so spoilt after Begum died."

"Who was the *gorah?* Philip, did you say his name was?"

"I don't know, Sal, but it was good to have a call from him. At least I know our little brother is safe."

"It sounds fishy to me, Raazia. *Dhal mey kuch Kala laagtaa hey*."

Saleena was astute. Almost suggested to Raazia that the *gorah* could possibly be his boyfriend but did not in case she may be wrong. They then talked about Nawaz. Raazia conjectured that he was only being nice now as he would be sucking up to Abdel through her for money.

Philip meanwhile decided to fly across to the Caribbean to join Abdel. His arrival at Grantley Adams International Airport had been delayed for five hours. Abdel waited anxiously in the lounge area for the arrival of Flight BA856, glancing at the overhead screen from time to time to check the arrival time. Though a little anxious about the delay, he did not mind the wait. He sat at the airport 'plane-watching'. It sure killed the time. Clearing through customs, Philip finally emerged in the arrivals area of BGI airport looking tired. They kissed each other as they met. Some passengers passing by gave them odd looks, then immediately turned their heads away seemingly in disgust. One particular man walking by with his family looked at them and shook his head. He was white, appeared to be in his mid-forties, quite plump, dressed in crumpled white shorts and a Hawaiian shirt, his belly hanging out with his shirt buttons undone, continued to stare at the two as they hugged.

"How was the flight?" Abdel asked.

"Long and tiring, I feel beat. The delay did not help. I could do with a nice long shower to be honest."

"Why was the flight delayed? The hotel is nice. You will like it I am sure," Abdel said.

"It was due to a stupid drunken passenger on board at Heathrow, would you believe? It was a young Brit, not surprisingly had far too much to drink. Apparently, he assaulted a male member of the cabin crew when he was asked to leave the aircraft. He naturally refused to get off the plane, insisting he had to get to his destination. He went and sat in someone's seat and refused to budge, pretended as though nothing had happened. The police eventually escorted him off the plane. Oh, what a twat I tell you."

"A bit of excitement on board then, huh?" Abdel said.

"Yes. I suppose you could call it that. It wasn't fun for the other passengers. Some were very frightened. Now let's get to the hotel. I am starving too."

Chapter 15

Autumn 1989 came around quickly. Tree foliage was beginning to change colour from lush green to a mixture of green, autumn gold and rust signalling an early change of season from summer to autumn. It was a vivid display of colours from nature changing seasons. Tons of letters addressed to Abdel had piled up in the living room to the point some had spilt onto the floor. The over-spilt ones began spreading outwards. Papaji kicked them back under the coffee table with his feet every time they were in the way. Surprisingly Papaji had kept his letters, not thrown them away which might have been expected. For some strange reason the envelope with his A Level results was kept on the mantle behind the old clock. He had longed for his only son to go to university. It would have made him proud, but that longing had paled into a forlorn hope after his stunt pulled winning the lottery. Abdel had been away for months. He had stopped counting the months his son had not been home. To an extent it did not matter anymore. There was no sign of Abdel returning home anytime soon.

Papaji did display some signs of worry about his son's disappearance when on occasions he paced up and down in the lounge in the evenings by himself just as he had done in the hospital when he had waited for his birth. His reputation lay in tatters, tarnished and in ruin. On occasions he showed signs of odd mental behaviour, demonstrating signs of disconnection with reality. At night he preferred to sit in the dark for hours talking to himself. *Amii* could hear him muttering gibberish as he sat on his favourite chair with a *tasbee* (rosary) in his hand, passing the beads between his fingers.

Most of the furniture in the house was still the same as when the children were small. Papaji had always been parsimonious when it came to changing furniture. *Amii* tried to join him on some occasions but he would snap at her if she said anything to him which was not to his liking, which left her frustrated. They constantly rowed over his odd behaviour. She said to Raazia on one occasion when speaking with her that she thought he had become *paaghal* (insane). He had stopped going for prayers at the mosque too; apart from work he had become a recluse. His self-imposed imprisonment, a complete detachment from the community, was odd. *Amii* thought depression had set in. The old guy looked tired and haggard. Old loyal friends Malik, Sheikh Ahmed paid him occasional visits, calling on him from time to time to enquire how he was doing as they had missed him at the daily prayers at the mosque.

Amii answered the front door one day.

"Please come in, Malikji and *Maulana sahib*. Come in. Do sit down. I shall call Faizali."

He took his time before he came downstairs. They both got off their seat to greet him. Normally he would greet them by hugging them first, but he no longer cared for old customs which, for him, seemed to have withered away. This time he shook hands only. They all sat down. Some minutes passed in silence.

"Faizali you should come to the mosque. It is no good you hiding away here," *Maulana* said, breaking the silence.

"Yes, yes you should," Malik added.

"I don't really feel up to it. All my energy has been sapped out of me. I am waiting for *His* call now," Faizali said in a low voice, head bowed, almost in tears.

Malik stood up and sat next to his old friend. He put one hand on his shoulder.

"You know life brings all sort of troubles in our daily lives. The Almighty helps us get through these tests he sets for us. I remember the day I came over when your dear Begum, God bless her soul, had passed away. You were so distraught at her loss. You then picked yourself up afterwards and carried on with life. You need to pick yourself up again, my old friend, and deal with the troubles, not shut yourself away from your community. It does not help you. It may not be easy, but you have to Faizali. Ask for forgiveness form Allah the Almighty and pray for your son. People are forgiving, you know, after all it was not your fault all this happened. Come to the mosque on Friday. *Juma* is a good day to ask for forgiveness from Him," Malik said.

"Thank you for your kindness. Your words mean a lot to me. I shall try."

The three of them sat for a while sipping tea, which Amii had made for them, enjoying the time together.

*

Faizali had a terrible migraine on *Juma* day. It was almost as though he was avoiding going to the mosque that day. Malik called for him to encourage him to pluck up enough courage to attend the local mosque. It would be his first time since his return from Pakistan. Naturally he was filled with trepidation. His nerves were on edge as he slowly climbed the short steps to the mosque. Strangely, whilst a most familiar place to him all the years he attended the mosque, it somehow seemed like a strange place that day. He could almost feel some eyes fixed on him. A few odd stares from some people here and there made him feel ill-at-ease. Malik counselled to ignore the stares. Some greeted him by offering '*salaams chacha*', others just glanced at him and looked away. *Amii* was just pleased to get him out of the house for a change.

*

January 1990. The four Louis Vuitton suitcases were left wide open on the double bed in the rented apartment. Philip was busy packing. They ended up staying in Bridgetown for seven months. Philip had exhausted his sabbatical from his employer, Abdel craved getting back home. He would be celebrating his eighteenth birthday in February and he wanted to share that day with his family at home no matter what. He had missed home terribly. Nothing would stop him going home to see his folks. The excitement of returning home was overwhelming for Abdel yet the feeling of trepidation had not been absent. He tried to hide it from Philip as it was truly time he faced up to the unknown waiting for him at home.

"I have loved this apartment a lot and I am going to miss it, Philip, but I can't wait to get home. My life has changed so much. I have had to grow up so fast before my eighteenth birthday. Sometimes I still think it is all a dream. I feel I shall wake up in my old bedroom penniless. I wish I could."

"Do you really? For one *you* would not have met me then, Abdel!"

"I don't mean it like that. I am happy we met. I miss home so terribly though."

"Yes, I know. It is all real, my boy. It's no dream. You all packed?" Philip asked.

"Yes I am. I am ready to fly home tomorrow. Have to, you know?" Abdel responded.

"Abdel shall we savour our last night here?"

"I think that is a good idea."

"Let's go sit and chill on the balcony," said Philip.

It was a perfect evening. The gentle sea breeze wafted through the open balcony doors. They sat on the balcony overlooking the glorious panoramic view of the Atlantic Ocean meeting the sky in the far distance. The calmness of the sea gave out that fresh slightly sulphur smell. It was lovely in the gentle breeze. The gentle wind whistled through blowing Philip's blond hair, slightly ruffling it only for him to brush it back, running through it with his fingers, patting it back in place with the palm of his hand. As the early evening wore on, the colour of the sky began gradually changing as the light slowly faded into the distant mist. Scattering of molecules in the air from the day's sunlight mingled with the warm air and the shimmering sea gave into the darkness that would soon follow. You could almost feel the intense change of nature as the sky slowly turned a shade of pink then red. Soon it would be dark. They sat next to each other holding hands sipping freshly squeezed chilled tropical juice, watching the sunset as the sky turned bright red in colour, the sun slowly ebbing away in the distance. The colour of the sea changed from blue to grey. The shimmering reflection of the sun on the sea died away far too quickly for the lovers.

"Isn't the sunset beautiful, Abdel?"

"It *is* amazingly beautiful," he replied.

"If I could, I would love to stay here forever. It's like paradise. So, what are your plans looking ahead? I know you have been homesick for a while, I can tell. You keep your distance both in mind and body. Don't you?" Philip said.

"Sorry, I don't mean to. *I* am homesick, Philip. I really am. I can't deny that. I am longing for home-made food. *Amii's* curries the most."

"Well tomorrow's the day, kiddo, when we get back home," said Philip.

"I cannot wait to get home," said Abdel.

"Are you ready to face your demons, you know, that you have feared all these past months?"

"No, not really but I have to face it sometime. As they say, have to face your demons sometimes."

"Yes, buddy. Do you think it will all be okay at

home for you? I am truly worrying about you."

"I don't know. I guess I won't really know until I get back and see for myself."

Philip placed his hand on Abdel's open palm, squeezing it slightly. With the other he lightly brushed his fingers through Abdel's hair ruffling it.

"Oi," Abdel retorted gently with a smile.

Both laughed at the same time. There was a momentary sudden silence as the conversation died away. They sat quietly for some minutes holding hands, enjoying the moment. Abdel was a troubled young man carrying on his young shoulders the burdens and troubles acquired, he knew, that lay ahead in life. He had let himself into some profound issues that he would need to deal with no matter what even though they were weighing him down. *Why is it so difficult, growing up?* he thought to himself. The intense feeling of guilt about the money was one thing, but the discovery of his sexuality was quite another to deal with. It was almost feelings of guilt that had started to eat away at him slowly. The momentary silence that had descended went on longer than necessary. Philip hated the eerie silence.

"So Abdel…" Philip said, breaking the silence, but before he could finish his sentence, Abdel interrupted.

"Philip, the one thing I know I have to keep absolutely secret is my sexuality. My family must never find out. No one must ever know."

"What is so terrible about being gay or bisexual, Abdel?"

"I am not sure you will understand, my friend. It's wrong to do this in my religion."

"So it is said of all religions. Not just yours. I was born a Catholic, I should know! God made us this way. Do you not think about that?" Philip said somewhat forcefully, defending his position.

"I don't really know what to think. I am so confused. But one thing I do know is for as long as I live this side of me stays a secret, our secret."

"Oh when you get back it will make headlines, especially in, *what* is your local paper in Leicester? Oh yes, the Leicester Mercury?"

"Please don't joke about this, Phil. I am serious."

"You just called me Phil. Wow, only my mum calls me that."

"You close to your mum?" Abdel asked.

"Yes, very. She knows too. I told her one day."

"Boy, really? How did she react? It must have been a bombshell for her!"

"She just said she always knew. She told me she was glad I told her. There are no secrets between me and my mum after that. I just came clean with the truth. She is superb, my mum. You should meet her. She will like you."

"You are so lucky."

"How about *your* mum? Why don't you talk to her?" asked Philip.

"I have a step-mum. She is not a very nice person. She definitely would not understand. She would tell my dad. My natural mother died a few days after giving birth to me. I never knew her."

"Oh kiddo, I am so sorry."

"It is okay. I was brought up by my step-mum and I do not think even though she had to bring me up, she would have those natural maternal traits as I am not from her womb," Abdel said.

"Abdel you do surprise me, you know, you come out with such precisely profound language, it makes me think you went to some private school."

"Very, very funny."

Chapter 16

The eighties drew to a close. Saleena for one was glad to see the back of the eighties as it was an absolutely dreadful decade for her. Life with Nawaz had been miserable. She was happy to leave it behind. She looked forward optimistically to the new decade hoping good things may come. Nawaz strangely was amicable in his relationship with her, so life had become a little bit more bearable. She started becoming used to it. Surprisingly he refrained from intimate contact with Saleena too, which suited her down to the ground. Whilst his odd behaviour was a blessing for her, she wondered how long it would last. She knew, felt it in her water, it wouldn't last long. Like leopards don't change their spots, why would he? She knew deep down he had some ulterior motive behind his change in behaviour.

One cold Sunday morning in January Saleena was busy getting ready for work. She was in the kitchen when Nawaz walked in. He asked to have some breakfast.

"Have you heard from Abdel, Saleena?" he asked

without any form of greeting out of the blue, though not least unexpectedly random.

Saleena had to pause and think about the unexpected question put to her. She looked at him without immediately responding. He waited for a response without repeating his question.

"No, still no sign of him," she responded.

"Any idea where he could be? He has been gone a long time," he said.

"No Nawaz, I don't know. I don't, honest," she said calmly.

Nawaz did not appear to believe her. He made a grunting sound. Saleena thought in her head that even if she knew where he was, Nawaz was the last person on earth she would tell.

"It is strange that he has taken off just like that without telling anyone in the family. Someone must know where he is, surely. Your dad phoned me last night and asked me if I knew where he was! Why should I know?" he stated with some aggression in his voice.

Saleena did not respond.

"Fancy just disappearing just like that after winning all that money and not letting even his family know where he is. That is strange. You must be worried about him as he is your only brother. Aren't you?"

Saleena just nodded as she was unsure whether she should respond.

"Did you hear what I said or are you ignoring me?" he said sharply.

"I was not ignoring you, *baba*. Allah looks after us all in one way or another and I am sure he is fine somewhere." A quietly cautious and measured response from Saleena.

"I can't believe he has so much money though, just like that. What a lucky bugger. I hope he shares it with the family when he decides to surface."

The conversation ended there. Nawaz knew Saleena was not about to be coerced into disclosing any more information about Abdel's whereabouts than she had imparted. He knew very well it would not be wise to pursue this any further at this time. The situation had become tense but abated when Nawaz left the house. As usual he went out without saying anything. Saleena was running late getting to the Centre as she had not anticipated being held back by his conversation. Driving to the Centre, she dwelt on the conversation with Nawaz.

"He is only nice to me as he wants a share of the pie through me!" she said aloud in the car. "What a bastard."

Abdel travelled first-class with Philip, travelling back home on a British Airways Boeing 747 which touched down at Heathrow airport around midday. The flight was comfortable with the cabin crew pampering the rich travellers who could afford to travel first-class in luxury. Philip and Abdel parted ways as Abdel caught a taxi to Leicester from the airport. He sat well back into the taxi seat, jet-lagged, leaning his head on the side of the window falling asleep. Returning felt great as he had missed home terribly. As the taxi was getting ever nearer to home, Abdel woke up suddenly. A feeling of dread returned.

His stomach began to churn. Deep anxiety mixed with a feeling of elation had gripped him. Adrenaline began pumping through his veins. Abdel pulled his coat up snugly, covering his body as he had begun to shake. The taxi driver was middle aged, short crew cut hair, English, with a short grey beard. His driving was good, mostly choosing to drive in the fast lane on the M1. Abdel wore a peaked cap, sunglasses to disguise his face, Armani jeans and a dark green coat hoping that would give him anonymity.

"You are the lad who won the £6.6 million jackpot on the lottery way back few months ago. Aren't you?" the taxi driver asked in a calm voice.

Abdel did not respond. He did not know what to say. After a momentary silence, Abdel responded to the question.

"How did you know?" Abdel asked.

"I remember you from the papers. Your story was all over the news. It was a wonderful story, mate, which was a whopping big one at that too."

"I was hoping not to be recognised, buddy."

"I have a trained eye, my friend. In this job I see many different types of people who sit in the back of my taxi. I see many different faces too. Some will do a bad job of not being recognised, some a good job, but your story was too massive to be missed by anyone. You had to be asleep to miss that one," the taxi driver said.

"Oh! I thought I'd done a good job with the gear."

"It's my trained eye, my friend," he said, pointing his index finger and middle finger, making a 'V' sign, towards his eyes.

The journey soon came to an end. Before he knew it Abdel was outside his home. He sat in the taxi for some ten minutes, the meter still running. Abdel had not worked out what he would say to Papaji or what he would do if things went horribly wrong. There was no plan 'B' in his head.

"We are here, buddy. The meter is still running."

"Oh, that's okay. How much do I owe you? Never mind, here, and keep the change."

Abdel took three £50 notes from his wallet and gave it to the driver.

"Thanks mate. That is very kind of you," he said as he unloaded the luggage from the back of the taxi.

Abdel used his set of keys to the house to let himself in. The familiar smell of stale curry mingled with the smell of burning incense made him smile. He stood there in the door frame inhaling that lovely familiar smell into his nostrils, stood in the spot for a few minutes, eyes closed, continuing to smile. As he stepped into the front room the first thing he spotted was the pile of mail stacked in the corner of the room. He went over, sat on the floor and waded through the thick pile of post. He did not find what he was looking for. Looking quizzical, he surveyed the room, spotting the envelope on the mantle. He picked it up, opened it and looked at the piece of paper for a few minutes. He smiled. "Yay," he said quietly. *Amii* came into the front room looking startled. She ran over to him, relieved to find the intruder was her step-son, got hold of him and hugged him.

"*Arrray...* where have you been *puttar*? We have been so worried about you. We have all missed you so much. And look at you? You have changed. I bet a million rupees you have a fancy car out there?" she said.

"No I haven't, *Amii.* I have not even passed my driving test yet so sorry to disappoint you, but no car, yet."

By the time he had finished his sentence she had rushed to the window of the lounge to look outside to see if a flash car was parked outside the house. She seemed a little disappointed there wasn't a flash car parked out there. For her it was all about showing off to the neighbours. She came back and hugged him again. She looked at him and smiled. Then suddenly she had tears in her eyes. Abdel had never seen her cry or be so emotional before.

"Is Papaji not home *Amii*?"

"No *betta,* he should be home soon, I think. Come sit here; tell me all about what you have been up to in the last few months. Did you find your envelope? It's over there on the mantle. Your Papaji had saved it especially for you on one side as it was getting lost in that horrible pile over there," she said, turning to look but the envelope was not there.

"So, what were your results then?"

"I got two As and a B."

"Papaji will be really proud of you *puttar.*"

"Will he?" Abdel asked, unconvinced.

At that moment the front door opened. Papaji walked in. The conversation stopped dead at that point between the two. The room was plunged into an icy cold silence on seeing Abdel, as his presence was unexpected. Faizali just stood there by the door, lifeless, not knowing what to say to his son. It was an awkward moment. The hostile look on his face was indescribable. Abdel stayed silent. He did not utter a word, expecting his Papaji to make the first move in saying something. He was his only son. Surely forgiveness would make everything fine. He was wrong. The strange atmosphere continued. Papaji's eyes turned bloodshot red as he continued to stare at his son intensely. The crows' feet next to his eyes became pronounced, he could see the pent-up anger was about to burst from his veins. Abdel was filled with fear as his skin perspired. The perspiration under his armpits began showing through the T-shirt he was wearing. Papaji then walked away. The months of absence had not softened his heart towards his only son. *Amii* placed her hand on Abdel's head and said.

"*Puttar* give him time to get used to it, you'll see he will come around."

Abdel had loved his father all his life. They had been inseparable. He remembered all the hugs and kisses Papaji used to shower on him. It seemed they were now strangers. Abdel sat on the sofa numb next to *Amii* for some minutes holding her hand. Neither said much for a good while.

"I don't know what you have been eating in the last few months, but you look very thin and pale. I bet you have missed *Amii's* cooking, haven't you? Come, you must be hungry. Would you like some lamb *sabzi* with *rotis*? "

The thought of homemade food brought a tiny smile to his face. He nodded.

"I would love to have some please, *Amii.* I have been eating fish, vegetarian pizzas and rice all the time and I am all fished out," Abdel said.

"Huh... *gorah* food not filling at all, is it? Come, I will feed you properly *Amii's* food. Nothing beats your mother's food."

Faizali had gone upstairs. Abdel had been yearning to get back home but had not really appreciated how angry his Papaji was with him. The house he had grown up in had for the first time become so uncomfortable that he felt like a stranger in it. It was *his* home at one time for seventeen years. It was a place that lovingly nurtured him to grow into a young man. Now it felt like a different place. A place he could not recognise as his home. *Amii* got hold of Abdel by his arm, gently guiding him to the dining table like someone would a blind person. The smell of lamb *sabzi* with freshly made *rotis* was delicious and inviting. Abdel looked at the food and pushed the plate away from him. He had longed for familiar food but had suddenly lost his appetite.

"*Array* what is the matter, Abdel? It is your favourite *sabzi* and *roti.* You always liked it very much."

"*Amii,* so sorry but I have lost my appetite."

"All of a sudden, surely it can't be so? You need to ignore Papaji. He will come around. Just be a little patient with him," *Amii* said.

"No, *Amii,* this time it is different. Did you see the look on his face? Those eyes were filled with anger. I have never seen him like that before."

"*Array* what are you talking about? It is all nonsense, Abdel."

"No *Amii* it is not. Those eyes said it all to me. 'You are not my son,' is what I read in them eyes, *Amii*. He has made me feel like a total stranger in my own home. *Mey tow parayah bunn geeya ees germey Amii*." He started to cry as he said those words that he was a stranger.

She put her hand on his head, looked at his sad face.

"No *bettay* you are totally wrong. Don't speak like that please."

She held him close to her, trying to comfort him. The conversation ended at that point. Neither said anything more for a while. *Amii* insisted he ate a little. Abdel took a couple of bites just to please her, but he could not eat so he went to his room. The room was exactly as he had left it. Nothing seemed to have been disturbed. His bed was made as it was the day he left the house.

The news of the return of the prodigal son had spread fast within the family. The whole Rehman family except Allia and Sara came to see Abdel the same evening. Papaji stayed in his room. *Amii* made a lame excuse, saying that he was unwell as he had a migraine. No one should disturb him. To Abdel the rejection was confirmed. Nawaz and Saleena had come too. Nawaz for one would not have missed this gathering. He was stuck to Abdel like glue that evening. He followed him like a dog following its master everywhere trying to have a conversation about investments as if he was suddenly an expert on the subject of making money. Abdel had never liked Nawaz. He knew the man was a pretentious idiot. A small-time taxi driver who had, maybe, dabbled in one or two small investments buying shares, but really knew nothing about investments of large sums of money. He talked about creating portfolios of stocks, shares and huge property investments, giving Abdel advice on it. *What a pretentious fucking bastard,* Abdel thought to himself. His attempts at trying to get away from him were futile. Nawaz followed Abdel like a poodle everywhere he went. Abdel had enough money to share some of the fortune. He announced that he would give everyone in the family £125,000 each as a gift to them.

Papaji remained resolute in his refusal to communicate with Abdel. Whenever he saw his father he greeted him as he had always done in the past when growing up out of his love for him as well as respect for him. He offered *Salaams* to him. Peace be upon him, but Papaji like a sulking kid simply ignored him. *Amii* found her husband's attitude churlish. Abdel tried his best to carry on life as normal but the consistent failure to change in his father's attitude towards him had made life difficult to the point Abdel felt intense unbearable rejection. He was like a stranger in his own house. Abdel was resigned to acceptance of his fate as a family member of the Rehman household, avoiding confrontation with his dad, spending most of his time in his room being bored to tears. A sense of loneliness slowly began creeping into his mind. His bedroom had a mini basketball net which had hung at the top of his door since he was about nine years old. It took him back to the days when he used to play with it. He used to stop playing when Papaji came home. He would jump off his bed and run downstairs to hug him. Tears filled his eyes when he looked back to those happy days.

Things were different. He was still his son. For hours Abdel stayed on his bed flicking the tiny ball towards the net; a few went into the net, the rest missed surprisingly. At one time he had completely mastered the art of netting the ball every time he flicked it towards the net. The tense home environment clearly changed his focus.

A small glimmer of hope was that Abdel's eighteenth birthday was only days away. There was a faint hope that Abdel reaching a milestone in his journey of life may wake him up, make him realise Abdel was his son and extend the arm of paternal loving care to him. He received birthday cards from all his sisters. He chuckled at the funny ones. One from Saleena made him laugh. She wrote:

'Happy birthday kid brother love you lots. Hope you have a splendid 18th birthday. I know you will! Many happy returns.'

She wrote a poem:

You were a little boy yesterday, my little brother,

Today you are a man, my little brother,

Tomorrow you will be someone, my brother,

Marriage with lots of children – a beautiful wife for life, still my brother,

Then as years go by your beautiful black locks will have a hint of grey hair, my beautiful brother,

Daddy of children that you nurture, still my brother,

But suddenly, before you know it comes membership of SAGA and with it a Zimmer frame for a present, but you will still be my beautiful little brother.

She signed off:

'With lots of love, your sister Saleena.'

Amii cooked special food for him. Nothing from Papaji, not even a card. Everyone came except Papaji. The celebration made it less than an ordinary day for Abdel for a change though he was sad Papaji was absent.

The next day Adel stayed in his room most of the day reflecting on the predicament. He picked up the extension telephone in his room when it rang. It was Philip on the phone as he said 'hello'. Abdel recognised his voice straightaway.

"Hi Philip, it's so nice to hear from you, I missed you yesterday. How are you?" Abdel said.

"Hey there kiddo, I am good thank you. Good to hear your voice, buddy. How are you doing? Happy eighteenth birthday, I hope you had a super time?"

"Afraid not Philip, my birthday was a non-event. Papaji did not even speak to me. He has hardly said two words to me since getting here. *Home* is not home anymore. The word 'home' has a hollow ring to it which is sad. I don't think he wants me here."

"No. You are kidding me, aren't you? What can honestly be the problem? I am really struggling to understand, Abdel. Most families would be delighted, if not delighted ecstatic, my man. Which one, the money or have you told them you are gay or both?"

"No, just the money. Don't joke about that. It is serious here. Papaji refuses to speak to me at all."

"Why what is his problem? Surely after all these

months things should have got better. You are his only son. Have you offered him some money, maybe you can bribe him? I am only joking. All I can say is sorry to hear things are as they are. Is there no way he can come around?" Philip asked.

"He will not accept. I don't know what to do now."

"Listen kiddo, you sound really down in the dumps at the moment. We most certainly can't have that. Can we now? Give me your address. I will be there in two to three hours' time."

"Meet me in town by the train station."

"Is that Leicester train station?"

"Yes."

"Okay kiddo, see you anon."

Late that afternoon Abdel caught a taxi to the train station. It was a cold, bleak February day. The station was busy bustling with people. The ticket booths had queues of travellers who waited patiently in lines to buy tickets. Abdel wore his favourite baseball cap, Gucci sunglasses, and a thick Armani coat with a hood which he pulled over his head. Apart from the Gucci sunglasses he looked like an everyday ordinary Joe, unrecognised. He sat on a bench with his suitcase on the side in the taxi rank area outside the station waiting. A few minutes later a red-coloured Mercedes pulled into the taxi rank. Abdel got on his feet as soon as he spotted Philip's car. He waved at him. Philip waved back. He then pulled up in a vacant spot right in front of where Abdel was waiting. The car was filled with bright-coloured balloons with number '18' printed all across them.

"C'mon, hop in," Philip said.

Abdel put the suitcase in the trunk and got into the passenger seat.

"Why have you got so many balloons?"

"You don't think I am going to let this one go by just like that, do you? Your birthday celebration is today, buddy. For me it's my friend's big birthday and we are going to celebrate it in style." With that he pulled out of the station and headed towards the M1 motorway.

The journey back to London took just over two hours' drive. Philip parked up his Mercedes in a reserved space behind a tall white building in Mayfair.

"Wow, this must be expensive living here? When did you move?" Abdel asked.

"Soon after we got back from the Indies, I found this place, loved it when I viewed it, so I bought it. I totally love it. I make money so I like living in style. You should too."

He pressed the buzzer at the main entrance door.

"Hi James, it's Philip here, could you let us in please?"

"Sure," said the doorman James.

A long walk through the marble floor foyer decorated in modern nineties-style decor, brightly lit, led to the lifts. Abdel stood quietly holding his suitcase. They took the lift to the sixth floor. As he opened the front door entrance to his flat, Abdel was in awe. Philip's place was kitted out in expensive furniture, the lot.

"Wow Philip, I never imagined your place to be so nice."

"I have taste, kiddo," said Philip.

"Yes, I see that," said Abdel.

"You have more money and can afford all these ten times over, believe me, you will see. C'mon, let's get freshened up, changed and hit the road. I have booked a table at a restaurant for us for seven."

"Seven people! Why have you invited so many?" Abdel asked, looking decidedly quizzical.

"No, silly, 7.00pm!"

A smartly dressed young Indian waiter in his early twenties greeted them at the 'Tamarind'. The waiter recognised Philip.

"Good evening Mr Benson, it's lovely to see you again. How are you?"

"I'm good, thank you Hassan, we have reservation table for two at seven."

"Of course, just follow me," said Hassan.

They followed Hassan just as the man said, to their table which had a 'reserved' sign on it. The restaurant was decorated in quaint interior design. A blend of Italian baroque mixed with traditional Indian style. A strange-looking place but it felt nice, cosy. A table in the corner away from the main part of the restaurant was perfect, Abdel preferring his privacy, especially when accompanied by a close friend. The evening was pleasant, the food delightfully delicious. Philip signalled Hassan by raising his hand which precipitated a flock of people joining them, restaurant staff mingled with patrons standing all around the table. Abdel was decidedly embarrassed as the crowd started singing.

"Happy birthday to you, happy birthday to you, happy birthday dear Abdel, happy birthday to yoooouuu..."

Hassan wheeled over a trolley draped in white cloth, with a huge birthday cake with 'Happy 18th' decorated on it with the number '18' lit up by candles. Abdel blushed at first in embarrassment as he had not expected it. It was a real surprise.

"C'mon Abdel, make a wish, blow them candles out." said Philip.

Abdel closed his eyes for a moment then bowed his head down, then with a big breath blew out all eighteen candles. A round of applause followed as everyone joined in singing the birthday chorus.

"Well how was that?" Philip enquired.

"That was superb. What a memorable occasion for me. I shall remember this always; I can't thank you enough."

"You are most welcome, kiddo. You don't need to thank me. Oh here, I almost forgot, I have something for you."

Philip took out a small gift box from his jacket pocket and handed it to Abdel. The tag hanging off it read 'To my handsome young friend happy 18th love Philip'.

"Open it," Philip said.

Abdel tore off the gift wrap discovering a beautiful silver ring with a small inscription on the inside of the ring which read: '18th love Phil'.

"Bloody hell, Philip, this is beautiful?"

"Well, it was made especially for you, Abdel, bespoke."

"Thank you so much," Abdel said.

"A kiss would be nice," Philip retorted.

Abdel shook his hand instead.

"C'mon, don't be a wuss man."

Philip stood up came closer to Abdel planted a little kiss on his cheek. Surprisingly Abdel did not flinch though looked decidedly embarrassed.

"Don't look embarrassed, it is fine honestly," Philip reassured his friend.

Abdel relaxed a little though conscious of being in a public place. Display of such affection was not for him.

Chapter 17

Spring came by quickly but before anyone blinked, it had passed by. Time seemed to fly by. Summer was nothing to write home about as it rained most days. The season was poor in contrast to the years before. Nature seemed to flourish, however, as always. Flowers were in full bloom showing off the season, working their magic without fail. Lush green foliage in abundance covered the trees everywhere. Grass grew at a faster pace as it absorbed the rainwater on the ground feeding it day by day.

Nawaz had been pacified for a while; the money from Abdel helped keep his mind occupied for some months on his business venture. He bought four new taxi cars. Hired staff to help run the business as well as getting involved in running it himself for a change. He stayed busy with his business, changed his car, and went on a holiday abroad to Pakistan by himself. The cash soon ran out. Then he reverted back to his habit, using drugs, which got worse. He had become a more regular user of cannabis.

Saleena was in the kitchen one morning pottering

around with household choirs. Nawaz came downstairs, sat down at the dining table. The kitchen door was ajar. He asked her to make him breakfast. She made him tea with warmed up buttered croissants, which she cut in half filling the middle with strawberry jam. The conversation seemed fairly random but amiable at first.

"Where is that brother of yours, Saleena? He keeps disappearing. No one knows where he is again. What is wrong with that boy? Can't he stay put in one place?" Nawaz asked in a calm voice.

She knew why the 'where' question was asked for, much to her annoyance.

"Nawaz, I do not know," Saleena said sharply.

"What do you mean you do not know?" he asked in a raised tone.

"Don't ask me. How would I know? He is a man, isn't he? Men don't share that kind of information with their wives or sisters," Saleena retorted with an equally sharp response.

"Doesn't that cow Raazia know?" he asked in an aggressive tone.

"I couldn't tell you, why you don't ask her yourself I don't know."

"Why are you so mouthy all of a sudden?" Nawaz said.

"I suppose you have spent all the money he gave you; which might I add you definitely did not deserve in the first place. Now you are going to suck up to him again for more, are you? Don't you have any shame begging for money?"

"What is that supposed to mean?" Nawaz said angrily.

"You know exactly what I said."

A, "Huh," sound came out from his mouth followed by a growling sound, then he stood up from the dining table chair, pushing it back under the table making a scratching sound on the floor. Saleena quickly retreated back into the kitchen, closing the door gently. There was a moment of fear in her mind, regretting her harsh tone. Nawaz flicked the butter knife on the floor, slammed the door shut behind him as he left the house. Saleena let out a heavy sigh of relief. Soon she settled down to finishing the household chores, and then she spent the day by herself mostly on the phone chatting with Raazia first then Allia, after that with Sameena about the *contretemps* with Nawaz. She spent the rest of the afternoon with her dear friend Doris.

It was about midnight when Nawaz arrived back home. He was drunk as a skunk. Most surprisingly he had managed to get home without being stopped by the police. He staggered in as he dragged himself into the house, slamming the front door shut, causing Saleena to awake from her sleep. He held onto the side rail tightly as he climbed up the stairs one by one, missing one step, nearly tripping backwards but managing to grab the handrail tightly to regain balance. He managed to stagger to the door of Saleenas's room then banged his fist on the door hard. She was still half asleep. The banging got louder, waking her up fully. The racket Nawaz was making was loud enough for neighbours to hear as some put their lights on. Saleena rubbed her eyes, rolled out of bed, finally relenting. As she was about to unbolt the door, it flung wide open. Nawaz forced it open by breaking it. A heated row ensued between the two. Nawaz's predisposition for physical violence surfaced with a vengeance. He wasn't going to settle for a verbal argument this time as he did in the morning. Worse for wear from drink, he pushed Saleena on the bed, forcing his body upon her. He punched her on her face. He raped her before he left.

Sadly, this was a start of endless nights of domestic abuse. The thirst for violence grew as each night went by. A resurgence of the same old pattern was developing day by day. He arrived home late at night drunk then would demand sex before leaving her room. Saleena soon began feeling bruised, psychologically tired as old scars began to surface. Pressure grew intense too to give into him and give him some information on Abdel. The vicious circle of violence continued as the nights passed. Lack of sleep began taking its toll on her. She began turning up late at work looking tired. Nadine had picked up the change in Saleena. When she asked her if all was well, Saleena said it was. But for Nadine it was déjà vu. She did suspect resumption of domestic violence as heavy bags under her eyes were obvious. Nadine was not going to give up as she persisted in asking Saleena if all was well but strangely, she said nothing.

One night Saleena barricaded the door after she locked it. She emptied her chest of drawers, dragged the heavy oak carcass across the room, positioning it against the door, then put the drawers back into the carcass, filing them with items to make it sturdy. "That will keep him out," She muttered loudly to herself. Tired, she fell asleep. Later that same night the noise of his car pulling up on the drive outside broke her sleep. The silence in the house was eerie at first. She put the bedside lamp on, rolled out of bed, glancing at the square red alarm clock to see the time. It was 3.25am. She lifted the curtain and peered through the window. Someone was disembarking from a taxi. She did not have the energy to investigate any further. Returning to bed, she fell asleep.

At 7.00am her alarm clock buzzed. She emptied the drawer contents before pulling the chest carcass away from the door. She opened the door quietly and tiptoed up to his bedroom. The door was ajar, his bed not slept in. She made her way downstairs, looked everywhere but there was no sign of him. The phone rang. She did not pick up immediately. It continued ringing. *Could it be the hospital?* she thought to herself. Maybe Nawaz was involved in a car crash, a thought which crossed her mind momentarily but was soon dismissed as she would not wish such a fate on her worst enemy. Saleena picked up the receiver slowly and held it to her ear.

"Hello," she said quietly, filled with a little trepidation.

"Saleena is that you? It is Nadine."

"Yes Nadine it is me," she replied as she stretched, yawned loudly, tilting her head one side then the other, stretching the muscles in her neck.

"Saleena I am worried about you. Are you alright, dear?" Nadine asked.

"Yes I am. I was just yawning, sorry."

"No, it is quite alright, as long as you are okay. I

was really worried about you all night last night, lovee. I tossed and turned in my bed but could not get to sleep thinking about you in the same house as Nawaz. Are you sure you are okay?" Nadine repeated her question.

"Yes Nadine, I am fine now," Saleena replied. "Oh Nawaz did not come home last night, not sure why, but for a moment when the phone rang, I thought it was the hospital."

"Well lovee, don't you worry about him. He can take care of himself, I am sure."

"Oh you truly are a gem, so good to me. Thank you as it means a lot to me."

"Saleena, lovee, you and Grace are both special to me."

"I will see you soon, Nadine. Got to dash, get ready and I shall see you anon. Bye."

That day Saleena got home from work at around 4.30pm. Nawaz's car was on the drive. Trepidation about going inside the house filled her from head to toe. *Why is he here at this time?* she thought to herself. As she slowly walked inside the house some official-looking papers were lying on the floor of the hallway. She walked a few paces, stopped where a blue-coloured one was at her feet. She picked it up. It was a charge sheet. He was on bail to appear at Manchester Magistrates court for a drink-driving offence on 18th September 1990.

"Ah, makes sense then why he did not come home last night," she muttered to herself. Nawaz had spent the night in a cell at the local police station for drink driving. She went upstairs and found him slumped on his bed with his clothes and shoes still on, snoring away.

Saleena showered, got changed and went into town. She bought some toiletries for herself from Boots then drove over to Nadine's. Early evening about 8.00pm she drove back into Manchester. On the way into town she spotted a large billboard poster advertising a new film release called 'Flatliners' which looked interesting. It had her favourite actors William Baldwin, Keifer Sutherland, Julia Roberts and of course Kevin Bacon. She had read some good reviews on the film and thought it worth watching on the big screen. Home life was dreary enough anyway, so it was an impromptu visit to the cinema that evening. As she drove home, she thought about those medical students seeking answers about the afterlife. The movie she thought was great. Well made in her opinion with great acting performances from the strong cast. It was about a Chicago medical student, Nelson, played by Sutherland, who persuaded his fellow medic colleagues to help him end his life and then resuscitate him in the nick of time. What a brilliant story she thought it was. She was a mere mortal. The only time she was personally affected by death was when Begum died in 1972. She thought about her mother and the afterlife after death. For a Muslim it is good deeds that help pave the way for a better afterlife, it is thought. Being a good Muslim earns oneself everlasting peace in the afterlife. She wondered if Begum was in a good place. *She must be,* she thought to herself, the poor woman had died after giving birth to Abdel. She could not imagine what it would be like, childbirth, but it could not be fun as she had seen women scream whilst in labour.

Nawaz was not at home as she pulled up her car onto the driveway. She felt good, letting out a huge sigh of relief. After tidying up downstairs Saleena went to her room. She did exactly what she had done the night before. She barricaded the door with the chest of drawers. It was about midnight she heard the noise of his car pull onto the driveway followed by the front door slamming shut which made a loud banging noise. Saleena, half asleep stayed in bed. Rubbing her eyes, she began to pray. "Please Allah let him just go to his room." Her prayers seemed answered at first as he did. But an hour passed, Saleena began dozing off only to be woken up by a hideously loud banging on her bedroom door. Nawaz was pounding his fist on it.

"Open the fucking door, Saleena, or I swear to God I will break it down," he yelled.

She stayed still. He continued banging on the door, turning the doorknob at the same time. The chest of drawers held fast as it kept him out. For a few minutes there was complete silence. Then, suddenly a huge bang on the door caused it to crack. Another blow caused the top part of the door to fold inwards. Debris flew everywhere. Saleena was petrified. He stood there looking incandescent. His silhouette in the light made Nawaz look like the incredible hulk standing in the hallway under the flickering light. He pushed the chest of drawers away, seemingly without much effort, climbed in through the open space of the broken door menacingly waving a cricket bat in the air whilst Saleena screamed for him to go away. A heated argument ensued between them both shouting at the top of their voices. He muttered something.

Nawaz swung the bat, attacking her. A hard blow to the head brought Saleena to the floor. She collapsed. She was on the ground unconscious. He kicked her repeatedly in the stomach with his right foot. A frenzy of violence perpetrated on a helpless woman finally stopped, leaving her on the floor bleeding from the head.

He stumbled as he pulled his body backwards, falling on a drawer which had been knocked out, and was lying on the floor. He got up, somehow staggered out of the room after dragging the chest of drawers away from the door. Saleena was unconsciousness. Blood seeped out from behind her left ear. An hour passed. She regained partial consciousness, managing to curl up in a foetal position still slumped on the floor. A little while later she began to move her right arm. She stretched out trying to reach the telephone cable. She managed to get hold of it; as she did, she yanked the cable hard from the skirting with one hard pull just in case she may not have the strength to have a second chance, causing the phone to tumble onto the ground. Then like a fisherman slowly reeling his catch towards him, Saleena pulled the phone towards her. She brought the telephone closer to her, picked the receiver up and listened to the dialling tone. She dialled Raazia's number. Raazia was fast asleep but disturbed from her sleep, she answered the phone. Although Saleena's number had displayed on the caller display screen the numbers appeared blurred to her. Rubbing her eyes, she picked up the phone. All she could hear was murmuring sounds with intermittent coughs in-between. She turned on the bedside lamp, a closer look at the display, she could read Saleena's number.

"Saleena I know you are there, baby. What is wrong? What is the matter, Sal? Saleena *are* you hurt, baby? What is wrong? Speak to me, Sal, please."

Saleena moved her hand up to her head and gently pressed her fingers on the left side. All she could feel was excruciating pain as she pressed her fingers inwards hoping for some relief. It felt tender. Fresh red blood covered her fingers and palm. Then she pressed the flat of her palm against the bruise hard to try to stop it from bleeding. She held it there tightly.

"Ouch... it hurts," she groaned.

She stayed in the foetal position on the floor unable to speak or move, then slowly pulled the handset by the side of her head. With the other hand she pressed her stomach which felt terribly tender with pain. Tears had begun rolling down her cheeks. Raazia by now was in a complete catatonic state. Saleena began sobbing loudly and uncontrollably.

"Raazia I'm really hurt. That bastard has completely done me in, Raaz, I can't even move. My ribs feel sore. My head, my face and legs just hurt so much. I am so much in pain Raazia. Please help me."

"I am here, baby. Don't speak. I am right here, baby. I will come to you as soon as I can. Let me ring for the ambulance. They will be able to get to you quicker than I can. Are you listening, Sal?"

Loud crying sounds could be heard from the other end of the telephone at first but soon faded away. Raazia began to cry not knowing what to do as Saleena was so far away from her.

"Sal listen to me very carefully. I am going to put the phone down as I need to call 999 to get an ambulance to you. Do you understand? I will get there as soon as I can, so stay right where you are, baby."

There was no response from Saleena. Raazia clicked the phone off, then immediately dialled for emergency help.

"It's Saleena, she is hurt. I am calling an ambulance for her," she said to Akeel who was wide awake by now as Raazia ended the call with Saleena.

"I bet it's that twat Nawaz. The fucking bastard, he is such an animal," Akeel said.

Raazia tried calling Saleena's number again after completing the emergency call but only got an engaged tone.

Raazia could not think straight, her mind all over the place, she started to pace up and down the room like a headless chicken. She began going here and there not knowing exactly what to do. Akeel managed to get her to sit down on the bed for five minutes.

"Raazia, c'mon, show some courage. Your sister needs you. It's no time for you to lose your head."

"Akeel I don't know what to do. She is so far away," Raazia muttered.

Akeel called Allia to get her over there whilst he made arrangements for their departure for Manchester. He managed to get a few things together in some plastic carrier bags. Raazia had not fully embraced the extent of the situation she faced. The worrying part for her was it was a two-hour drive to get to Manchester. Panic had set in. She could not think. Raazia paced up and down in the lounge waiting for Allia to arrive. Her pacing got faster as valuable time ticked on. She went to the lounge window to see if there was any sign of her sister.

"Oh Allia please c'mon," she kept repeating over and over. The minute she spotted headlights of a car approaching the house she called Akeel who was in the kitchen.

"Akeel, c'mon, let's go. I think Allia is here."

"What do you mean you think?"

"Don't argue, not now, just get the car started."

Akeel cleared the wet windows, caused by overnight dew. He kept the engine running to warm up the car. Allia pulled up her car behind his, got out and walked over to Akeel. Before she had chance to speak, Raazia dashed over to them.

"Allia what kept you? We need to get to Saleena quickly. I don't know how bad she is hurt but I will call you when we get there okay? Please look after my girls."

Allia had no chance to speak or ask what had happened. Raazia and Akeel seemed to be in a hurry as they got into the car.

An ambulance had arrived outside Saleena's house, followed by a police car. Two young officers had been despatched responding to calls from neighbours about a domestic incident. The ambulance crew could not gain entry into the house despite knocking hard on the front door. Nawaz was out cold on the lounge sofa. Saleena was still unable to move. One of the neighbours came over speaking to the ambulance crew, stating she had heard the occupants of the house engaged in a domestic as she heard them shouting at first then followed by screams coming from the house, and then it all went completely quiet afterwards.

*

"Let me try the back gate, see if I can get in without having to break in," said the young male officer whilst the ambulance crew waited.

"Please be careful," his female colleague cautioned him.

"Don't worry, I'll be fine," he said.

The male officer climbed over the gate, soon emerging some minutes later at the front door, opening it from inside. A small crowd which had gathered outside cheered and clapped. Fortuitously the kitchen window had been left slightly ajar. The ambulance crew rushed up the staircase finding debris strewn everywhere in the landing area. Instinct guided them to Saleena's room as they headed for the room with the broken door.

"Blimey, looks like a bomb has exploded in here," commented one crew member.

"God, I dread to think what is in there," the other responded.

The crew got to Saleena through the mess, pulling away the door and pulling the chest of drawers into the landing area. A visual examination of her state seemed bad. Her head was bloodstained. There was no sign of any movement. It looked hopeless as she lay there lifeless. A paramedic checked her wrist first, detecting a faint pulse.

"Hello, can you hear me? I am a paramedic," he

said three, four times as he tapped Saleena gently on her cheeks with his fingers. Saleena groaned as she made a slight movement. Her breathing was quite faint. He could see a blood stain on the carpet where her head lay on the floor. After checking her airway, she was put in the recovery position. The paramedic continued talking to her trying to keep her conscious. The wound to her head was seen to first. Saleena groaned, holding her stomach tightly as the crew treated her head.

The crowd of people outside had swelled slightly. A young, quite attractive-looking English woman in her late twenties with long dark hair had come out to see what the commotion was about. She jostled through the crowd to get closer to the house trying to get a better view, as Abdel had when the old lady had been knocked down. She then tried to look through the glass bay window as the light was on. She could not see much. Then another police car arrived at the scene. Two older male officers, one in his thirties, the other much older, disembarked from their vehicle. They immediately began to push the crowd back.

"C'mon now, there isn't much to see here. C'mon, move along please." The older officer tried to disburse the crowd.

"It's that Indian fella's house isn't it?" the attractive woman said. "I know he lives there as I seen him a few times. Corr blimey, he gets home late at night drunk as a skunk. I see him stagger into the house. He just about manages to get through that front door of his. I am surprised he ain't been nicked by the coppers when he is drivin' home in that shocking state. It's criminal I tell you!"

"Is that so?" one bystander asked.

"Yeh, any rod up I've heard some terrible noises from the house too. It's almost every night. You can hear them rowin'. Flippen heck, he must be bashing her too, poor thing that wife of his. She is real pretty. I've seen her a few times. She is friendly too. Often says hello when I see her, real friendly like, you know. I bet he has done her in. He looks like a right sod to me."

Another bystander, a man in his forties, salt and pepper hair, standing next to her simply nodded.

"Do you know them then?" he asked.

"Noo, I dunno who they are really as I never met them proper to be honest. The chap looks a bit dodgy to me. I have seen him about a few times. Never speaks. Strange fella, keeps himself to himself. The Indian lady seems nice though," repeating some words.

"Yeh, I have seen that guy a few times meeself. He is a massive bloke. I'd say he is not the sort you trifle with or meet up in a dark alley at night," the man said.

The attractive woman nodded agreeing with him.

"Ay Officer why don't you go arrest that Indian guy?" the woman shouted.

A couple of youths in their late teens to early twenties, who had just joined the crowd, one Asian, another English, listening to the conversation started to chuckle.

"You people like to gossip don't yaa? People have privacy you know and are entitled to it."

The woman rolled her eyes turning her head away sharply as she tutted.

"What do ya kids know about life anyways?"

"Plenty more than you, missus."

"Oi, you cheeky thing, and stop callin me 'missus'. I am only twenty-four."

"Yeh you look it too!"

The young boys continued laughing as she ignored them.

The ambulance crew emerged from the house carrying Saleena on a stretcher. She was covered with a blanket. The two young officers went downstairs into the lounge. Nawaz was slumped on the sofa snoring away loudly. He looked dishevelled.

"Blimey, this one reeks of booze. He looks completely out of it too!" said the female officer.

"Aai yai yai, bloody hell, you are right. It's going to be a hella'va job arresting this one, Libby, look at the bloody size of him. He seems to be in cloud cookoo land, this one," the male officer said as he covered his nose with his hand.

"Hey mister, wake up. C'mon, lad." The male officer tapped Nawaz on his cheeks whilst kneeling down on the floor next to him then continuing to shake him by the arm. Nawaz stirred a little, moving his arms about. The officer persisted in waking him up.

"Who the fucks are you and what do you want? How did you get in the house?" Nawaz asked, his speech completely slurred.

"You are under arrest, buddy. You do not have to say anything unless you wish to do so, but what you say may be given in evidence."

"Fuck off, you motherfucking prats. Get the fuck out of my house!" Nawaz shouted at them.

"Mind your language, sir, there is a female officer here."

"Fuck off," Nawaz replied.

"Sarge down at the station is gonna love this one, I can tell you that!" the female officer said as she tried to handcuff him. Nawaz struggled, breaking free for a moment. The two police officers then pinned him down on the floor face down, while the male officer sat on top of him. The female officer cuffed him securely this time.

Using her communication device, she requested backup from officers standing outside. They were straight in. They got hold of him by his arms, dragging him out of the house. The younger two officers breathed a sigh of relief as Nawaz was not only drunk but was heavy as an ox to lift. It took four officers to finally get him into the back of a police van. The crowd outside cheered once Nawaz was securely in the back of the police van. The drama over the crowd dispersed.

Raazia and Akeel arrived at Saleena's house a couple of hours later. The light in the lounge was lit. Raazia rang the bell a few times but there was no response. She peered through the window but there was no sign of anyone in the front room. Still tense and frantic she called out to her husband.

"Akeel I can't see anyone in the house. What shall we do? Shall we ask the neighbours, Akeel?"

Akeel nodded. Raazia made her way to the house on the right-hand side as the light downstairs was on.

It was nearly 3.30am. She knocked on the door apprehensively. A while later a young man answered the door.

"Can I help you? Do you know what time it is, lady, knocking on people's doors at this hour?" he said very curtly, keeping the door open very slightly ajar, his foot wedged firmly behind the door. The lad looked about seventeen years old.

"I am so sorry to disturb you, but I hope you can help please. My sister Saleena lives next door. I've knocked on the door but there is no response. Please, I am desperate for help. Do you know anything at all about your neighbours? I saw the light was on and so thought I would knock and ask. I know it's late. My husband is over there by the car, he thought we could ask the neighbours too."

"Who is it at the door lovee, at this hour? How many times have I told you not to open the door to strangers?"

A woman's voice which sounded like it came from upstairs boomed downstairs, telling him off.

"Mum, it's only about the neighbours, you know the police thing. I can handle it," he said, turning his head as he shouted back at her.

Raazia could hear sounds of footsteps approaching. A woman in her late thirties with short brown hair cut in a bobbed shape opened the door wider.

"Hello love, can I help you?" she said.

The boy rolled his eyes as he walked away inside before disappearing out of sight in the darkness. Raazia was still in a completely frantic state. She attempted to explain but her speech was garbled, she made no sense.

"My dear, what is the matter? Please come inside the hallway. Besides, love, it is not nice speaking on the doorstep. Come in," said the woman.

Raazia stepped into the hallway. It was dark. The woman switched the hallway light on as she closed the front door.

"We can speak properly here. Sit down, lovee," she said.

She moved a magazine off the small pink chaise telephone table seat to make room for Raazia to sit.

"Ryan, love, could you get a glass of water from the kitchen for me please?" she shouted out to her boy. "Did you say to Ryan the lady next door is your sister? Ryan is my lad; ever so good, he is. Only seventeen, you know. Teenagers, they don't seem to sleep at night these days."

"Yes, Saleena is her name. I spoke to her over two hours ago on the telephone. My husband and I have driven up from Leicester to get here."

"Oh, lovee, the police, the ambulance, they were all here about an hour or so ago. A few of the neighbours were standing outside. We did not know what was going on at first. We saw your sister being taken to hospital on a stretcher. The man next door, well he seemed out of it, you know, drunk like, and the coppers had handcuffed him. They took him away in a Panda car, I presume he was under arrest."

"Would you know which hospital she may have been taken to, please? My husband and I are strangers in town here."

"Yes, love, it would probably be the Manchester Royal Infirmary in town as it is the nearest one that has an A & E Department. I suggest best to follow the signs to Manchester University which is on Oxford Road and then watch out for the signs for the hospital which is on The Boulevard. If you get stuck just stop and ask someone."

"Thank you so much," said Raazia.

"I hope your sister is okay, lovee. Good luck," the woman said.

Akeel was adept at following traffic signs. They reached the hospital within twenty minutes. The roads on the outskirts of Manchester were quiet though the town was a little busier. Some night-time revellers were milling around in the city area. Akeel followed the woman's directions accurately to the tee. As soon as he pulled up in the hospital car park, Raazia opened the car door quickly dashing out in a hurry. She looked around for the A&E sign.

"C'mon Akeel, hurry please!" Raazia yelled.

Raazia was still in a state of panic. Akeel secured the car before they headed for the A&E department. A middle-aged female assistant behind the Perspex barrier came to the window. Raazia was out of breath; she raised her body to get to the circular dots cut into the Perspex to speak through it.

"Can I help you?" she said.

"Yes please. My sister was brought here by ambulance about an hour ago. Her name is Saleena Khan. Can you tell me where she has been taken to?"

"If it's ambulance, dear, she would be in the A&E department. Just follow the red line on the ground through those double doors there and keep going. You will come to it. You can't miss it."

"Thank you," Raazia said.

Akeel walked at a normal pace while Raazia dashed at a fast pace along the long corridors following the red line painted on the ground. It was early hours of the morning, but the hospital was busy. It was like the place never sleeps. They walked past the wide wooden double doors with a sign overhead which read 'Accident & Emergency' approaching a counter facing directly opposite them. A young man behind it, ruffled hair, wearing black trousers and green top was sat on a low chair which he rolled forward without getting up and approached the desk. Raazia explained. The man turned his head round one hundred and eighty degrees then glanced at the white board on the wall behind him. The emergency admission patients' names had been written on it in a blue marker. Pointing in the directions of the cubicles, he said, "She is in cubicle 10. Over there across along that way." as he pointed the direction.

"Thank you," Akeel said.

Raazia walked with trepidation following the direction just given by the young man, not knowing what she would find as she approached cubicle 10 slowly. As she got to the cubicle, she could see Saleena had a bandage wrapped round her head. Her face was black all over. Raazia stepped back, put her hand over her mouth, leant backwards, nearly falling over but luckily Akeel was directly behind and prevented her fall. He held her tight round the shoulders with both his hands.

"Hi rey Allah, what has this bastard done to my sister? Akeel just look at her. Look at the state of her."

She approached the bed slowly. Saleena had her eyes closed. Raazia took hold of her sister's hand and squeezed it tight. Tears just rolled down her cheeks. She sat down on a chair and kept hold of Saleena's hand as tightly as she could. Raazia then began to sob loudly. Akeel moved over to his wife's side. He held her. She rested her head against him.

"Sshhh Raazia, you will not help Saleena if you keep crying," Akeel cautioned his wife.

"*Hi rey* Akeel, look at my sister. She should not be here like this. I don't know what we will do if she goes."

"Sshhh... she will be fine. You'll sec. She is now in a place where she will be looked after properly, Raazia," Akeel reassured her.

Raazia continued crying. The pain of seeing her sister in a dreadfully critical state in hospital at death's door seemed unfathomable to her. Her pain was indescribable. Saleena looked as though she had been in a boxing ring with someone crushing his opponent completely. Her eyes were swollen. A white bandage wrapped round her head covered most of her hair and head; a small red blood patch behind her ear was prominent. The swelling looked terrible. They both stood there quietly overawed by the sight of Sal's injuries. A little while later a Chinese doctor came into the cubicle.

"I am Doctor Katherine Chang," she introduced herself, then after a quick shake of hands with Akeel and Raazia she picked up some papers which were on Saleena's side to read the information.

"Are you the patient's relative, ma'am?" the doctor asked.

"Yes, I am her sister Raazia. This is my husband Akeel. Is my sister going to be okay, doctor?"

"We have yet to take some x-rays of the head. It was a vicious attack she was subjected to. She has head injuries, with severe trauma. Domestic violence I understand. These incidents can end up in serious consequences for victims sometimes. So far signs are good as she has responded well so far. Main thing is she is alive! Once the x-rays are done, we will have a better idea of the head injury. She seems like a strong lady, your sister, ma'am."

"She has had to put up with a lot in her marriage. The husband is a brute," Raazia responded.

Doctor Chang then left. A hospital orderly came a couple minutes later to move Saleena to x-ray.

The two young officers who attended the house arrived some minutes later at the hospital. They met Raazia and Akeel.

"Hello, I am PC Ryan Dodd, and this is my colleague WPC Libby France. I understand you are relatives of this victim?"

"Saleena is my sister," Raazia replied.

"We were called out to your sister's house. She was found in one of the bedrooms of the house lying on the floor. She looked in a bad way when we attended. We are here is to find out her condition and to see if we can get a statement from her. Her husband at the moment is at the police station locked up in a cell. We are making further enquiries as we would like to charge that man for what he did to your sister," said PC Dodd.

"How can *I* help?" Raazia asked.

"Well we would like to try and build a picture here. I mean a history of the relationship between these two would help to begin with as we need to understand the background. This man seems to be a violent man capable of extreme violence. Your sister seems to be lucky to be alive," WPC France said.

Raazia felt the need to sit down as she suddenly felt dizzy, completely overcome by what she heard, breaking down in tears again.

"Miss, you okay? Sit down here." The woman officer sat with her on the next chair, whilst PC Dodd went to get some water.

WPC France comforted her. She placed her hand on Raazia's shoulder. Akeel was standing beside his wife. Seeing her upset, he put his hand on her other shoulder to buttress the comfort already provided by the officer. Raazia took a few minutes before gaining composure. Raazia was a strong woman. She mustered up her inner strength soon, wanting not to display weakness, just as Begum had done when the children had visited her in hospital in 1972. She pulled herself together. PC Dodd returned with a glass of water.

"Thank you." Raazia showed appreciation for the water before she took a few sips out of the plastic cup. "Alright, what do you need from me?" Raazia said.

She began detailing the history from her conversations with Saleena as WPC France jotted down some notes on a notepad.

Saleena was moved to a room. It was relatively quiet, comfortable too for her needs, and she was very lucky to be allocated a single room. Raazia had decided she would stay the night with Saleena at the hospital whilst Akeel would make tracks to get back home, for the twins. It turned out to be a long night. A night duty doctor popped in briefly to check in on her. He was a young doctor, brown hair, wore round silver glasses, a white coat and a stethoscope hung around his neck. He checked her notes, glanced cursorily at the patient, gave Raazia a nod before leaving the room. Apart from a faint, "Hi," which he almost whispered, he did not say anything. Saleena, heavily dosed up with morphine seemed comfortable as she slept. Raazia sat on a chair. She catnapped on and off, turning side to side in the hope of getting a comfortable position so she could get some sleep. She managed to get sleep for an hour or so. It was 6.00am when Saleena opened her eyes. The first thing she saw was her sister Raazia sitting in a crouched position with a blanket over her. An involuntary cough, trying to clear her lungs made Raazia jump out of her seat. She came over to the bedside and straightaway held her sister's hand. Saleena squeezed it back gently but tightly. Raazia reciprocated. Saleena's eyes filled up with tears.

"Raazia I am in so much pain, could you call the nurse?" was the first thing she said.

"Of course, sweetie, don't go away, be right back," she said, making Saleena smile a little.

Raazia hurried out of the room to see if she could get help. A hive of activity in the main ward area, apparently a change of shift for hospital staff taking place, made it difficult for Raazia to get someone straightaway. Night-time staff getting off their duties were handing over as doctors, nurses hurriedly performed handovers to the day-shift staff. Cleaners were in the corridor areas busy cleaning away. Raazia managed to attract a young nurse's attention.

"Please, my sister is in pain, can you come quickly?" Raazia pleaded with her.

"Yes, I will do in a minute, as soon as the handover is complete," the nurse responded.

A little while later she returned with a small vial containing one white, one pink tablet with a glass of water. Saleena gradually managed to swallow the tablets helped with a few sips of water. She tried to gulp the water sips, but she coughed it out. The nurse put her hand on Saleena's back to comfort her.

"Easy, easy Saleena, don't hurry. I guarantee you, the tablet will work itself down, you'll see," the nurse said.

Saleena put her hand up to her neck; she pressed her fingers into the neck muscles to ease the pain of swallowing the tablets. At that point she realised why she was in hospital. Her subjugation at the hands of her husband Nawaz dawned on her with the enormity of the suffering she had endured over many years, finally resulting in her ending in hospital with death almost staring right in her face. Floods of tears started to run from her eyes down her cheeks.

"Sshhhhh... Sweetie, let it all out. Cry as much as you want, it is good for you," Raazia said as she reached for her handbag. She fished out some tissues, slowly and gently wiping them over Saleena's face, being careful, trying to avoid causing pain to her swollen eyes.

"I am here now, Sal. So, don't you worry. You can stay with me for as long as you want. I will take care of you. That *haram zaada* idiot is not worth wasting your tears on. Be brave. We will sort this out, trust me."

Raazia sat by her sister's side holding her hand. Both women looked sad. The same nurse came back an hour later to check in on Saleena. This time Saleena managed a smile.

"The pain any better?" the nurse enquired.

Saleena nodded.

"Good girl, they are strong painkillers. Helps, doesn't it?" the nurse responded as she winked at Saleena.

"Thank you so much," Saleena said.

"If you need anything else just call me, okay?"

Saleena nodded.

Around 2.00pm Nadine stopped by at the hospital to see Saleena. Before she saw the state of Saleena, she braced herself, conjuring an image of her friend in a state of peril coupled with a strong feeling of déjà vu. A shiver ran down her spine. She slowly approached the room, poking her head round the door. She witnessed the sight of her friend who was black and blue from the bruises, not to mention the bandage round her head, partially looking like a 'mummy' with a dried blood stain on the side of her head. A frightening sight for her, she approached Saleena, immediately holding her hand as she got closer to her, looking incredulous that Saleena was still in the vicious circle of domestic violence bringing her into hospital.

"I don't really know what to say, Saleena, I must confess," she said, shaking her head. "You need to deal with this now. I am not going to let you go back to that house again. Look at you, my love. You can't. My friend Grace was just like you – stubborn. Please don't make me feel helpless. I have finally again found a good friend. I know you are much younger than me and a lot prettier than me, but I like you as much as I did Grace. Let me help you, Saleena."

Saleena had tears in her eyes. Nadine picked up a soft tissue and wiped her tears away. Nadine smiled at her friend, managing to get her to display a smile on her face. They held hands.

"Saleena, I mean it, I will help you. I will not take no for an answer. All you have to do is reach out to me or anyone who will help you. If you keep going back there you will end up like Grace."

"You must be Nadine?" Raazia asked.

"I am, and you must be Raazia?" Nadine asked.

They shook hands. Outside in the corridor two officers who had attended the scene had come to see Saleena. Nadine stayed in the room whilst Raazia went over to speak to them.

"How is your sister feeling, Miss?" asked PC Dodd.

"Not sure yet. We are waiting for Dr Chang to come see her with the results from the x-rays," Raazia responded.

"Is she up for giving us a statement?" PC Dodd asked.

"No, please give her time. Is he still at the station, you know, Nawaz?" Raazia enquired.

"Yes he is but we can only detain him for twenty-four hours max, and then will have to let him go. So, the sooner we get a statement from your sister the better. We will have pleasure in charging him after that."

"Okay, let me go see if Saleena is up to it," Raazia said.

Saleena nodded when asked. The police officers stepped into the room then slowly she recounted the events of the night bit at a time, faltering in places, but her account seemed credible.

"Thank you Miss, we will take this back to the station and speak to our superior back at the station."

"Good girl, Saleena. Now let the police do their job. It will teach him a lesson I hope," Nadine said.

*

"He is a bloody liar, that guy," WPC France said as they walked through the long hospital corridor towards the exit. "He said in the interview his wife slipped down the stairs is how she got her injuries. But when we got into the house she was still upstairs on the floor in the bedroom!"

"We can put that to him before speaking to the Sarge and see what he wants to do about charging him," PC Dodd said.

It was mid-afternoon, Dr Chang came by to see Saleena.

"Good afternoon, Miss. How is the patient today?" she asked Saleena directly whilst she picked up the chart hanging on a clipboard on the metal bar at the end of the bed which had been hooked onto the metal frame. She turned her head slightly, looking at the chart. Saleena saw the doctor raise her right eyebrow slightly but smiled. A visual cursory examination of the head injury followed as she nodded her head. Doctor Chang then gently pressed the area with her fingers. Saleena flinched a little. The blood stain had turned a darker shade of brown on the outside. A good sign.

"Good, the bleeding has stopped," she said whilst she looked at the notes again.

"The x-rays are fine, you will be happy to hear."

Both Raazia and Nadine breathed a massive sigh of relief.

"Thank you, Doctor," Raazia said.

"There is no sign of any break or fracture which is good. She has had a bad trauma to the head though. I fear the blow to the head may have caused concussion as a result. She will need a lot of rest. I feel it would be a good idea to monitor her for the next twenty-four hours here so I will not be discharging her just yet. Last night was stable for her and her heart rate and blood pressure are back to normal which are good signs."

"Is she going to be okay, Doctor?" Raazia asked.

"All the signs are good, so expect so. I must say the injury sustained to the head was of concern to me, but the x-rays look fine to me. I am more concerned about her psychological wellbeing now. This is important too as scarring that is not visible to the naked eye can equally be worse. Women are good at hiding psychological problems, especially domestic violence victims. She is a survivor. I would urge she be removed to a safe place once she leaves here. Counselling could help. The police have asked me for a statement about your sister's injuries which I am happy to give. Like I said, we will monitor her for one more night, possibly two, see how she is. Assuming all is well I will consider discharging her tomorrow or the day after. Let's cross the bridge when we come to it okay, I'd say?"

"Thank you, Dr Chang," Raazia said.

"You are most welcome," replied Dr Chang. "I repeat, I don't think it is a good idea for her to return to the house after she is discharged. She needs a break from routine environment. So where will she be staying?"

"She can stay..." Raazia began to say.

"She can stay with me." It was a simultaneous reaction by both Raazia and Nadine to the question.

"Good to have caring friends and relations," Dr Chang said.

"Sure, Doctor, and thank you again," said Raazia.

"It's my pleasure. Please, I urge you to take this seriously. I hope I don't have to see your sister back here again. I will be back tomorrow to finally check on her. Goodbye for now."

The words: 'survivor' and 'victim' were strong nouns Dr Chang had used which reverberated in Raazia's head. Her sister Saleena had been labelled a 'survivor', a victim of domestic violence. Raazia tried to fathom the power of the words as they were unfamiliar to her. Akeel had never raised his hand to her, ever, not that she could remember anyway. The only memories of physical violence she had experienced were with *Amii* as a child. She remembered Allia being struck with a rolling pin when she could not shape the chapattis into round shapes. That was then, a long time ago. The memory of that day with the passage of time had paled into a distant memory with her, perhaps not Allia. Raazia really had to begin to understand the enormity of the situation here. She reflected upon the injuries she had witnessed with her own eyes. They were dreadful. Saleena could have died. *But how could this happen to my sister?* she thought to herself. Raazia could not shake off the word 'survivor' as it played on her mind constantly.

There was no shortage of visitors the next day. Early evening a senior worker, Maleeka, from a local refuge, the Manchester Women's Refuge Centre (MWRC) for women suffering domestic violence visited Saleena. A small, stout, slightly porky lady, overboard with facial makeup, wore large dangly earrings and a clingy dress which just did not look right on her. She shuffled as she walked.

"You must be Saleena? I am Maleeka. I was told you were in this room. How are you, my dear?"

Saleena managed a miniscule smile but said nothing, just looked a little bewildered at the unknown visitor.

"Don't have that worried look on your face, dear, I am not from the hospital. I am here to help you, my dear. Nadine called me yesterday afternoon. I am here to help you from your terrible situation. You will let us help, won't you my dear?" asked Maleeka.

Before Saleena even had a chance to respond to the question...

"Of course you will. Most of the women who come to us do let us help. And you are?" she asked somewhat abruptly, turning to Raazia.

"Raazia, Saleena's sister."

"Oh, very good to meet you, my dear." Maleeka responded, extending her hand towards Raazia to shake it in order to greet her.

"Do you need help to change your position, my dear?" asked Maleeka.

A nod from Saleena spurred Maleeka into action.

"Raazia if you grab hold of her arm I will do the same on this side. Saleena can change position then."

Saleena adjusted her body to turn sideways, and then forward, slightly facing Maleeka who then plumped up the pillows vigorously behind Saleena before letting her return.

"There, feel okay now? Oh, dear, sorry to see you like this but that must be painful for you? Listen, if you let us help, this will never happen to you again. It was good to meet you today and I shall return tomorrow to see you. Raazia, come walk with me and we can speak. Raazia, you know women in domestic violence relationships are in grave danger. I myself am a survivor. I know first-hand what it was like to be a victim, a survivor. My husband used to come home drunk every single night, demand sex and used to beat me up. He abused me terribly. My parents did not help when I informed them. I ended up in hospital just like your sister. That was it for me, the final straw that broke the camel's back so to speak. I swore to myself then, he would never touch me again. He didn't as I did something positive about it. I made sure he was prosecuted for assault too."

"What did you do?" Raazia asked.

"Simple, I reported it to the police. I got him prosecuted. He went to jail for six months. I wish the courts had thrown away the key. He was a terrible man. I was that angry, I not only left him, I left behind the house with all my possessions including all my clothes too. But with the help of the local council providing some funds I founded a refuge for survivors like me. That set me up. We currently have thirty-six women staying at our refuge. Saleena will be thirty-seventh if she comes to stay. We have helped hundreds of women over the years. They don't stay forever. We help set them up to be independent, help take control of their lives and they move on to better things. My aim is to get women out of danger first, my dear. That is priority. Home Office figures on deaths are staggering. One in three women ends up in a morgue."

"Wow. I had not realised this," Raazia said.

"You are a lucky woman, I can tell. You have not experienced it," Maleeka said astutely.

"My Akeel has never raised a hand at me, ever. I did not even know what 'survivor' meant until today," Raazia responded.

"It really is wonderful to hear that from a woman, my dear. Men can be such ugly brutes. Women are easy targets for letting out their pent-up aggression. All that built-up testosterone they have turns into violence at some stage. It is power, control and dominance of the weaker gender. That is what it is all about with men. You should come and hear some of the horror stories my girls tell you at the refuge, my dear. It is a real eye-opener when you hear their stories. Our Asian women in particular are more vulnerable. But due to cultural traditions, being taught to be subservient since childhood, fear of bringing down family reputations often means women just put up with it. They fail to spot the potential danger signs until sadly it is sometimes simply too late. They end up dead. You have not experienced it, I can see. You have to be in our shoes to realise what it is like to be helpless. The refuge centre will protect Saleena and she will be safe. As she gets better and stronger, we will help her settle somewhere. Here, by the way, is my card, my dear. I shall come tomorrow. Will you be here?"

"Yes, I will be," Raazia responded.

"Goodbye for now."

Raazia found a chair to sit on in the corridor of the hospital. She sat down quickly; her mind was in turmoil as she reflected upon the short, but very profound conversation with Maleeka. She had used some very powerful emotive language that had blown her mind into tiny smithereens. For a while she appeared to be dazed. After a while as she reflected upon the situation, Maleeka's words did help Raazia understand some more about being a 'survivor'.

Raazia had never thought about women's refuge organisations before. She never had to. It was naivety maybe. She began to realise how lucky she was with Akeel. The Malik family were gems compared to Saleena's. To her, domestic violence was a new phenomenon. She knew women were often subservient to their husbands and sometimes the in-laws, but never imagined the depth of it before today. Raazia got up off the seat suddenly. She hurried back into the room to speak to Saleena but she had dozed off to sleep.

Raazia found a payphone nearby. She made long-awaited calls to Akeel, Allia and Sameena.

Chapter 18

Saleena woke up from her sleep feeling slightly better. Resting coupled with the strong painkillers helped the pain and headache subside. She stretched a little, letting out a yawn, then opened her eyes wide. Raazia appeared blurry at first but after rubbing her eyes vigorously she came into clear focus. She smiled, Raazia smiled back. They both held hands.

"Hi," Saleena said in a low voice.

"Hi *meri jaan*. Have I got you back?" Raazia asked her sister, tears flowing from her eyes.

"You can't get rid of me that easily," Saleena responded with a smile.

"I wouldn't want that to happen to you again, sweetie. Are you hungry? I am."

"Yes, I am."

"You want to walk to the cafeteria with me?" asked Raazia.

"Yes. Help me out of the bed, will you?"

"Of course, come," Raazia said, happy to oblige.

The hospital cafeteria was busy buzzing with patients, hospital staff and visitors. Raazia was ravenous as it had been over forty-eight hours; she had not eaten apart from some chocolate bars from the vending machine. She ordered some chips with a cheese pasty, a cheese and tomato sandwich too for Sal, which Saleena tucked into though slowly, managing to chew it, getting it down gradually despite her painful jaw hurting still. Nadine arrived to join them, as did PCs Ryan Dodd and Libby France. Nadine got coffee for all of them, insisting the two police officers join them and partake in coffee whilst they talked.

"It is good to see you up and about, Miss. You are eating too, I see, that is a good sign. Give you some strength, it will," said WPC France.

"Thank you. Do you need another statement?" asked Saleena.

"No, we really came by to inform you, and we are sure you will be pleased to hear, that Mr Khan has been charged with assault, causing you actual bodily harm. He has been remanded in custody to appear at Manchester Magistrates Court tomorrow."

"Oh! Do I need to attend court?" Saleena enquired, feeling panicked.

"No, the court will only deal with the remand situation tomorrow. You do not need to attend court just yet. The case will be dealt with another time."

"Phew, that is a relief. I thought I would have to face him so soon," said Saleena.

"No, no, don't panic. We will let you know when you have to go so don't worry just now," PC France reassured her.

The officers then left, thanking Nadine for the coffee. Nadine shared with Raazia her story about Grace. None of the three women had a dry eye as she finished telling Grace's story. Raazia was stunned into silence.

Saleena stayed in hospital for two more days before being discharged. Maleeka visited her each day in the afternoon without fail. Papaji visited Saleena. He had travelled with Akeel up to Manchester when Akeel went to collect Raazia. Papaji had heard about Maleeka offering Saleena refuge. Strange that all Papaji seemed to be concerned about was his reputation. He was oblivious to the serious risks his daughter was exposed to living with his son-in-law, and expressed no real concern or appreciation of the gravity of the situation his daughter had been placed in or that she was at risk of potential serious harm. Instead he had nothing more to say about the whole matter except giving his daughter a lecture about marriage, respect and loyalty. He went on and on about the importance of family life. Obeying one's husband as it was a duty for a woman. That she was duty bound by their culture to return to her home. Saleena simply shut her mind to the utter nonsense spewing from his mouth, for a while choosing not to listen to the old man's rantings. Raazia could not bear to listen to the ranting of an old man anymore. Raazia suddenly sharpened her tongue and let loose all the pent emotional anger built up inside her for years.

"Papaji, I have heard enough of this cultural

rubbish from you. Do you not see the danger, Saleena is in? You must be either totally blind or you just don't give a damn about your kids. What kind of a father are you? The whole of our lives we have lived in fear of you, your damn traditions and culture is all that has mattered to you. Have you ever considered our feelings, ever? All you were ever interested in was getting your daughters married off no sooner we turned sixteen. What a life we have had, totally subjugated life by men!"

"*Betti,* it is what we are," Papaji said in a low voice, completely dumbstruck for any more words.

"No, Papaji, no *bus kuro,* enough is enough. All you men want is women to be your slaves, for us to be subservient to men and your masculine power ego. Saleena is a grown woman. She can decide what she wants to do without you lecturing her like this. How dare you? You are a fine one to talk, aren't you? Look what you did to our mother. You wanted a son. Begum died because of you. Our childhood was robbed when our mother was taken from us. So, don't meddle in Saleena's affairs now, Papaji. You would do well to leave her alone."

Papaji was stunned into silence. Raazia had bottled up her anger for years and suddenly she lashed out, telling him exactly what he deserved to hear. She wanted to say it sooner but had always restrained herself out of respect for him. This time not even wild horses would have stopped her. Akeel gave out a grin happy that finally his wife had given the old man a mouthful and he thought he deserved it too. Papaji uttered not a single word after that.

"Sweetie, Maleeka will come for you this

afternoon. Make sure you go with her. If you need anything, anything at all, just let me know. Whatever you do, do not call either that idiot Nawaz or Papaji." Raazia said her farewell, then both hugged which was emotional.

"I will be okay. Don't worry," Saleena said.

The journey back to Leicester was awkward. Raazia said not a single word to her father. She felt disgusted with his lecture to Saleena, not appreciating the danger she had been put in. Neither did Papaji say anything back to her for that matter. Akeel tried to break the deadly silence between the two by asking if Papaji wanted to make a stopover at a service area for a comfort break, but Papaji wanted to get back to Leicester as quickly as possible. Akeel did not give up, he still tried to make conversation but the atmosphere for the whole two-hour journey remained completely tense.

After being discharged from hospital Saleena did not return home. Only Raazia, Akeel and Allia knew Saleena's whereabouts. Her stay at the Women's Refuge Centre was an enjoyable experience for her. Maleeka could not have been more pleased with Saleena staying there. To Maleeka, Saleena was like finding gold dust. She was smart, friendly and her expertise in working for charitable organisations helped the Centre raise much needed funds. Soon the Centre began to plan to expand its facility. Saleena was there to help as well as playing a pivotal role in the organisation. She helped the Centre devise a computer system for efficient handling of administrative and financial tasks which had become cumbersome to perform manually.

Papaji had become aware Saleena had not returned home. Nawaz phoned almost every day to complain about his wayward daughter who had dishonoured him by failing to return to the matrimonial home. He told him it was his fault as it was down to his bad upbringing. She was not a good woman to marry as she had disobeyed him many times and he regretted marrying her. He accused Faizali and his family of being dishonest, misleading him as to how good their daughter was when she was not.

"Your fucking bitch of a daughter has got me to go to court for me assaulting her. *Me*, would you believe it? The bloody nerve, I tell you, of the woman when I have done nothing wrong," he shouted down the phone a few times to Papaji.

Papaji hated hearing the harsh words as they were untrue. *How dare he criticise my parenting skills?* he thought. It bruised Papaji's ego extensively. It dented it, in fact, to the extent that he now had to prove Nawaz wrong, even though he was on his side.

To Papaji the mere fact that Saleena had not just disobeyed him but her husband too was a disgraceful affront to his culture which could not be forgiven. Saleena had been misguided, he thought. He knew her mind was being poisoned by misguided women who were leading her astray. He called them a 'bunch of no do-gooders' who themselves were misguided feminists who knew nothing about culture, family life, and were dangerous. He was determined to find her. Daily, relentlessly, he phoned Raazia and Sameena to question them about his daughter's whereabouts. Tense relations between him and Raazia reached boiling point one day when Raazia told him to leave her alone, to stop harassing her and not to phone her again, hanging up the telephone on him abruptly. He was not deterred. The next day he went over to confront Raazia about the aggressive phone call. Raazia sent him off packing with a flea in his ear. She told him to leave her house as he was a selfish man. He had robed all his children of their childhood by his slavish following of his culture and his anachronistic traditions. He was not worthy of being addressed as a father anymore.

Papaji's ego was bruised beyond doubt; first Nawaz criticising him, now his own daughter. He had demanded respect from his eldest daughter, lecturing her on family values. Raazia was not having any of it anymore. Her sister's wellbeing was more important than traditions which did not benefit any of them. He sulked for days at home afterwards. Faizali tossed and turned in bed at night. He couldn't sleep. His situation weighed heavy on his mind. How was he to try and mend the mammoth rift in the family? He kept thinking. For a brief moment he began questioning his own values. The fabric of life as he knew it had disintegrated to a point of no return. He confided in his old friend Malik who listened with a sympathetic ear. Malik's advice was to leave things be as the children were grown adults who had made their own lives. He strongly advised his friend to let go, cut the umbilical cord and let them alone. He should be there only as a symbol of the Rehman family. Living in western countries was difficult enough. He admitted he let go of the old traditions long ago himself as they were simply not in keeping with their chosen life in England. Things were better that way, was his experience. He was happy at least not carrying what he called 'the baggage' of the past. The rapid changes of modern-day life Malik believed had eroded their old ways, which he believed were no longer possible to sustain. Papaji disagreed with his friend vociferously. Culture was core to his upbringing. It was his duty to keep the long line of tradition going.

Chapter 19

Nawaz appeared at Manchester Magistrates Court on the morning of his trial on a charge of assault on Saleena as well as answering a charge of driving with excess alcohol. Papaji was there early waiting outside the courthouse for Saleena. Nawaz was convinced his wife would not turn up at court that morning. Banking on her not turning up to give evidence, he had maintained a not guilty plea. He was wrong. He watched, somewhat stunned and entirely surprised; his wife walked to the courthouse flanked by five women from MWRC, Maleeka leading the way. Papaji made his approach. Saleena saw him but avoided eye contact. Maleeka stood in front of Papaji preventing him from speaking to her. A minor scuffle broke out between the two of them. Maleeka was not going let him speak to Saleena no matter what. Papaji pushed Maleeka hard on her shoulders, making contact with her. Something a man could not do in his culture to a woman. He was *na mahram* to her. She was a stranger to him, not his kin, such contact was not permissible as *haram*. Maleeka pushed him back hard, defending herself. A court security office approached to separate them. Papaji changed tact.

"*Betti,* Saleena, you cannot do this as this is not our way of life, *betti* please," he implored her.

"You are a selfish, evil man allowing your daughter to be abused by her husband. He is a monster," Maleeka retorted angrily.

"You women are an affront to our culture poking your nose into other people's affairs. You should mind your own business and stop corrupting my daughter to your nasty ways. *Sharram honi chayey na?* You should be ashamed. Why don't you stay at home with your husbands?" Papaji stated.

Maleeka did not rise to the provocative words. She turned away from him; the girls then walked away, soon disappearing into the court building. Nawaz smugly walked up to his father-in-law and tersely greeted him by nodding his head in a peculiar way.

"*Salaam alaiykum* Nawaz, *bettay,* how are you?" Papaji asked.

"See, I told you on the phone. That's *your* fucking daughter!" he said as he walked away.

"What the fuck is she doing here?" he asked his solicitor angrily.

"Calm down, Mr Khan. You are in the courthouse and attracting attention. It will not help you to be aggressive," his solicitor Mr Adams advised.

Court security on CCTV had already homed in on his behaviour. A security officer approached Nawaz who decided to walk away towards one of the interview rooms which had just become vacant. He rolled his eyes as he walked away. Mr Adams followed like a poodle following his master. Mr Adams was a young solicitor in his mid-twenties, smartly dressed in a suit.

"I want you to fix this. You are my lawyer. You are supposed to be on my side, not theirs," Nawaz said indignantly.

"I am a lawyer, sir, not a miracle worker. I am here to assist you with your case," Mr Adams responded swiftly. "Besides, you took a big gamble. Yes, had your wife not turned up then you would have been walking out of the court today free. However, her attendance changes everything. I must say she has given a very credible statement of her account to the Crown. I can most certainly cross-examine her, test her evidence and try my utmost best in employing my sharp legal skills to cast doubt on her credibility. Test her story. But I know how the Justices' minds work. Your wife's injuries were terrible. The reality of the matter is I suspect they will convict you. The Crown Prosecutor Mr Weiss is very punctilious."

"What does that mean? You lawyers are always using big fucking words!"

"It means he will pay a lot of attention to minute detail, in particular her injuries she sustained, how she sustained them and more importantly the court will hear of the history of violence which is not going to help you at all, in my opinion."

"I told you she accidently fell when we were arguing," Nawaz asserted.

"Mr Khan, I believe you. You are my client, but will the Justices believe you? That is the question. I am terribly concerned you will lose your temper in the witness box and that would be suicide in there for you. Mr Weiss will not give you an easy time in the witness box either. Under his cross-examination I rather suspect you will lose your temper. He is a clever lawyer. He will break you in the witness box. Once you have shown your aggressive side to the court your case will tumble downhill like a slalom skier," explained Mr Adams as he continued. "Look, you took a chance. If your wife had not come to court, then the case would have collapsed. However, you have to face reality. She *is* here. She will give evidence about what happened that night. The Justices will prefer to believe her version, I suspect. The Crown's evidence is significant which worries me. I strongly urge you to reconsider your position. Looking at the evidence, even though it is your word against hers, you would be taking a very big chance as it will boil down to a question of fact. The Justices trying the case will weigh up the evidence before them, decide whom they will find to be a credible witness and make their finding accordingly. My legal advice is to change your plea to guilty. Change of plea coupled with mitigation before the court may make things somewhat easier for you, at least you may have a chance of avoiding prison."

Nawaz sat quietly pondering on the strong advice tendered to him.

"I would seriously urge you to reconsider your position. Change your plea to guilty today, get the matter over and done with. If you go ahead with your not guilty plea and you are convicted, I am almost certain you will go to jail. The trial will not be easy to win." Nawaz's brief reiterated his advice to his client.

Nawaz grunted, leaning forward, bowing his head as low as he could, shaking it vigorously.

"You lawyers are all the fucking same. No bottle whatsoever."

"It's not a case of that, I assure you sir. I have good skills and can equally cross-examine your wife, attacking her credibility. Attacking a Crown witness has risks attached to it. It may well open the door for the prosecution to question you about your guilty plea for the drink-drive matter. Once that comes out in the open you will not stand a chance, I can tell you that for sure. If you change the plea to guilty at this stage, you may well get a suspended sentence rather than going to jail. I urge you to reconsider."

Saleena was seated in one of the witness rooms situated on the opposite side of the court building away from the defendant's waiting area. PCs Dodd and France were seated outside in the main waiting area of the court as they too had been warned to attend court to give evidence. Papaji was wandering around hoping to catch Saleena, speak to her before it was too late. He tried to pretend he did not know where he was as he went around having a peep through the slim glass windows looking for his daughter. As he approached the room Saleena was in, PC Dodd stood up from his seated position.

"Can I help you, sir?" he asked.

"Oh, I am trying to find my way round as I am new here. I have never been inside a court building before."

"I should ask one of those ushers over there," as he spotted one and pointed towards the usher, "I am sure he will put you right," PC Dodd said.

"Thank you, Officer," Papaji responded as his plan to catch Saleena had truly been foiled for sure now.

Saleena sat nervously in the witness room when the Crown Prosecutor popped in to see her. The Prosecutor was a young chap, looked to be in his late twenties, blond hair, softly spoken. He seemed nice. He sat down across the table from Saleena.

"Good morning, Mrs Khan. My name is Aaron Weiss. I will be prosecuting your husband today. Are you feeling alright?"

"I am very nervous," Saleena responded.

"There is nothing for you to worry about. I will be taking you through the evidence. It is as you stated it in your statement you gave to the police. Here is a copy. Please could you read it to refresh your memory, and don't worry I will be there to help as you are my witness."

Saleena nodded. Mr Weiss quickly ran through the procedure with her, what the court room layout was like, when she would be called to give evidence. Maleeka had been sitting right next to her providing the much-needed moral support. Saleena had begun to perspire profusely. Her make-up started to run a little. Maleeka helped her freshen up.

"All rise," the court usher's voice boomed in Court Room 1. "All present and having business with the court please stand," he continued, giving the proceedings the gravitas and formality.

The court room had oak panelling all round it, a high ceiling with chandeliers beaming bright white lights into the room. A coat of arms plaque with the words: 'Dieu et mon droit' (God and my right) etched on it hung high prominently on one of the walls behind the Justices' bench.

Three Justices walked in from a side door into the court room, walking in a row as they made their way to their seats. Two white middle-aged women flanked the chairman of the bench.

"Good morning all. Please take a seat. Miss Jenks are we ready to proceed?" the chair asked the court clerk who was white, in her mid-thirties with heavy spectacles covering her face. Her hair neatly breaded in French plaits.

"Yes sir, I believe the first case being called is R vs Khan. This was down for a trial today, but the defence have requested the charge be put to the defendant again today. May I, sir?"

"Please proceed, Miss Jenks."

She turned to Nawaz, who was by now sitting in the defendant's box.

"Nawaz Khan, stand up." The chair requested he stand in a firm tone.

As Nawaz rose to his feet the Clerk read the charge:

"It is said that on the night of 25th August 1990 you assaulted Saleena Khan by beating her and causing her actual bodily harm contrary to Section 47 of the Offences Against the Persons Act 1861. How do you plead?"

He paused. There was no response as he stood in silence continuing to stare intensely at the Justices.

"Mr Khan the court is waiting for your response to the charge. Are you maintaining your not-guilty plea today?" the Chairman asked.

"Guilty," he responded in a terse manner.

"Sir the file indicates that Mr Khan previously pleaded guilty when he last appeared in court to a further charge of driving whilst under the influence of drink. Mr Weiss will no doubt give you the details shortly. I shall read the charge in open court, sir."

Mr Weiss nodded. Nawaz, standing in the witness box rolled his eyes then put both his hands in his trouser pockets looking up at the ceiling, seemingly amused much to the annoyance of the Chairman. Saleena with her friends from the MWRC walked into the court room followed by the young police officers as well as observers. Raazia was there and so too was Nadine. The proceedings momentarily halted with the hubbub whilst everyone took their seats in the court's public gallery. Papaji had already been sitting in the court room from the start of the proceedings. He stared at Saleena with piercing eyes as she came in his view. Saleena avoided looking at him. The court proceedings continued.

"Now that members of the public have settled in, shall we continue Miss Jenks?" the Chair requested.

"Yes sir, apologies for that. I understand the victim has just stepped into court now that there has been a change of plea to the assault charge. I believe the two officers present were involved in the investigation of the matter. They were Crown witnesses, sir."

The officers nodded in acknowledgment.

*

"Nawaz Khan, it is also said that on the 22nd of August 1990 you drove a motor vehicle on Moss Lane East at 11.48pm when the level of alcohol exceeded the prescribed legal limit in your breath. The reading was 148 micrograms contrary to section 5 of the Road Traffic Act 1988. You entered a guilty plea to that charge on 18th September 1990?"

"Yes," Nawaz acknowledged tersely.

"Sit down for the moment, Mr Khan, whilst we hear from the Prosecutor, and wipe that grin off your face, Mr Khan, this is a court room," looking away from him. "Mr Weiss?" the Chairman said, addressing him.

"Sir. Morning, Your Worships, may it please the court. I appear for the Crown."

"Morning, Mr Weiss." The two women Justices on the wings greeted him too.

"Sir I have to say this case is sadly a horrible case of domestic violence where it seems very much to be a case of a man exercising power over his victim. The victim is his wife, Mrs Saleena Khan, who was viciously attacked by him on the night in question. In her statement given to the police, she states that throughout her marriage Mr Khan has been belligerent towards her and on many occasions, she has suffered extreme physical abuse and violence from him. She describes him as a selfish evil man. On the night of 25th August Mrs Khan had retired for the night. In order to protect her from unrelenting sexual demands, physical attacks upon her and constant abuse, she had barricaded the door by pushing a chest of drawers against it. She had filled it with items to make it robust. Sometime just after midnight the defendant staggered home in a drunken state. He made his way up the stairs, standing outside the door of her bedroom, banging on the door incessantly. The noise was heard by some of the neighbours; a witness had stated to the police officers attending that night that she had heard loud noises. Sounded like an argument. She heard it as it was a summer's night and had kept her windows open.

"Mrs Khan did not open the door as he demanded. She told him to go away as he was drunk and disturbing the neighbours and as it was late at night. What Mrs Khan did not expect was the defendant was armed with a cricket bat which was used to break down the door. This is the aggravating feature here, Your Worships, the use of a weapon against a defenceless woman. When deliberating upon your sentence I do ask that you consider the fact that he was armed with a weapon. He forced his way into the room. The force applied to the door resulted in the top part breaking in half. It flew wide open with debris from the door flying everywhere. He climbed in through the open space of the broken door as he menacingly advanced towards her waving a cricket bat in the air whilst Mrs Khan screamed for him to go away. A heated argument ensued between the two of them. Then totally out of the blue the defendant swung the bat, attacking her. He struck three blows to her head in quick succession which brought Mrs Khan tumbling down to the floor. As she collapsed onto the ground unconscious, he kicked her repeatedly in the stomach. A frenzy of violence perpetrated on a helpless woman.

"When finally, he stopped, it left her on the floor

bleeding from the head. Mrs Khan lay in her room unconscious with blood pouring out from behind her left ear. When after a while she regained partial consciousness, she says she does not know how, but somehow, she managed to grab the telephone cable, reeled it towards her like a fisherman catching fish on a line, to get the telephone near her. She dialled her sister's number. The sister is Mrs Raazia Malik who lives in Leicester. It was Mrs Malik who called 999 for help. When help arrived Mrs Khan was in a terrible state. Initially the paramedic thought she was not alive as there was no movement. The police took photographs of the victim's injuries which I hand over to you to look. They depict the severity of the injuries inflicted upon her."

The court usher came over, took the pictures and handed them over to the Clerk of the court. She glanced at them quickly before passing them to the Justices. Mr Weiss continued.

"They are graphic, Your Worships, but they show you the outcome of the ferocity with which this defendant attached a helpless woman that night. She was taken to Manchester Royal hospital by ambulance and she received treatment there. Sir, the victim is here today in court. She is the lady seated behind over there in the public gallery behind the two police officers who had attended the scene on the night. What was even worse was that the defendant simply did not care. The police officers attending the house found him slumped on the sofa downstairs, fast asleep, after the brutal attack whilst his wife lay bleeding upstairs."

The three Justices in sync looked towards the back

of the court room to see if they could spot her amongst the crowd of people in court. Saleena lifted her hand up slightly in the air to identify who she was. The Chair of the Bench acknowledged her presence in court by a nod.

"As you can see, sir, she still bears some scars from the vicious attack on her. In addition to the assault charge Mr Khan also faces a drink-drive matter. Very simply on the night of 22nd August Officers Adams and Kendrick were on duty when they spotted the Defendant's BMW being driven erratically, headlights were off, on Moss Lane East at around 11.48 that night. When stopped by the officers, they could smell alcohol on his breath quite strongly. A positive roadside breath test resulted in his arrest. At the station he was asked to give breath samples on the Lion intoximeter. The lower of the two readings produced a staggering 148 micrograms reading in his breath. The legal limit is 35. He was over four times above the legal limit, sir. This defendant is a man who clearly is not wishing to obey the laws. Thank you, Your Worships."

"Mr Adams," the Chairman said.

"Your Worships, thank you. May it please the court, I appear for Mr Khan. This is a very sad case of a man whose marriage had failed. Sadly, Mr Khan turned to drink for solace. Mrs Khan had for reasons only known to her been sleeping apart from the defendant for many months. I will say this to the court that he does apologise for his lack of judgment in relation to both matters he has been charged with. He completely regrets what happened that night. He has tried several times to say how deeply sorry he was to his wife but regrettably has not had chance. He offers it now to her here today, publicly in court through me. He is full of remorse. He regrets his shameful behaviour. He says what happened was completely out of character for him. He is willing to attend a domestic violence rehabilitation course which will help him realise the importance of treating partners with respect. It will help educate him and to help build trust in a relationship. I would ask Your Worships to be lenient when considering the sanction to be imposed by the court. Thank you, Your Worships."

"We will retire to consider our sentence," the Chair of the Bench announced.

"All rise." The Ushers' loud voice carried all round in the room with a slight echo.

The Justices returned following a short break to pronounce sentence.

"Stand up, Mr Khan." Nawaz stood up from his seat, making a grunting sound. "We were shocked to see how bad the injuries Mrs Khan had suffered were at your hands. More concerning was that not only were you under the influence of drink, you used a weapon to break the door down. Whilst we have considered the points offered by your solicitor to us in mitigation, we find it hard to accept that your behaviour that night can be justified. You viciously attacked a defenceless woman with a bat and embarked upon inflicting gratuitous violence upon your wife."

Whilst the Chair of the Bench was pronouncing the sentence a burly man dressed in a blue uniform with handcuffs hanging out from the side of his belt appeared. He strategically positioned himself directly behind Nawaz.

"You were highly intoxicated. You must have driven home in that state. You also face a charge of driving with excess alcohol in your body on 22nd August. You took a big risk. Our view is that the two matters taken together are so serious they warrant a custodial sentence. Therefore, for the assault matter you will serve a prison sentence of six months and a concurrent sentence of six months for the drink-drive charge. You will be disqualified from driving for three years. Jailer, take him away."

No sooner had the Chair finished pronouncing the sentence, the court room descended into mayhem. Women from MWRC cheered loudly. They whistled. They clapped. Nawaz struggled with the jailer as he tried to handcuff him, at the same time Nawaz began shouting obscenities towards the women in the public gallery. The court clerk picked up the telephone summoning security to come into the courtroom and restore order.

"All rise," the Usher said loudly as the Justices stood up off their seats, leaving the courtroom in a hurry.

Saleena went back to the house that afternoon to collect her things. A feeling of emptiness in her life looking at the house which had brought her so much misery unfolded in her mind, considering what a loss of her life it was for her. She surveyed the house which was in a chaotic state. Maleeka had parked her car on the drive taking her time folding the rear seats, moving stuff around, making room for Saleena's things, then entered the house. She commented on the pungent, stale smell of takeaway food mixed with the stench of alcohol emanating from the lounge. Empty bottles of beer were strewn everywhere. The place was littered with rubbish lying around. Saleena went into autopilot mode and began picking up the rubbish.

"What are you doing, my dear?" Maleeka asked.

"Cleaning the house," Saleena responded.

"What the bloody hell for? Leave it, he can clean his bloody mess when he gets out of prison."

As they went upstairs the place was still the same as was left the night Nawaz attacked her.

"Oh my god, my dear, you are so lucky to be alive. This looks like a warzone to me. Just look at the mess he has left. He is an animal. You are well out of it, my dear," Maleeka reassured her.

Saleena sat down on her bed staring at the chest of drawers carcass, her clothes strewn everywhere. Though the mess had left her room bereft of life. It was a place she would not miss.

"My dear, c'mon, pack up as quickly as you can and let's get out of here. This place is creepy."

Saleena relocated to Leeds three months later. With help from Raazia and Maleeka she bought a small studio apartment close to Blenheim Primary School where she worked as a teaching assistant for the next three months. She became fond of one of her pupils, Lela, aged seven. She reminded her of Allia not least because of her humour but she had an uncanny resemblance to Allia. Lela was not shy at all, slightly timid similar in mannerism compared to Allia. One day Lela arrived at school seemingly withdrawn, not unnoticeable. A small bruise mark on her left cheek she tried to hide with her long dark hair.

"Lela I just want to have a quick word, sweetie. Could you come here please? Don't worry, it's nothing for you to worry about. I just want to make sure you are okay, darling. Is everything alright at home?"

"Of course, Miss. Why do you ask?"

"How did you get that bruise on your cheek? You have been hiding it with your hair all day today?"

"Will I get into trouble if I tell you, Miss?"

"No darling, you will not get into any trouble, I promise you."

Lela hesitated at first. Waited for a few minutes, then she opened up just as Allia would have.

"My mom was showing me how to shape the chapattis into a round shape and no matter how hard I tried, I just could not get them shaped. She got really frustrated about it. She had a rolling pin in her hand and she wacked me one on my face."

"Oh, that is terrible. Come here, sweetie." Saleena immediately hugged Lela tightly.

"You know the exact thing happened to my sister Allia too when she was about your age."

"Really?" Lela asked, looking surprised.

"It is not right. Your mother should not hit you. She should teach you without hurting you. Do you want me to have a word with her, Lela?"

"No Miss, she will tell my dad and he will smack me for telling the teacher."

"Okay, I won't, but if it happens again you must tell me, okay?"

"Sure, Miss, I will."

That night Saleena could not sleep. She stayed awake in her bed thinking about her childhood. How it was wasted. How Allia's childhood had been annihilated by *Amii,* as was Raazia's. Lela telling her story today was déjà vu about the chapatti incident. Being compelled to learn something at such a tender age with the threat of physical violence brought it all back to her. *So what if she* did *get it wrong?* Saleena thought. *It wasn't the end of the world. She is a child. Why do people have to be so cultural? These outdated idiosyncratic principles they follow have to stop.*

Saleena just could not get off to sleep that night. She tossed and turned in bed trying to get to sleep but it just played on her mind all night. She woke up in the morning with a sore head which necessitated taking paracetamol before heading off to school. As she drove to work a feeling of uneasiness continued to trouble her, a feeling of premonition. Lela was not at school that day. The school office had been notified by Lela's parents that she was unwell. A whole week went by but there was no sign of Lela. One afternoon Saleena finished school early and called at Lela's house. She drove to Hyde Park, a densely populated working-class area of Leeds with tightly packed terraced council houses. Saleena rang the bell. She waited nervously but no one answered the door. She used the door knocker. A while later a pale-looking Asian woman dressed in *shalwar kameez* answered. She had jet-black hair and wore thick framed eyeglasses.

"Hello, I am Saleena Khan from Lela's school. I was just wondering how Lela was. She has not been in school for a whole week and I was on my way home so I thought I would call in and ask."

"Cee fine. Cee not here. Cee gone Pakistan with father."

"Oh, the school were not told about this. Why?" Saleena asked, looking incredulous.

"No English. Now you go," the woman said.

"But—"

Before she could ask any more the woman slammed the door shut.

Saleena drove home with a feeling of dread in her stomach. That evening she phoned Nadine to chat about Lela as she felt intensely depressed about it.

Chapter 20

Lela did not return to school. Saleena could not take her mind off Lela's predicament. Her disappearance was unbearable. The same evening Maleeka phoned Saleena bearing bad news. Nawaz was out of prison and was asking around for her whereabouts. She warned her to be vigilant. The grim news came at a bad time. She was already very worried about Lela and now this was something else to also worry about. The long winter nights exacerbated her depression. Loneliness made her uneasy. The thought of Nawaz turning up at her doorstep one day filled her with utter dread. Each day that went by she hated living life being on edge.

She was at work one day at the Red Cross shop. Ellie, the shop manager, asked her if she would be interested in working at an orphanage in Soroti, Uganda. The opportunity was timely. Without hesitation she accepted it straightaway.

After his release from prison Nawaz came out a bitter man harbouring a grudge and consumed with feelings of retribution. He phoned Papaji daily wanting to know where his wayward daughter was. Papaji could not help him. Raazia was still not on talking terms with Papaji. Every time Nawaz phoned, Papaji had to listen to his son-in-law's whining. As if his whining wasn't bad enough Nawaz continually addressed him as 'old man' which he loathed. Faizali stopped answering the phone after a while.

Saleena arrived at Entebbe International airport at 6.30am that morning. She sailed through customs check.

"*Habbari Mamma, Karibu.*" A customs official greeted her after checking her passport.

A young African man standing behind Saleena in the queue said, "He said, 'How you are, madam, welcome,' in Swahili."

"Oh, I am well and thank you. How do you say thank you in Swahili?" she asked.

"*Asante sana.*"

"*Asante sana,*" Saleena repeated. The official nodded and smiled at her.

It was hot. The early morning sun was beating down. Outside the airport, she could see a hive of activity. The traffic was building up, lots of cars rushing past, some lifting dust off the road into a cloud. Long queues of taxis waited just outside the arrival entrance for their fares from the three flight arrivals landed in the last hour. Saleena alighted one of the taxis whilst the driver loaded her luggage into the back of his Nissan Primera. The driver was about five foot six in height, youngish-looking guy. He wore a white *topi* on his head.

"*Salaama*," Saleena greeted him.

"*Wa alaiykum salaam mamma*," the driver replied in a soft voice.

"You speak any English?"

"Yes madam, I speak a little English. Where are you wanting to go, madam? I am your driver today, my name is Rasheedi."

"Thank you Rasheedi, can you take me to the Emin Pasha Hotel in Kampala please? Is it far?"

"Okay, madam, it is about forty-one kilometres and it takes about one hour. Just sit back please. I take you there."

"Thank you, Rasheedi."

The driver niftily negotiated his car from the one-way system from the airport onto the busy Kampala Road heading towards the capital, gaining speed intermittently then slowing down for cars as he approached traffic. The ride was bumpy in places as he went over the potholes. Uganda seemed beautiful but at the same time she could see the indigenous people not being well off. In the distance she could see people walking barefoot which saddened her. Rasheedi was a good driver. He knew his route well. His time estimate was good. They were outside the Emin Pasha Hotel in exactly an hour.

Kampala looked like a typical capital city, sprawling with traffic and people everywhere. Saleena was surprised to see badly rundown buildings in the capital probably dating back to the colonial days, if not older, some looking terribly shabby now from neglect. They must have been superb in their heydays but many years of neglect since their masters had left them, especially the Asians in 1972 when General Idi Amin kicked them out, showed visibly. Some looked desperately in need of a good facelift, others a lick of paint would do the job. She rang Raazia from the hotel room to let her know she had arrived safely. After spending a comfortable night at the hotel, she flew into Soroti airport in a Cessna. A very handsome young African chap by the name of Calvin met her at the airport. She saw her name written on a piece of cardboard he was holding.

"Hello, I am Calvin," as they shook hands, "welcome to Soroti."

"I am Saleena, *asante sana*."

"I know who you are, Mamma, and you already speak Swahili! Please come this way. I will take your luggage for you," he said, looking pleased.

Soroti was a small town in Eastern Uganda near Lake Kyoga with a population of 48,000. Calvin drove his Jeep through Main Street which had mainly single-storey buildings. Main Street was the hub of the shopping area for the people of Soroti. The reality of what a third world place looked like hit Saleena as she looked all around her on the streets. Many people seemed quite poor. There were women dressed in old clothes, children wearing torn clothes, some wearing flip-flops on their feet, others walking around barefoot; the buildings all looked terribly run down.

"Oh my god, Calvin, this is depressing looking at how poor people are here."

"Yes, Uganda is a rich country but looking at the people all around us here you would not think so.

Well this is how people live here and our job is to help them in whatever way we can," Calvin said as he smiled. "Don't worry, you will get used to it and there are good things you can do here which lots of people will appreciate. You have impressed me as you already know some Swahili. You will need to get used to the heat and mosquitoes at night, though," Calvin said, laughing loudly.

"You make it sound dreadful. I am sure it's not that bad?" Saleena said, smiling.

"Temperatures some days reach as high as 30 degrees Celsius in the daytime, you know, it's not like England."

The Raffiki Orphanage Centre was an old-style double-storey building dating back to probably the colonial days. Though an old building, quite run down too, it was home to some two hundred orphaned children. The building was on Juma Bhai Road in Soroti which was conveniently central enough for some key facilities, shops, markets and schools nearby. There was a primary school as well as a secondary school, Saleena was surprised to learn. The children were poor, some hardly clothed properly, wearing ragged and torn clothes. Saleena cried when she saw the state of some children having to grow up without their parents which was heart-breaking for her. Her childhood, though difficult, looking from the very different perspective now seemed miles better and she was fortunate to have had parents around her. The orphaned children left behind had nothing except the Centre. The catastrophic spread of HIV virus and AIDS had taken many lives. The key cause of the children's plight she was witnessing was down to the spread of the disease. For many, trying to access clinics from remote areas was a major task. By the time the patients walked miles to the clinics life had been completely sapped out of them. AIDs, HIV sufferers had dropped dead like flies during the height of the spread of the disease in the late nineteen eighties into the nineties. Many children whose parents had fallen victim to the horrible disease had been left orphaned with no one to care for them. Donations from charities like the Red Cross helped build orphanages to house the unwanted children left behind.

Calvin worked at the Centre. He was twenty-eight years old, handsome, muscular, could easily pass as an Adonis type. He was unmarried. Saleena was reserved and a relationship so soon after her marriage breakdown was not contemplated particularly as her state of mind was still fragile. Calvin showed signs of fondness towards her. Some days he would flirt with her by just smiling in a particular way whenever he made eye contact with Saleena. A wink occasionally coupled with a particular cute smile made Saleena feel good.

Raazia spoke to Saleena almost every other day. They exchanged information about their day: how the day went, anything interesting that had happened, families, Saleena's work at the Centre. Saleena did not, however, let on about Calvin. As far as she was concerned the flirting by him was simply flirting and nothing more. Almost every single day Papaji asked the same question about where Saleena was to the point that Raazia ignored his question every time he asked.

The volunteers at the Raffiki Centre one evening organised a barbecue outdoors for the children. As the sun set in the distance, dusk began to fall. Sparks of embers from the burning charcoal sprayed the air intermittently in strikingly beautiful patterns with intense heat emanating from the burning logs. Older children lined up to help cook burgers, marinated fish and corn on the cob on charcoal fires. Long queues of children lined up clutching their plates in their hands, patiently waiting to be served. They sat outside on the ground with their legs crossed in a circle, singing songs. First, they sang in the local dialect, Teso, and then Swahili mixed with some English words. The workers joined in, holding hands with the children as they all sang together. Lucy a fourteen-year-old, picked up her guitar and began singing 'Kumbaaya my Lord, kumbaya,' in her distinct African accent. It was beautiful. Calvin sat opposite Saleena smiling all the while as they all sang together. Saleena felt intensely happy for once. She felt at home. It made her forget the horrible married life in Manchester.

Soon, as the night wore on, tired and sleepy the children went off to bed few at a time until just Calvin and Saleena were left sitting by the burning wood fire. Being comfortable talking with each other led to Saleena pouring her heart out about her miserable married life. Calvin listened intently then just hugged her. It felt good as he gazed into her eyes. She averted her gaze straightaway, remembering her vows to Nawaz.

"I think I will go to bed now as it's been a long day. *Asante sana*." She yawned as she bade him goodnight.

"Can you not stay for a bit longer? I like your company, Saleena," Calvin asked.

"No, I best be getting off to bed."

"Okay, I see you in the morning. Goodnight."

Saleena became close to the children at the Centre, trying her best tirelessly as a substitute parent, looking after their needs, building bonds with the children, seeing them grow up happy and learning to speak Swahili as well as English too. Providing love as a substitute parent was all she could do. She often visited Kampala to lobby ministers for financial funding for the Centre. During one trip she was introduced to Anisha Ali, a Member of Parliament. Anisha was a lawyer from England. She had left Uganda in 1972 when her family had been kicked out of the country by Idi Amin. She grew up in London, was educated and had qualified as a barrister, then returned to Uganda later to reclaim her father's land and property. Anisha had become one of the few women in the country wielding some power. She was never without her bodyguard, Charlie, who accompanied his employer wherever she went. Charlie was a well-built African man in his late twenties; six foot four, strong, not someone you would mess with or meet down a dark alleyway.

Anisha had one day arranged for Saleena a special visitor pass to Uganda's Parliament. The building dated back to the nineteen sixties, colonial times. Overawed by the imposing building somewhat resembling the House of Commons back home, much to her surprise the whole house rose to its feet as she walked into the public gallery. She was received in the House by a standing ovation by its honourable

Members including President Augustus Otambu who was on his feet too. Members took their seats as the house fell silent.

"We welcome a special guest to the House today," he said in a short delivery. "Saleena Khan, we are indeed honoured by your presence today in the House of Uganda's Parliament. I can tell you the House is united in not only welcoming you to our country but is indebted to you, madam, for the important work you have undertaken in Soroti. The children talk about you fondly I hear and call you 'Mama' as you are like their mother. Might I add with great fondness too. You love them like your own. Well, ma'am, Uganda loves you too. I salute you. *Centi sana*, Saleena," the President said.

The House rose to its feet again, Saleena receiving a five-minute standing ovation. It was a moving moment for her as she wiped her eyes dry, echoes of, "*Speech, speech, speech...*" echoed around the house. She was the first non-member of the chamber invited to deliver a speech from the President's box.

"I am truly honoured, Mr President, members of this House, to be invited to speak here today. I have never done this before," she said, shaking.

Members clapped.

"Making a speech in front of so many important people here today is by no means easy for me, but I thank you, *asante sana,* for your very kind welcome extended to me today. I love all my children at the Raffiki Centre. They are special to me. Let's not forget they are the future of your country. Without the Centre those children would have nowhere to go and would probably just die. It is important to keep the Centre going as those children are Uganda's future. Please Mr President, I urge you to keep the funding from your government coming and support the work we do at the Centre. I thank you for your support. Thank you."

Another resounding standing ovation followed. Saleena was presented a key of freedom to the town of Soroti as recognition of her contribution, by the President.

Saleena had a great day. She could not believe the recognition for her work had come from the very top of the Government of Uganda. She could not wait to phone Raazia to tell her all about her exciting day. She learnt fairly quickly, it was who you know, and knowing powerful people in the country paid off. It was useful in securing ongoing funding for the Centre. Mrs Ayende, the Director of Raffiki, too, was quick at recognising her invaluable work which did not go unnoticed. Her contribution reaped a reward of a seat on the Board of the Charity. She came to love Uganda as much as she loved her charitable work, happy to make her new abode a permanent home. Saleena and Anisha became good, close friends. They shared everything with each other, often visiting each other, spending time talking about old times in England every time they met up on occasions, conversing in Swahili!

Chapter 21

In the spring of 1997, Calvin proposed to Saleena. Calvin was a perfect partner. Her happiness seemed almost perfect, unparalleled to her life beforehand, which seemed a distant memory. Happiness at last, at the age of thirty-three, but she was not free to marry. Her return to England was imperative. Would Nawaz give her a divorce, was the question. She no longer cared for her father's archaic traditions anymore, but she knew Nawaz would be stubborn, an insurmountable obstacle to her freedom. She knew it was difficult for a Muslim woman to get a *Talaq*, a divorce, if the husband did not consent. Saleena would have to petition a Sharia court for a *Talaq*. That would be difficult. A hope she held was that he might even have re-married, or better still, had a priest pronounce *Talaq* in her absence. She would not have objected as it would be convenient as well as just the ticket. Maybe with the passage of time Nawaz may have mellowed. He may want to get rid of her forever, consent to both the *Talaq* as well as a divorce without raising an eyebrow. She desperately longed to be free of him.

Saleena flew into Manchester International airport with Calvin. Her old friend Maleeka met them at the airport. The minute Maleeka spotted her old friend come out of the Arrivals gate she ran towards Saleena arms open. They hugged.

"Oh my god, Saleena, look at you! You look wonderful, my dear. Uganda has agreed with you. I hear you are a celebrity over there," Maleeka said as they both hugged for a good few minutes. "And *who* might this handsome man be?"

"This is Calvin, *a friend only*," Saleena responded.

"Hello Calvin, I am Maleeka," introducing herself as they shook hands.

"I have heard a lot about you, Maleeka," Calvin said.

"All good things, I hope my dear," she said with a cackle.

"Of course, yes Maleeka. You are a star and a saviour of our dear Saleena. If you had not been there, Saleena would never have come to Uganda," he said, smiling.

"C'mon, my dears. I will drive you to Leeds. We can catch up in the car, Saleena," Maleeka said.

*

Edward Bernstein practised mainly family law in Leeds, taking the crème of the domestic violence cases from the Women's Refuge centre to court. He was a hell of a good legal aid lawyer, came recommended by no less than Maleeka. He was a short man, five foot four in height but a tenacious divorce lawyer. He had an uncanny resemblance to

Mahatma Gandhi with his gold-rimmed spectacles firmly placed close to his eyes, bald head and same height. Saleena and Calvin talked in his office as he took instructions, quietly making notes whilst Saleena detailed her long history of violence and abuse during her marriage. Bernstein was surrounded by hundreds of law books that were stacked tightly together on shelves all round his quaint little office. "Five years' separation is the best bet," he advised.

Nawaz's life, with his continued drug habit, had spiralled into complete chaos. Family had cut off all ties with him after his mother passed on in 1995. The house had deteriorated in a squalid state. Rubbish built up over months had piled everywhere. Most days he would be high on drugs. Prison life had turned him into a bitter man harbouring feelings of retribution that festered inside him. A grudge he was not going to let go of easily. His taxi business had gone too. Often, he just stayed in bed until late in the afternoon. A pile of unopened letters had built up behind the front door. He would just leave them there until they got in the way of opening the front door only to kick them to the side of the hallway. Fresh mail delivered one day, he spotted a crisp white envelope which had a Willingtons & Mace Solicitors stamp on the front. It caught his eye. He grabbed it off the floor, ripping the envelope open, read it then flung it across the hallway in a fit of rage. His wife was seeking a divorce from him.

Nawaz picked up the phone, dialled the numbers on his phone with haste.

"Hello," Papaji said.

"Your bitch daughter has just sent me a letter from

lawyers telling me she is divorcing me. She first sends me to prison and now this? You must take care of this, old man. See to it that there is no divorce or else..." He hung up, slamming the handset before Papaji had even chance to say *Salaams*.

"Who was that, dear?" asked Fauzia.

"Nawaz, I don't know what is wrong with that man, but he has no respect for his elders. He was abrupt, rude and called me an old man. Saleena has sent some legal papers for divorce. He was angry. But what can I do? *She* is his wife, his responsibility, not mine," Papaji said in a sullen voice to her.

"Saleena is here? I heard she had gone abroad," Fauzia said.

"What do I care? None of the children care about their old *Abbah* anymore. Apart from Akeel no one comes to see me anymore. What kind of children are they?" Papaji said in a sad tone.

The phone rang again. Papaji answered.

"Is that you, old man?"

"*Arrrayy... salaa...*" Papaji stuttered.

"I am going to come see you this weekend. I want this sorted!" Nawaz said abruptly, slamming the handset on the phone base.

"O' Allah why have I got this man as my son-in-law? He is so rude," he moaned.

"Who was it, dear?" Fauzia asked.

"It was Nawaz again! He is bent on just tormenting me, now has threatened to come down here at the weekend. All he said rather rudely was that he wants the matter sorted out."

"*Mutlub?*" (Meaning) Fauzia asked.

"I don't know, dear. Let me see if Raazia knows where Saleena is so we can go see her and see if we can sort the matter out. I don't know what has happened to our children. First, we have Sara disappearing, then Abdel running off and now Saleena is doing this. I am very tired of all this. I am getting old and tired of all this ugly business. I thought when the children are all grown up, they will have their own lives. I can retire in peace. But look at my grey hair. It's all because of them, I went grey early," Papaji complained.

"They are *your* children. Aren't they? Why are you complaining to me?" Fauzia muttered.

"Even you are nasty to me. I miss my Begum so much," he groaned.

"Papaji, for the last time I told you I do not know where Saleena is. She has not been in touch with me." Raazia almost wanted to slam the phone down but stayed on the phone a little longer, rolling her eyes with a disgusted look on her face.

"Do you know that *bey sharram* sister of yours has done, hmmm? She has got lawyers involved now. She wants a divorce. This is getting out of hand. We have to deal with this as a family issue, Raazia, *betti.*"

"Papaji I do not know anything. You married me off when I was only sixteen. I don't owe you anything. Besides, I have my own problems. Can you leave me alone please?" She hung up the phone feeling completely exasperated.

Raazia felt she was not going to be railroaded by

him anymore. Respect and honour for the elders was one thing but to be obsessed with it at the expense of your children was quite another, such that was intolerable to her. Besides, she was not going to betray the trust Saleena had placed in her even though she was lying to Papaji. Yes, it would be *haram.* But protecting her sister qualified in her mind as sufficient justification for which she hoped *Allah* would forgive her.

Papaji had his suspicions that Raazia was protecting Saleena. He knew she knew Saleena's whereabouts. This issue weighed quite heavily on his mind, so much so he could not concentrate on his prayers. Whilst he was praying *namaaz* suddenly his mind would wander off and he would forget if he was in his second *rakaat* or third. He would start again but, in the end, give up. His mind felt burdened with troubles. Later on, that same evening he went to see Raazia after evening prayers finished at the mosque. He rang the front doorbell but there was no answer. He knocked on the door three times. Akeel answered the door.

"*Salaam alaiykum*, Akeel *betta.* I have come to see Raazia," Papaji declared at the door.

"*Waa alaiykum salaam,* Papaji. You look troubled; agitated in fact, is there anything wrong?" Akeel asked.

"No, nothing urgent but something important I need to ask her."

"Raazia has gone to bed, Papaji. She is feeling unwell. Has a migraine. She has gone to sleep. Shall I wake her and ask her to come down?"

"Oh, no *betta,* I shall come back tomorrow to see her. Just tell her I came by after *namaaz* to see her."

"Yes of course I will. *Khudaa hafeez.*"

The old man had a restless night tossing and turning all night in bed that night. He could not sleep. Nawaz's words "*See to it that there is no divorce or else*" and "*I want this sorted.*" kept going around and round in his head.

"This is a conspiracy of silence, I tell you," he muttered to himself the next morning as he tried to get out of bed at the same time as he unruffled his hair with his fingers. Getting out of bed was a struggle for him. A sharp pain in his knee joints caused him to sit back on the bed. For a good few minutes he sat rubbing his knees with both his hands. The pain subsided a little. Breathing heavily, he slowly got up, putting pressure on his legs, managing to slowly hobble a few steps, making his way to the bathroom, walking slowly with his back hunched making groaning sounds.

"You must not let them get away with it," Fauzia said to Papaji.

"But what can I do, my dear? I am old, helpless now. Just look at me, I am old. My knees play up all the time," Papaji said.

"*Baywakoof.* Don't bark at me. I have not done anything wrong," Fauzia responded sharply.

"*What* did you call me?"

"I am your husband, *benchodd*, not *bey wakoof.* I will show you who is a man in this house," he growled, slamming the door behind him.

Fauzia sat on the bed in amazement as Papaji had never before sworn at her like that.

That morning Papaji spent a great deal of time on the telephone. He called Raazia first but no answer, then Sameena but no response there either. Allia, he hesitated to call as she had not spoken to him in years. She was his last resort. Allia recognised his voice and hung up the phone. Frustrated, he paced up and down in his living room for hours just like he did in the hospital when waiting for Abdel to be born.

Raazia felt no loyalty towards her father, nor did any of her sisters. Robbed of her education, Raazia had not forgotten the hard work attending night school after she married Akeel to obtain some educational qualifications. She was proud of her achievement, her struggle to become a primary school teacher, teaching maths at the local Fresh-Fields primary school, work she enjoyed immensely. She was firmly in control of her life. She felt blessed too, having Akeel as a husband, who was a lovely father to their twin daughters Meesha and Sakeela.

It was late Saturday evening, about 10.30pm. Papaji breathed a sigh of relief as there had been no sign of Nawaz when suddenly there was a loud knock on the front door. Papaji answered the door.

"*Salaam alaiykum*, Nawaz, *betta aaiyay putter,* it is very late. How are you?" Papaji asked him politely as he struggled to sit.

"Don't 'how are you me', old man. Do you know what your stupid daughter has done to me? She has ruined my life. She sent me to prison when I have done nothing wrong to her. She has now got herself a lawyer who says he will be sending divorce papers through. What kind of a bloody woman is she? Your daughter! Her behaviour is shocking, I tell you," Nawaz growled.

"But, but, buut *putta...*" Papaji struggled to get his words out.

"What must be our own community saying about this, I wonder. Only if they knew what your family was like. She is bringing dishonour to me and to you. Don't you see or care? I want this sorted straightaway. Are you listening to me, old man?"

"*Apney bado sey addub sey baat key jaati hay bettay* (You have to speak to your elders with respect)," Papaji retorted.

"Ah, fuck that respect business, old man. She is your fucking daughter. She has screwed my life over. Sort it out or else I will ruin you and your reputation. Your name will be dragged in mud, I can promise you that. You know how our community gossip. The information I will put out about you and your family will spread like wildfire. You will be ruined."

"You are so malicious, Nawaz?"

"Do I look as though I care, old man?" Nawaz stood up and walked to the door, leaving the house by slamming the door shut. Papaji stood there with his mouth wide open, dumbfounded. He was speechless at his son-in-law's incredulous, appalling and disrespectful behaviour. His threats to ruin him made him tremble.

"Surely you can't let him get away with this?" Fauzia said.

"If our name is tarnished again, we will be finished. I have managed to get things back to normal after Abdel's lottery business. Now we have this *bay wakoof*'s business plaguing us. I have always prayed on time, been a good man, Fauzia. Why is this happening to me?"

He sat on the sofa, buried his head in his hands began to sob loudly. Fauzia was taken aback with surprise as she had never seen him break down, when she thought him to be as tough as steel, or cry before. The harsh words were a bitter pill for him to swallow but swallow he had to. Nawaz had made it personal. The personal attack Nawaz had launched was vicious.

Chapter 22

Eight years had passed Abdel had been away from home. Abdel and Philp had remained good friends, keeping in touch almost once a week; usually they met up for a meal at their favourite haunt in London. Abdel had found it difficult being away from his family. He lived on his own on the outskirts of the capital city, owning a five bedroomed detached house. A beautiful house set six hundred yards from the front road, accessed via metal gates. It was a beautiful property in suburbia with two acres of land. He had six thoroughbred stallions with stables in the vast, lush green acres of his land. Horse racing had become another vice, which Papaji would hate him for if he knew, but racing thoroughbreds had become a passion for him, a hobby for a rich young man. Winning major horseracing prizes on three occasions had given him a real buzz.

Papaji was growing old in years, but he was still headstrong, refusing to speak with Abdel. Abdel had never given up hope of one day becoming reconciled with his father. Though Papaji's refusal to even come to the phone to speak to his son seemed to be a forlorn hope, Abdel did not give up. He telephoned once a week hoping to catch Papaji one day, picking up the receiver, and he would at least hear his dad's voice. He avoided the phone. Abdel only managed to speak to Fauzia each time he telephoned. He longed for Papaji to one day call him up and speak to him as a son.

Nawaz was served with divorce papers personally by a court bailiff one afternoon, as he was about to leave the house. He swore at the bailiff then threw the brown envelope into the long bushes in the front garden. Not surprisingly this geared him into an angry mood. Days following the service of papers, Nawaz spent endless amounts of time waiting in his car outside the refuge centre; he lay in wait for Saleena. Empty coffee cups kept piling up day by day in the foot wells of his Nissan. His stakeout one afternoon paid off. He spotted Saleena and Calvin entering the centre. A few hours later they emerged boarding a private taxi. Nawaz followed them.

*

18th December 1997 turned out to be a perfect day Christmas shopping on Oxford Street. London was buzzing with hordes of Christmas shoppers rushing about for last-minute shopping. Christmas decorations and festive lights lit up the streets everywhere. Sounds of Christmas songs and carols played in every shop. Carol singers singing away in the main shopping precincts gave it a Christmas feel. Stores were packed with people, as were tube trains. Calvin and Saleena enjoyed spending their day together shopping. Saleena loved shopping for presents the kids back at the Centre would love to receive. She bought every single child a present for Christmas. She couldn't wait to see their faces light up when she got back and handed them the gifts.

Calvin was pleased to get on the train as he could rest. He had been heavily laden with bags full of Christmas presents. They got the train back to Leeds. Back at home they settled down in front of the television to watch festive programmes. They watched an old movie, Now Voyager with Bette Davis on BBC 2. The channel was running a Bette Davis season of movies for the festive time. Saleena loved old romantic movies. She sat close to Calvin on the sofa, huddled next to him with a bowl of popcorn as they watched the movie. Boston heiress Charlotte Vale played by Bette Davis in the movie is a neurotic woman in complete mess, largely because of her domineering mother. Following a stint in a sanatorium where she receives the attention of Dr Jasquith, Charlotte comes out of her shell, then electing to go on a cruise. On board the ship she meets Jerry played by Paul Henreid. It was a romantic genre, as expected. Charlotte Vale falls in love with Jerry who happens to be a married man. They enjoy a brief tryst in Rio before returning to the States where Charlotte struggles to forget him, but she is unable to find happiness. Saleena loved the power, the romantic element of the movie. She picked a tissue up from the box next to her and wiped the tears from her eyes as the movie ended. Calvin smiled at her as she blew her nose.

About 2.00am Saleena heard a strange sound. It sounded like glass breaking. She lifted her head up off the pillow to see if she could hear it again. Calvin was fast asleep on the sofa bed. There was no sound after that. She thought nothing of it, falling back to sleep. Suddenly a heavy blow was struck to Calvin's head by an intruder. The blows continued. Saleena got out of bed screaming as the intruder grabbed her.

"Shut the fuck up, bitch. If you scream, I will kill you and your *kala* boyfriend," said the intruder in a muffled voice. She continued screaming. Calvin lay there lifeless; his white Calvin Kleins were drenched in blood. Saleena was struck on the head. She fell to the ground. The ferocity of the attack was vicious. Arterial spurts of blood splattered everywhere. The intruder then turned the place upside down before leaving, taking Saleena's jewellery and Calvin's wallet before disappearing in the dark dead of night. A neighbour hearing Saleena's screams dialled 999.

The police on arrival forced entry through the door discovering a hideously gruesome crime scene with two bodies covered in blood. CID arrived declaring a murder investigation. A hive of police activity followed, attracting attention of the curious neighbours wondering what was going on. It looked serious as the police donned plastic jumpsuits outside by their police vehicles, with masks on for preservation of the crime scene evidence – fibres, DNA and any other evidence to be found. The area surrounding the flat had been cordoned off with police tape.

Chief CID investigation officer Detective Constable Benjamin McLean, known by his nickname Sherlock to his colleagues, arrived first on the scene, then colleague DCI Kiki Slater arriving some minutes later. Sherlock smoked a pipe and wore a hat resembling Sherlock Holmes. It explained the nickname. Though it was the early hours of the morning he was smartly dressed in a suit with a smoke pipe in his mouth. He spoke with a heavy Scottish accent, mid-forties, and wore spectacles. Kiki was of South African descent, spoke with a slight Afrikaans accent, and was in her late thirties. She was an experienced police officer having worked in the serious crime squad for six years. Forensics arrived too, beginning the painstaking task of photographing the crime scene, collecting evidence, looking for even the tiniest particle or fibre that could be crucial in providing clues. Sherlock and Kiki carefully surveyed the scene looking for visual signs of evidence that could establish motive.

"Oh my, something I was not expecting to see a few days before Christmas I must say, Kiki. Any ideas on motive?"

"Looks like a burglary gone wrong, Gov. The occupants were disturbed. Looks as though the female victim's jewellery is missing, the male victim's wallet too," she said.

"I don't know, you know, something does not feel right to me here. There seems to be more to it than meets the eye," Sherlock responded.

"Really, sir, what do you think may be the motive then?"

"I don't exactly know at this stage, it's only a hunch, but it sure ain't a burglary, if you ask me! The weapon used was heavy, blunt, the attack frenzied to say the least. Pre-planned, I'd say. Why these two, is another question. Could it be a racial attack, I wonder? Who knows?"

"Okay, well let's work on the theory then, Gov. Homicide, you reckon?"

"Let's reserve judgment on that one, Kiki."

The bodies were bagged and moved as soon as forensics had finished, leaving hollow sketches painted on the floor where the bodies were discovered.

The story made national news that morning as dawn broke. Early morning BBC and ITV news bulletins reported the incident, relaying the grim news, withholding the names of the victims which had not been released by the police yet. Raazia was at home making preparations ready for Christmas. She was up early pottering around the house cleaning mostly. She had the radio on.

"We have some breaking news coming from our reporter Ben Leon from Leeds this morning. Police were called out to a flat in the Woodhouse area. A man and a woman were found dead in the flat and police have opened a murder enquiry. Let's go over to Ben in Leeds. Ben, what's the story there?"

"Chris, as you said police were indeed called out in the very early hours of the morning, around 3.30am in the Woodhouse area of Leeds. A neighbour had heard some disturbing sounds and had dialled 999 to report the incident. The police as yet have not revealed exact information or the identities of the two victims, but they are believed to be an Asian woman and a man of African origin..."

Raazia dropped the duster from her hand. She stood there motionless. Her visceral instinct since the day she had the phone call from Saleena when Nawaz had nearly killed her, was to expect the unexpected. She knew Saleena was back with Calvin staying at her flat in the Woodhouse area. Raazia rushed to the radio, turning the volume up. She sat on the chair by the radio.

"...the bodies have been moved to the nearby mortuary. What the police have said is that there was a break-in at the flat in the early hours of the morning but whilst only some items were stolen the principal motive, they say, seems to be possibly racial and they have consequently declared it to be a murder enquiry. Police have carried out the painstaking job of trying to find the weapon used to kill the victims by carefully combing the area, have been making door-to-door enquiries and are appealing for any witnesses. If we have more, we will come back to you later."

Raazia switched the radio off, walked over to the telephone, picked up the handset and dialled Saleena's number. She started to shake as the phone began ringing. She stared at the decorated Christmas tree as the phoned continued ringing. Someone picked up the phone, much to her relief.

"Hello Saleena, is that you? Happy Christmas, sweetie, I was so worried when I heard the news. There has been an incident in your area."

"Madam, may I enquire who you are, please?"

"Sorry? Who is this?"

"Police, madam."

"Police? What is going on? Where is my sister Saleena? I am Raazia," she said as she began shaking uncontrollably. "My sister is staying at that address."

"Please wait a moment."

The police officer called Detective Mclean over by waving at him to come to the phone.

"Sir, I have a lady on the other end of the line, says she is the female victim's sister."

"Thank you. Hello, Detective Benjamin McLean here, Miss. Are you a relative?"

"What has happened to my sister Saleena? Why are the police there?"

"Ma'am I am very sorry to advise you that this is a police crime area as there were two bodies discovered here. One is a female, the other a male. We are anxious to identify them, could you help us please? Hello, hello, Miss, you there?"

Raazia collapsed on the floor hearing the news of Saleena's death confirmed. She was unconscious.

"Madam, are you there?"

There was no reply. Ben asked a police officer to put a trace on the caller's phone number. He disconnected, then dialled the number again, but got an engaged tone. Ben arranged for a local police car to be despatched to Raazia's address for enquiries.

Raazia came to five minutes later. Akeel used smelling salts to bring her around. The news of her sister's violent death was so unexpectedly shocking; Raazia could neither fathom the situation nor think. Akeel sat next to Raazia, holding her, trying to comfort her. Minutes later there was a knock on the front door. The police got there quickly. Akeel did much of the talking as Raazia wept uncontrollably.

Papaji was visited next by the police. Surprisingly, he did not react, flinch, or display any grief upon hearing the news of the death of his daughter. The tragic news of her death had spread within the local community as people began making their way to Papaji's house to pay their respects. Raazia and Akeel arrived at the house shortly afterwards. Loud wailing sounds were heard from the house. The profound feeling of intense loss pervaded the atmosphere. The crowd gathered outside the house began a vigil, holding candles. The crowd swelled minute by minute. Some were curious, simply eager to learn about what had happened, others had come to pay their respects. Death had brought the community together as the crowd grew larger, demonstrating community solidarity in the family's time of grief. How strange, a few years before Papaji had been shunned by the community as an outcast, but the pendulum had swung right across the other way in his favour. He sat in the lounge looking a little pale but remarkably composed in demeanour. The news media vans arrived on the street, setting up their sophisticated equipment at the location near Papaji's house ready for their reports.

When the police visited Nawaz to inform him of the news, he displayed absolutely no emotion whatsoever when given the grim news of the death of his wife. His demeanour much to their surprise, quite candidly, was disinterested, stating that as she had left him some years ago, he was not interested.

*

Sherlock and Kiki visited Raazia, Papaji, Maleeka and Nadine numerous times to get a better insight into at least Saleena's background to see if clues would emerge so the investigation could focus on direction. Raazia, Nadine and Maleeka regurgitated detailed accounts of the violent relationship Saleena had endured during her marriage. Raazia made an off-the-cuff remark to the police stating she would not be surprised at all if Nawaz had done it. She believed he was capable of it or if he had not done it himself, she felt he had a hand in her sister's death somehow. Both Maleeka and Nadine concurred with this opinion.

Nawaz was visited three times. Arrested once and interviewed at the station. Vigorously defending himself, he refuted any allegation, stating she had gone from his life by leaving him. Why would he want to kill her? Sherlock confronted him in one of the interviews with the history of domestic violence in his marriage, but Nawaz remained steadfast in defending himself. He maintained he had no motive. In fact, he rebuked the police for disturbing his civil rights and liberty. Seventy-two hours passed by quickly. There was little evidence for maintaining a murder enquiry. Sherlock called a press conference.

"I am Detective Benjamin McLean. This is my colleague DCI Kiki Slater. Thank you, ladies and gentlemen, for attending this press conference. We have a short statement to make about the tragic deaths of Saleena Khan and Calvin Lenton. We have carried out extensive enquiries and at this time there is no reason to believe the deaths were racially motivated as previously reported in the media. There is no evidence to suggest that. Our enquiry is therefore focussing on the investigation being a burglary of domestic premises where unfortunately the two occupants disturbed the burglar or burglars whilst the flat was being ransacked. At this time, we believe the intruder or intruders attacked them with a claw hammer which sadly resulted in their death. We are of course appealing for witnesses. If anyone has any information at all about this enquiry please contact the police. Anything at all, however small it may be, we urge you to call us on this number on the card below. Thank you."

"Officer, Jamie Fryer, BBC news, could you explain why the two victims were butchered in the most horrific way possible?"

"We do not have the autopsy report from the coroner yet. When the precise details are known I may be in a better position to answer that question." Somewhat of a diplomatic response from Sherlock.

"Rita Benson, ITN news. Was the crime related to family honour? As the Asian lady seemed to be living with a black man."

"We do not believe so. Again, there is no evidence to suggest that to be the case," Ben asserted.

"Thank you, ladies and gentlemen, for you time. That will be all for now."

Chief Constable Hathaway telephoned Sherlock after the press briefing and thanked him for his excellent diplomatic handling of it that afternoon, which helped ease off the pressure on him from his superiors and probably even higher. A racial killing, apart from causing disquiet in the local community, would have heavily impacted on police resources. He was anxious to not just save resources but to dispel any disquiet among the ethnic community of Leeds that it was racially motivated, and have police protection extended to everyone whatever the race, colour or creed.

Chapter 23

Calvin's body was flown to Soroti for burial following release by the coroner two weeks after death. Saleena's funeral was a poignant affair. For Abdel this was the first family funeral he had attended. Philip accompanied him. Sara attended too though she could only vaguely remember her mother's funeral as she was five at the time Begum passed away. Sara was seen for the first time after many years since her disappearance. Abdel was only a few days old when Begum died. Nawaz did not attend. Papaji seemed surprisingly composed. He did not acknowledge Abdel's presence. Raazia, Allia, Sameena and Sara were completely devastated at the loss. Raazia cried and wept uncontrollably. Nadine travelled from Manchester for the funeral, as did Maleeka with some of the women from the refuge who knew Saleena. Nadine held Raazia's hand tightly, offering her comfort. Memories of Grace came flooding back as she fought back her tears.

Hundreds of mourners from the local community attended the mosque, then after for the burial. Sheikh Ahmed was about to begin the funeral rites when a cavalcade of black limousines pulled up at Saffron Hill Cemetery. Someone important maybe was being buried too, the mourners thought, but a heavy police presence signified something strange. President Augustus Otambu accompanied by Anisha disembarked from a long black limo flanked by several of his bodyguards dressed in black suits and dark glasses as they slowly approached the burial site.

"I am sorry," someone said, "this is a private funeral."

"Yes, my friend, we are here for the funeral of Uganda's daughter Saleena Khan," the President responded sternly in his African accent as the mourners looked on in complete amazement. They continued slightly moving away slowly from the graveside, perceiving that the group of strangers, dressed as they were, as well as the heavy presence of so many black men seemed awkwardly hostile, or at least the heavy force in which they appeared suddenly gave that perception of a threatening presence to the mourners. Completely bewildered, the mourners looked on. They stared at them intensely, wondering who the people intruding on a private funeral were.

"Please continue with the rites, my dear friend," the President instructed Sheikh Ahmed.

The Sheikh did as he instructed. The group began to hum a sombre tune as Saleena's coffin was lowered into the hole dug out into the earth.

As the mourners lamented at the graveside, President Otambu delivered his short but moving eulogy.

"I am most sad to be standing here today

mourning the passing of Uganda's beloved daughter Saleena Khan. It pains me to be here delivering this eulogy for our dear, dear Saleena. I can tell you Saleena had a kind heart. A woman who had a heart of gold. It is not often you meet a woman like our dear sister. She left her home seven years ago to look after orphans in Uganda's Raffiki Refuge Centre and she adopted them like she was their mother. She had a heart of gold, a kind heart found rarely in people. It is a quality very few have and my dear friends, this lady had that very quality. Her children will miss her dearly. They lament her passing with pain in their hearts. Her work here on earth has been prematurely cut short, but done. This is a sad day for Uganda and her families both here and in Uganda. I pledge, my friends, I will not rest until her killers are brought to justice. I wish Uganda's daughter, Saleena Khan, farewell. I salute her and I thank Allah for granting this lady to us for a short time. I pray to Allah *He* grants her peace and to rest in peace as her work here is done."

The President stood for one minute in silence, arm firmly held high, and his hand touching his forehead in a salute posture. So did his entourage. The moment seemed remarkably to resemble a military style farewell. He then laid a wreath and a bouquet of roses on the ground before leaving. Apart from Papaji there was not a single dry eye.

Nadine and Maleeka had attended the cemetery for the burial, later returning to the mosque. The day following her funeral Raazia led the women of the Rehman household, her friends and some women from the community, to attend the cemetery to pay their respects. Muslim women by tradition do not attend the actual burial ceremony.

Just as her funeral was a moving moment, today was equally moving. Raazia placed a bouquet of flowers made up of white roses with pink carnations on her sister's grave. Her card read:

To my dearest sister Saleena, I truly Love you & will miss you so much sweetie. You were very brave in life. But now rest in peace my love. Allah will take care of you. We miss you very much with all our love

Raazia, Allia, Sameena, Sara and your nieces' Misha and Shakila. xxxx.

Your loving sister Raazia, forever.

You were my grace. I have lost you too my love. My lovely Saleena I shall miss you terribly. I wish I could have done more to protect you. R.I.P. you are in the arms of my Lord and he will protect you. With fond memories,

Nadine.

Forty days of continuous lamentation and recitation of prayers from the Koran at the Rehman house followed. Time ticked on.

The police enquiries continued. The coroner's report eventually delivered read:

This statement has been compiled by me Dr Craig Summers. I am the pathologist who performed the autopsy on two victims of crime from Woodside, Leeds. I formally state as follows:

My name is Doctor Craig Summers. I am a Home Office Pathologist. My qualifications are:

MSc.Biochem, University of Edinburgh.

M.D., University of Edinburgh.

F.R.C.P, Internal Medicine and Pathology, Princeton University NJ (US)

Clinical Professor and Chair, Dept. Of Pathology and Biophysics, Royal London Hospital.

On 28th December 1997, I performed autopsies on a male and a female. The male was a black male in his late twenties and the female of Asian origin in her mid to late thirties. Both the male and female had identical and similar injuries which in my opinion had led to their ultimate deaths.

Upon the examination I performed on the bodies, they were found to have contusions and extremely deep lacerations to mostly the upper part of their bodies. The head, in particular the skull area had received very severe and sustained blows from a blunt object, possibly a hammer. I describe the injuries to be as follows:

The skull had a left parietal depressed fracture with underlying epidural haematoma of maximum 5.1cm thickness, a right frontal open comminute fracture with associated subdural haematoma of maximum 3.3cm thickness, along with substantial blood collection within the subarachnoid space, both lateral ventricles and basal cisterns.

The wrists of both victims exhibited deep linear ischemic dermal abrasions which could only be caused by a tight constrictive device that strangulated blood circulation to the skin immediately underneath the constrictive device.

The time of death I confirm was between 3 and 4 a.m.

In my opinion death would have been within minutes of the trauma. The blows from the injuries described above would most certainly have led to death within minutes. I think it would have been highly improbable for the victims to have survived for much longer than maybe 5 to 10 minutes following the blows to the skull.

Dr Craig Summers

28th December 1997

Bereft of any clues as months went by, no arrests, Sherlock and Kiki came under heavy pressure to wrap up the case, as police resources committed to the enquiry with senior officers working on the case seemed to be a drain on the Force's resources, as the case was at a standstill. The police were nowhere near approaching any arrests; the paperwork was bagged up and shipped to the basement, a label at the side and top in black marker pen marked 'cold case'.

"I am sad to be walking away from this case, lass, I have to say. They were a nice couple and I just feel justice has not been done." Sherlock shared his regret.

"Yes, true boss. I agree. Have to say there is something that has been bugging me about this case all along," said Kiki.

"Go on."

"Remember the ITN reporter at the conference, Rita Benson?"

"Somewhat vaguely, Kiki... and...?"

"She had mentioned a phrase – 'family honour', do you recall?"

"My memory is a little bit fuzzy there, remind me."

"The notes stated when I read them back somewhere that Dad showed no emotion when told about the death of his daughter, neither did the husband who was in fact very belligerent and was completely disinterested when the police visited him and in the police interview too. I believe he did not bother attending the funeral which to me was very strange to say the least. That says something to *me,* boss, does it not to you?" she asked.

"Not evidence, Kiki, that could convict your possible suspects you just identified! I take it they are your prime suspects, are they?"

"Well yes, if we had more time my enquiries would have focussed on those two. To me there is something definitely strange about them. Does that not strike to you as strange, the responses displayed by the two when told about the violent death of their near and dearest? Does to me, boss, for what it's worth," Kiki asserted.

"This is a tough one, Kiki. We have an unsolved murder case. We have our gut instinct but that sadly is not enough to takes us in that direction, lassie."

"Ben, we cannot let this go. It is not right. Can we not follow it up surreptitiously?"

"No."

"I am deeply disappointed, sir," Kiki stated.

"But I do know someone who owes me a favour up in Manchester. I will speak to him. We can put a tail on him see what happens."

Raazia finished tidying up in the kitchen at Papaji's house after a short memorial *majaalis* service at home in memory of Saleena a year later. The kitchen door was slightly ajar. Raised voices attracted her attention. Eavesdropping on the argument between Papaji and Fauzia seemed to disclose a surprising, totally unexpected revelation.

THE END

About the Author

I was born in Soroti, Uganda, as a refugee, arrived in the UK as a child and settled in Birmingham in the early 1970s. My secondary education was at a comprehensive school there.

Following obtaining a law degree from Wolverhampton Polytechnic in the 80s, I attended the College of Law in Chester, in 1991 qualified as a solicitor and have since worked in the legal profession. I settled in Leicester in 1995. Currently I am a Director in a law firm.

During my long career, one of my proudest moments, apart from the birth of my two children, was that it was an absolute honour to serve the community as a JP. I was appointed a magistrate in 2005 and sat on many cases in the magistrate's court, dealing with adult criminal cases at that level. One particular case concerned honour killing. A very interesting case which is where the idea about writing my book – *The Price of Honour* – came from.

I have two children, Ali and Mariam.